The World at Noon

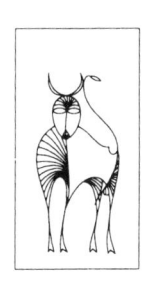

Guernica

Toronto / Montreal / New York
1994

Copyright © 1994, Eugene Mirabelli and Guernica Editions Inc.
All rights reserved.

Two chapters from this work appeared in
The Michigan Quarterly and *The American Poetry Review*.

'Friday on My Mind' by Harry Vanda and George Young.
Copyright © 1966, 1967 J. Albert & Son Pty. Ltd.
c/o EMI Unart Catalog Inc. Reprinted by permission of
CPP/BELWIN, Inc. Miami, FL. All rights reserved.

Antonio D'Alfonso, Editor
Guernica Editions Inc.
P.O. Box 117, Station P, Toronto (Ontario), Canada M5S 2S6
P.O. Box 633, Station N.D.G., Montreal (Quebec), Canada H4A 3R1
340 Nagel Drive, Cheektowaga, N.Y. 14225-4731 USA

Legal Deposit — Second Quarter
National Library of Canada
Bibliothèque nationale du Québec
Library of Congress Catalog Card Number: 93-80680

Canadian Cataloguing in Publication Data
Mirabelli, Eugene
The World at Noon
(Prose series; 29)
ISBN 1-55071-000-1
I. Title. II. Series.
PS3563.I68W67   1994   813'.54   C93-090591-1

For Francesca & Gabriella & Gino

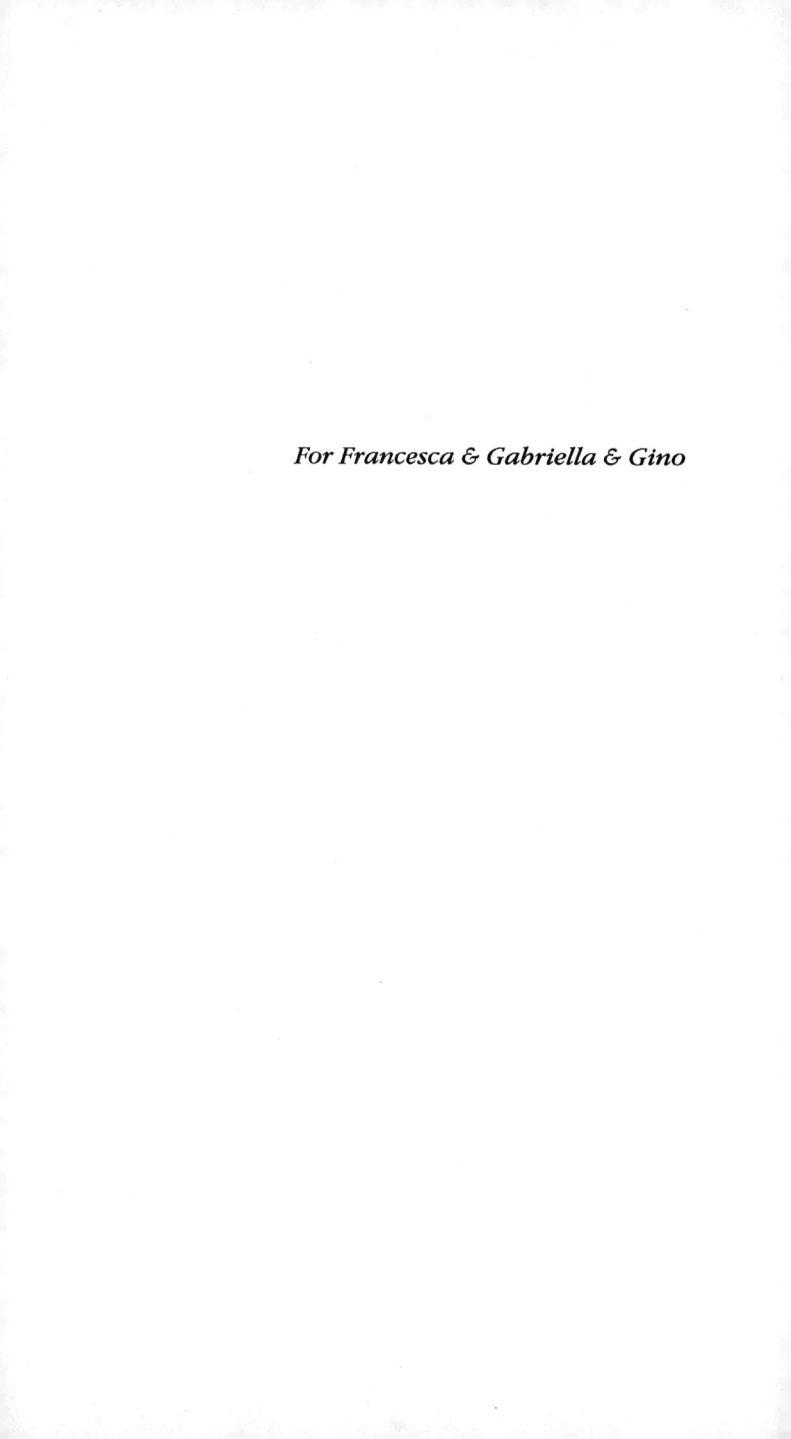

Ecco ridente in cielo
Spunta la bella aurora,
E tu non sorgi ancora,
E puoi dormir così?

Il Barbiere di Siviglia

I'm gonna have fun in the city,
Be with my girl, she's so pretty.
She looks right tonight
She looks outta sight
To me.

'Friday on My Mind'

1

Angelo Cavallù, born with the flanks and hind legs of a horse, died of old age under a tree in Palermo in 1900. Stella DiMare, a goddess so beautiful her looks could stun, was carried away by the tidal wave which swept the port of Reggio in 1908. Angelo's son Pacifico married Stella's daughter Marianna on the dock in Boston, Massachusetts. Pacifico made a fortune in Boston while Marianna bore him nine children — five girls and four boys, all of them reckless. He built a villa in Palermo and his children grew up in the breezy fields of New England and the walled gardens of Sicily. The second world war caught him over there in Palermo and his wife, Marianna, over here and they didn't get together again until the war was out of the way. Pacifico died at his dinner table in Palermo in 1950 after a good meal, his beard pressed into his chest and the blueprints for a cargo ship spread out in front of him, just as Marianna returned from the kitchen with his coffee. Most of his money was gone by then and the villa was a mess of cracked tiles and leaky plumbing, but he had been making plans to get rich once more. As for Marianna, her children travelled to Palermo to visit, and some grandchildren came, too, so she was never alone. She died early one morning in 1955, a few hours after having seen her own dead mother — the goddess — standing on tiptoe, as if she weighed nothing at all, standing and beckoning from a large scallop shell which floated off shore.

2

Marianna's nine children were Lucia and Marissa and Bianca and Candida and Dante and Sandro and Silvio and Mercurio and Regina. Those are their first names, at least. The boys were handsome and the girls beautiful and all of them were wild. Now take Marissa, that slender young woman with a river of shining black hair. She fell in love with a jaunty aeronautical engineer named Nicolo Pellegrino. Nicolo had worked a couple of years for a steel fabricating company in sooty Pittsburgh, then returned to MIT to begin teaching, a clean young man in a white flannel suit and a Panama straw hat. *Nicolo Pellegrino, permit me to introduce you to Marissa Cavallù.* They were married in 1929. Marissa and Nicolo Pellegrino had two children — boys. Rafe, the youngest, grew up to be even-tempered, steady, loving, prudent, wise and good. But Nicolo, the oldest, grew up to be me.

I found myself happily at the center of the universe on a broad sunny floor bounded by the stove, where a row of white enamel knobs perched this way and that on the gas pipe, a high sink with a glittering stream of water, and a wooden icebox which offered a multitude of doors and snappy latches. All this was presided over by my mother and more distantly by my father. She stayed here, he went everywhere. I had lots of good-smelling crayons, white oblong cardboards from the shirt laundry, a set of wood blocks (also cylindrical wood pillars, thin boards, some squares which were actually two triangular pediments put side by side, and an arch with the semi-circular cutout tucked into it) a toy sailboat, a red rubber racing car, a tray of rainbow watercolors, mittens, a large wood snow shovel, bowls of yummy alphabet soup, a tricycle, and chunks of brilliant ice to suck at on hot days. My uncles liked to joke and toss me around, sweeping me past the stove and up past the icebox to the ceiling where it was so high it was scary. My aunts were dazzling women with sharp red fingernails who would try to hug the breath out of me, or they would kiss my neck and slyly pinch my bottom, then kiss me quickly again before I could cry.

Skip the boyhood, the youth and young manhood — here I am, a man with a wife and three kids and no control over anything. A few years ago, when I turned fifty, I wanted to stop and think, wanted to reflect on my life and what I had done and what had happened to me, wanted to decide how to spend the second half. But there wasn't time. There hasn't been time to tear out the sink and rebuild the kitchen, hasn't been time to replaster the kids' rooms, or to break ground for a new garden, hasn't been time to get ready for the Merrimack five-kilometer run (veteran class), nor time to make love at leisure with no kids around, hasn't been time to keep a journal or write good letters or learn how to paint, no time to figure out God, console my mother, reassure the children, no time to sort through the photos, pick out the good ones and arrange them properly in albums.

And there hasn't been money, either. I chose a scholar's life. My father was a professor who taught through the gray months and raised tomatoes all summer long, and it looked like a decent way to make a living. Of course, he taught aeronautical engineering and not the flimsy historical rhetorical nonsense I labor with. Anyway, it was only a stratagem to make money until I was able to throw off my disguise and reveal my true self — the great lover, the author of a great book, the founder of a great religion, you name it. So we bought a VW bug and headed West and I taught at Cascadia College in Washington State. The pay was low but we hoped to live on enriched language, toasting a slice for breakfast on the end of a fork while punctuation marks fell off like meteors, at noontime eating a dish of yogurt with verbs (lots of protein in verbs) and for dessert, fresh apple trope and rhetoric. After three years of starvation, we packed the VW and headed East.

Now I teach in Boston and Maeve runs her editing and publishing companies from our kitchen table. We live an hour from the city over bad country roads. We are not going to build that house with the pine-floored kitchen and bunches of herbs on the walls, the neat orchard and wild flower fields. No. We shall stay in this same leaky wreck amid these rotting apple trees, tall grass and lazy boulders. We shall stay broke. We had our children too late or too far apart, or we had too many or too few. The creaky house will grow bigger and more hollow as the children leave. I'm fifty-three. We have two daughters and a son. One daughter is at Harvard, an unworldly young woman, sifting for wisdom in the accumulated rot of centuries, and the other (miniskirts, eye-shadow) is in high school, and our son, the youngest of the three, is already too old to be kissed on the sweet nape of his neck, a prince of the eighth grade.

3

The rain was falling softly, maybe not at all, and there wasn't any sky. The Charles River was gray as glass. As I was coming off the bridge I glanced into the rearview mirror and saw my father, dead these past three years, at the wheel of the car behind me. He had on his gray fedora and his rimless glasses and was focused on driving, unaware that I was just in front of him. The traffic was fast and I had to watch where I was going, but when I looked into the mirror again he was still there. Maybe he was going to visit mother at the hospital, too. I deliberately turned my eyes away, stared at the truck in front, and when I looked back some other car had shifted in behind me. I relaxed: I had been imagining things, that's all. Then father's old Ford rattled up on my left and as it sailed by I had a last glimpse — it was him, all right, serious and alert — before he vanished into the traffic ahead. My car went into a skid and I wrenched the wheel, slewed crazily into a side street and came to a halt. The tenements and storefronts looked gray as fog in the drizzle. I didn't know precisely where I was. I rubbed the windshield with the back of my hand and began to drive slowly, stopping to look around at each corner, and when I came to Mass Avenue I turned onto it and headed toward Harvard Square.

The rain had ceased by the time I walked into the college yard. I trotted along toward the library, the path slippery with fallen leaves. And there was my daughter Nina coming down the wet stone steps: a young woman in a yellow raincoat with a dark green canvas shoulder bag. She saw me and waved, smiling. "Hi, dad," she said. "Our timing is perfect."

"You're going to break someone's heart with that smile," I told her.

"You think so? So far I've had no luck at all."

"I'm supposed to remember to ask if you want your winter coat."

"Not now. I'll pick it up when I see you guys at Thanksgiving. I'll come home and get it."

"That's a month away. More than a month. You'll freeze."

"Don't worry about it, dad," she said sharply.

I glanced sideways at her as we walked. She hung her canvas bag from her other shoulder and took my arm. "Sorry," she said, apologetically.

"All right, Thanksgiving," I said. We came

out of the yard onto Mass Avenue, people everywhere. "The car's down this way."

We drove the mile or so to the hospital. The door to my mother's room was ajar. I knocked but there was no answer, so I pushed it gently open and put my head in. Mother was lying on her side, propped up a bit on pillows — still alive, thank God — reading a book. Her face didn't look as slack and baggy as it had yesterday, and now her thin hair was brushed into shape and she wore a touch of lipstick. "Hi, mother," I said from the doorway. She glanced up, looked over her glasses at me, her face blank.

"Ah, Nicolo," she said, pleased.

I walked in, Nina following.

"And Mariannina. How beautiful you look," she said, cautiously lifting her head to see more.

"How are you feeling, nana?"

"Much better, dear. — Come here. Over here," she told her.

I kissed mother's cheek and it was warm, not hot and damp as it had been yesterday. Nina went around to the other side of the bed, tossing her yellow slicker on the window sill.

"See. There's the card you sent," mother said slowly to Nina. A flock of get-well cards was taped to the wall where she could see them across the foot of her bed. Among them was a studiously detailed drawing of a space ship by my son, and a handpainted sign which said *Get better soon* by my brother's two kids. Nina's card was there someplace. "I knew it was from you as soon as I saw the whales," mother explained, removing her glasses.

"Yes, that's the one," Nina said, putting a cheerful lilt into her voice.

"I remember when you used to like unicorns," mother added.

"That was a long time ago," Nina said flatly.

"How are you feeling today?" I asked.

It hurt in her back, she said, down where the surgeon had done his work. I asked had she taken any pain killers. No, she said, she didn't want to take any of those drugs, they were habit forming. "Yesterday I was tired from all the coughing they made me do. That's why I was so sleepy when you came in yesterday." She hesitated an instant, looking at me. "I remember your visit. I remember."

"You weren't feeling so well," I said. I wondered if she remembered both me and Maeve, or just me.

"Both of you," mother continued. "And the pills make me sleepy, too." She put the book she had been reading onto the bedside table. The hospital identification bracelet was a loop of white plastic ribbon with her name on it, rather like a little girl's make-believe jewelry, and it made her wrist look terribly narrow and frail.

"The coughing is good for you. It clears out your lungs," I told her.

"That's right, nana."

"I know, I know. They have a machine I blow into. — Sit over here, dear," she said to Nina. "I want to look at you. Bring the chair. I hope you're not studying too hard."

I slid mother's reading glasses into their embroidered case and put them on the bedside table on top of the book about Verdi. There were three raggedly torn envelopes with the greeting cards thrust part way back inside, a plastic dinner knife, an open box of pastel-colored mints, a box of paper tissues, and the small oval picture frame which held two photographs of father. Mother had trimmed the two snapshots (an old black-and-white photo which showed him laughing and a modern color print taken at his eightieth birthday party) and had put them, one overlapping the other, in the gray silver case which she now carried with her whenever she took a trip. In the color photo dad looked horribly old, his eyes glistening and sad. While my mother and daughter conversed I went out to the hall and walked down to the nurses' station.

I recognized Brenda, a short cheerful woman, behind the counter. My mother was doing well, she told me. Her temperature was down from yesterday. Her lungs were much clearer. Every day she was feeling less pain in her back. My mother had been talking about her granddaughter all morning, Brenda told me. I smiled back and thanked her and walked up the hall. The tan linoleum floor, the cork bulletin board, the tall cart loaded with towels and bandage rolls and packets of this and that — everything was disagreeably familiar though mother had been here only a week. I wondered if I should tell her about my having seen dad earlier in the day. Her own dead father still visited her in dreams from time to time and she always awoke comforted. When I entered the room Nina was telling her something about her house or her housemates, and mother was listening attentively.

"Your daughter is baking twelve loaves of bread today," mother informed me.

"Is that right?"

"I made the dough this morning before class," Nina said.

"I think your daughter works too hard. She has classes and her library job and now she cooks."

"I don't cook every night, nana."

"Do the boys cook?" she asked, curious.

"Some do. No one has to cook. They can do other things, like clean-up."

"Well, I think it's a wonderful thing, the boys and girls living together in that dormitory," she said decisively.

"House," Nina corrected her.

"House," her grandmother said.

We talked about making bread and what mother had eaten for lunch and how far you could see out the window from up here. We talked of this and that and I asked mother if she was tired. No, she was just resting with her eyes closed, she said. Then she opened her eyes and began talking again. She said that she thanked God for her wonderful friends and her family. My brother Rafe phoned her every day from Washington. "And he was just up here for a whole week," she reminded me.

"I talk to Rafe every day, too," I told her. "We talk about you."

"And your uncle Mercurio," she continued. "Mercurio calls every morning from Florida. And his voice is so strong. So — So —" Now her own voice wavered, ceased.

On the margin of my sight Nina shifted uneasily, for she knew as well as I where this talk was going.

"Yes," I said.

"He always says, How's my big sister? How's my Marissa —" She broke off, her eyes filling as she looked at me.

"Mercurio is doing well," I told her. "Mercurio is doing all right."

Her fingers were groping stiffly at the bedside table and now they knocked over the oval picture case. I snatched up the handkerchief box, plucked out some paper tissues and gave them to her. She carefully wiped her eyes, the blue string-like veins standing out on the back of her crooked hand. She blew her nose. She sighed. "He told me he walks every day. He keeps up his strength," she said at last.

Nina was watching us, her eyes glistening and her cheeks flushed as if from a hard run. She came and righted the oval picture frame.

"Mother —" I began.

"By the way," mother said to me. "Your aunt Regina would like to see you once in a while."

"I'll stop by her place someday soon."

"It's only a hop, skip and a jump from here," she added.

"Maybe today. But I don't think there's enough time. We've got to go and you need some —"

"She'd like that," mother told me. Then she cautiously rolled onto her back and sighed and closed her eyes. Her face was fallen and tired, sad in repose, ancient.

"I'll come by here tomorrow, but Nina has lots to do and won't be able to come."

She opened her yes, cleared her throat and spoke quietly. "I know. She can come another day. — You can come another day," she told her granddaughter.

"I will. I promise," said Nina. Then she leaned forward, the heavy glazed fabric of her yellow rain slicker crackling as she gave her grandmother a kiss on the cheek.

4

It was raining when we came out the hospital door. We ran to the car and I drove us away to the Square, guilty pleasure flooding my veins. "Have you had lunch?" I asked her.

"No. Have you?"

"Let's eat."

"Yay!" she said. I swung into a muddy parking lot and rolled down the window, the rain blowing in. A man with a Jamaican accent said, "Put it away down there, sah." I took the wet ticket, rolled up the window and drove cautiously down the crooked aisle of cars to the end of the lot. This had been my favorite city and now I barely recognized it. "I can't remember what used to be here," I told Nina.

"Does it matter?"

"I used to walk by here all the time. It used to be a building."

"Well, it's a nice parking lot now. — Your umbrella or mine?"

We jogged to the Square hunched under my umbrella, the rain slashing at our legs. I liked being close with her. We dodged around a big square stack of loose bricks and trotted past long pieces of freshly cut granite which lay in the gutter like a giant dashed line. A brick pillar or monument of some sort had been built on one of the traffic islands. I remarked about how new everything was. "Because they never finish building it," Nina cried, lifting her voice against the rush of rain and the hiss of passing cars. We came to a restaurant and I started to turn in but Nina, tugging at my arm the way she used to when she was seven, said she knew a better place, so we kept going.

Da Ponte's had a huge glass pastry case by the door, but what filled your eyes were three white walls of roughcast plaster and the neatly squared rows of butcher block tables. It was past lunch time and there were a lot of empty squares, as if we were walking onto a chessboard near the end of the game. We chose a table near the front and sat down beside a red and brown art nouveau poster for Rajah coffee. "Isn't this nice?" Nina said, tossing back her wet hair.

"Very nice." It was bright and fresh, even if it wasn't what I had in mind. "Do you ever go to Rossini's Café? It's still there, isn't it?"

"Of course it's still there. Yeah, we go there once in a while."

"And Sally's Waffle Shop?"

"That's kind of out of the way. I know you and mom like it. But it's still the Sixties in there." She squeezed a long heavy twist of inky hair in her fingers and studied the water that began to drip from it.

"Well, this is a nice place," I said.

I looked beyond the window at the rain falling. The air in Da Ponte's was warm and held the yeasty odor of rising dough, an odor I've always enjoyed. It was pleasant to sit there with Nina and to watch the rain falling on the street outside and to smell the pastry dough and not do anything at all. After a while I thought about mother lying in the hospital bed, the little room like a cube suspended in the rainy air a mile away, and I began to wonder if I was doing enough to make things come out right, wondered if I should talk more with the nurses, wondered if I should visit the neurosurgeon again. I thought of dad in bed, his arms and legs as pale as old sticks with the bark fallen off, arms and legs moving ceaselessly. I wondered what he meant, driving along in the car that way. I watched Nina drying a sheaf of her hair with a wadded paper napkin. She saw me and smiled. She laid aside the soggy ball of paper and slid her hands lightly, ever so lightly, over mine on the table top.

"Don't worry," she told me. "I think nana's doing very well. Really."

"You make her happy," I said. "You make all the difference in the world."

She lowered her eyes and began to spread my fingers flat on the table. Her hands were flawless, the veins just visible beneath the surface like a subtly worked design, the joints magically supple, the nails translucent — all so unlike my mother's aged hands. I told Nina that now she should think of her own work and her own life. "And enjoy things. Don't worry about your grandmother," I said. "I'll look after her. You look after yourself."

She glanced up, smiled briefly. "Mom already told me that."

She squeezed my fingers, then the waitress came and I pulled my hands back, embarrassed. "What's good here?" I asked Nina.

"Whatever you like," she said, brisk once more. "I'm going to have salad because I don't have much time." She had been a vegetarian since her fifteenth birthday.

Nina's salad came shortly but my croque-monsieur did not. "I can catch up," I told her. "Go on with what you were saying about Mark and why he isn't eligible."

She jabbed her fork murderously into a tomato slice. "He isn't eligible because I don't like his stupid face and I don't like his stupid politics and I especially don't like his stupid attitude toward women."

I asked how she had gotten involved with him.

"I *didn't* get involved with him!" she cried. "I was polite to him and he's been pestering me ever since!"

"You've got to be impolite. It will simplify

your life. Speak from the heart. Tell him he's a pest. Tell him he's a bore. Tell him to —" I gestured as if to brush away a fly.

"— To fuck off? That's not as easy as it sounds." Her cheeks reddened at the word, but so slightly you might not have noticed.

"Memorize a few simple phrases and have them ready the next time he calls."

Nina smiled. "Like those other phrases you gave me? Like, I'm not ready for that yet. Or, I'm not in the mood for that. —Did I tell you about this Felix Stout? He has a grant and he's writing a book on anthropology or mythology or something like that. He's nice."

"A student?"

"Felix?" She laughed as if I had said something hilarious. "No, no. He's out in the real world. He's been around."

I watched her attacking the salad and wondered how much I could ask. "How old is he?"

She shrugged. "I don't know. Thirty something. Does it matter? You said it wouldn't make any difference who I went out with so long as he was right for me. Remember?"

"That sounds like something I might say." And now I figured I was going to regret it.

"Anyway, he's good company," she said lightly. "He's funny and he's not a pest."

Then the waitress brought my croque-monsieur and, of course, I burned my tongue on the melted cheese, grabbed a glass of water, began drinking.

"Don't rush," Nina said. "I've got time."

My daughter and I met for lunch, just the two of us alone, only three or four times during the academic year and we had agreed that this one didn't count. On the ones that counted we not only ate lunch and had idle conversation, we also took a walk and looked into this or that shop and bought nothing at all, or maybe a record or just a wire bracelet inlaid with chips of colored stone. As I said, this wasn't one of those lunches but it was a good one all the same. She recited a few lines in Anglo-Saxon from a poem she liked, told me about a British rock group I hadn't heard of and her foreign language course and about the effects of a one-megaton atomic bomb blast over the city of Boston. (Years ago she had embarrassed herself by weeping in class when they showed a movie about the desolation of Hiroshima.) For a while we talked politics and in the moment when I was most happily aware of loving her I recognized over again, with a twinge in my chest, that she was marvelously grown up and hardly mine at all. We were discussing a movie by Bergman, one which I had enjoyed but which Nina hated, when we were distracted by a young woman. Her hair was streaming rainwater and now she seated herself at the next table, one hand still clutching shut the collar of her yellow jacket. Yellow was the color for rain gear that season. The jacket was a sporty thing slashed here and there with huge black zippers, even the sleeves had zippers. It looked just right for keeping off the spray when you headed upwind in your yacht, but it was no good at all in a rainstorm. Her corduroy jeans were dark with water.

"Hey," Nina said. "It's Roxane."

The drenched one looked over at us and brightened. "Hi, Nina."

"This is my father," Nina told her. "And this is Roxane Beach. Remember?"

I didn't remember and didn't want to be introduced.

"Hello," the young woman said. She let go of her floppy collar and shook my hand.

They spoke briefly about how they were doing (Not bad. Same as ever.) and how long it had been since they had last seen each other (Six months? Yes, six months!) Then Nina, being Nina and wanting the whole world to be friends, said, "Want to sit with us?" And Roxane Beach smiled at us and said, "Sure. I'd like that." She pulled open half a dozen zippers on her jacket, then tugged the loosened garment up over her face and off. She shook her head as vigorously as any dog, spraying us.

"Roxane's a photographer," my daughter informed me, as if it were a marvel.

I said that was nice.

"Actually, my boss does most of the interesting stuff. I put the lights where he tells me to. Mostly I answer the phone."

"Don't you get to take any pictures?" Nina asked.

"I did a lot last summer. Shot group photos of every soccer team in every suburban town in eastern Massachusetts." She smiled.

Beach gave the waitress her order and we ate and talked of one thing or another. I didn't do much of the talking. I hadn't wanted anyone to join us and now I felt shut out. Our table was meant for two and Beach sat at the side, between Nina and me, her wet knees bumping mine. She looked about twenty-six, maybe twenty-seven, had pale gray eyes and wax-white hair which appeared to have been chopped at rather than cut. The wet hair looked awful and I quit trying to recall who she was. Nina was sweeping the inside of her salad bowl with the last crust of bread which she now popped into her mouth. Did I mention that when she was fifteen Nina had tried to live on pure air alone and no gross food at all? She had fretted the patience of her mother and father, frightened her kid sister and starved herself ugly. A few months of that and the bones of her spine showed like teeth, her breasts dried up, her menses ceased to flow and her skin turned to sand. Now she was talking eagerly, her hand poised just above the table, and now she made a swift soaring gesture between the brimming glassware. It was a pleasure to watch her. I ordered another cup of coffee and desert.

"Listen, you guys," Nina said. "I've got to go. I'm late."

"I'll give you a ride —" I began.

"I'm sorry I won't see you when you come in tomorrow," she told me. "But I'll be thinking about you. This is a nice place, isn't it?"

"Very nice. Now let me give you a ride."

But she said she didn't need a ride, she was going back to the house on the shuttle. I should stay put, finish my desert, keep Roxane company. Then she flung on her slicker, pulled her umbrella from her shoulder bag, waved a kiss and went out the door. I looked out the window at the noiseless falling rain and the cars going silently past and wished I had been better at letting her go just then.

"I'll be through in half a sec," the young woman said hurriedly.

"Oh. Well. Take your time. It doesn't matter."

A trickle of water had crept down her temple and sparkled now beside the earlobe in which she wore three tiny wire earrings. Seen this way, from the side, she displayed a tightly contained profile with a somewhat narrowed eye and a stiff jaw, and maybe for that reason she reminded me of an athlete, a powerful swimmer about to hurl herself into a race. I wondered what kind of a friend she had been to my daughter. Then I sensed that I was making her uncomfortable, so I looked around at the classy posters on the far wall and began to study the one for LA MAISON MODERNE, 2 RUE DE LA PAIX 1905.

"It smells good in here, doesn't it?" she said, catching me unaware.

I agreed that it did smell good.

"Sometimes I like to look out a window and watch it raining," she continued. "What about you?"

So we talked about the weather until she had finished her soup, then she dove expertly into the billows of her yellow rain jacket, swam up through the head hole, her hands surfacing at the same moment, and began to pull shut the zippers here and here and here. "I know this thing isn't very efficient but I got it for nothing after a photo session," she explained. At the door we both hesitated to step into the downpour. I asked if she needed a ride, but she had already started to turn away and now she smiled and waved goodbye, much like Nina, and I trotted off to my car to do errands.

5

You can keep dry if you walk directly from the garage through a long narrow connecting room whose walls have sagged out of plumb, then hop up a stone step into the kitchen. Our kids used to play in the room and some of their early artwork is still tacked along the wall above the forgotten toys. The kitchen itself is big enough to hold an auction in. It contains a huge cast iron stove with fancy nickel trim, as well as the gas stove we cook on, the refrigerator, the leaky sinks, racks of pots and pans, cabinets (each door with its bright piece of painting or watercolor or pen drawing), our old table, a school of cardboard whales swimming overhead, two worn benches and, if you step around the crocks and baskets and old Calico lapping at her saucer of milk, there's Maeve's pine desk (typewriter, purse, note pad) and the jelly cupboard where she stores her stuffed file folders. When I got home the windows were white with steam and Maeve was at the stove, lifting a ladle full of soup from the pot, a sheaf of papers in her other hand. She was barefoot, her big soles numb on the chilly stone floor, because she loved summer and refused to admit that it had changed to fall. "How did it go?" she asked, looking up.

"Mother was better, Nina was fine. What about you?"

She cautiously emptied the ladle back into the pot. "Busy day. Dinner is going to be a little late."

I looked over Nico's shoulder at the TV. "It's the one where they reverse time so they can go back and write on daVinci's canvasses and tell which ones are fakes. I've seen it before," he said without turning. I put my arm around his neck and kissed his thick mop which had the same comforting odor as my childhood teddy bear. "I'm hungry," he added.

"Fisher came by to drop off the graphics. That delayed everything," Maeve told me.

"Who?" I asked. The kitchen table was a mess of loose typewritten pages. There was also a beanbag frog used as a paperweight on our letters, a mug with half an inch of black tea, a couple of computer disks, Maeve's reading glasses, a red clay flower pot with something growing in it, Nico's school books and a pair of polyfaceted ruby dice from one of his games. I began to sort through our letters.

"You remember Fisher. You said you liked him. He does beautiful graphic work."

"Fisher is all right, but too sweet-tempered for me. This all the mail?"

"That's it."

There was Maeve's note that one of my graduate students had called, but the only real mail was the bill for Maeve's mammogram and a letter from Charlotte Squire, a former student of mine. "You could have opened Charlotte's letter. It's addressed to both of us," I said.

"I have my scruples. What does she say?" Then Maeve turned her back and began grating cheese.

"There's a map and — It's a wedding invitation. Charlotte is getting married. That's a surprise. She's getting married."

"Young women still do that, even pretty ones," she said flatly. "When's the wedding?"

"December. I wonder if she'll still write letters after she's married."

"Why not? You do." Maeve tapped the loose cheese crumbs from the grater and turned to me with a smile.

"The ants are coming in," Nico informed us. "And do we have to wait for Morgan? I'm starving."

"You can speed things up by setting the table," Maeve told him.

"Where's Morgan Kathleen?" I asked.

"Field hockey," she said.

"In this rain?"

"It's a crucial game. — Here. Taste this and tell me what you think."

The three of us had just seated ourselves at the diningroom table when we heard

Morgan Kathleen, heard the door swing open, heard her bookbag go thud and her hockey stick fall rattling to the stone floor. "How did you make out? How did it go?" we called to her. She stood a moment in the diningroom doorway, her hair drenched flat and her face streaked with mud. "We lost," she said hoarsely, her eyes brimming. Then she wheeled around and tramped up the stairs. Maeve called after her to wash her face and come down to eat. *"We tied them in the last quarter and then lost in the shitty flick off!"* Morgan shouted back at us. The bathroom door crashed shut. Nico cleared his throat and said, softly, that he thought we should not ask her anything more about the game. And then, to break the silence, he began to talk about his weird English teacher.

Later in the evening Morgan Kathleen showed me her physics problems, due tomorrow morning. They were nice problems, I remarked. "Well, I don't think so," Morgan said, irritably. We were sitting across from each other at the kitchen table, her books between us.

"They're beautiful. Where are your formulas?" I asked her.

"Right here." She opened her notebook and began to flip through the pages, humming. She was in her rose-colored bathrobe, the one my mother had made for her, and her hair was up in a thick white towel which was wrapped about her head like a turban. She turned the notebook to me. "Here they are," she said.

"How can you read that? Can't you write any better than that?"

"I can read them fine, daddy. And I've already done the first three problems and number seven. Do number four."

"Let's start with a fresh sheet of paper."

"Here." She tore a fresh page from the notebook, slid it to me.

"And a pencil."

She slapped a pencil briskly onto the table top.

"Now read the problem out loud," I said.

"A ball is thrown vertically upward at forty-eight feet per second," she began. I drew the diagram as she continued aloud, and after some calculations we came up with the right answer. "I told you it was easy," I said, pleasantly surprised.

"Let's do the others," Morgan said crisply.

Nico came into the kitchen. "*Excusez-moi*," he said. He tucked a folded sheet of paper into the French textbook which lay beside me on the bench. "*C'est la vocabulaire pour demain*," he explained. He left and we went through the remaining physics problems. Morgan did the mathematics on a calculator the size of a playing card, her large fingers arching and stabbing at the tiny buttons without a miss, her pointed nails glittering with red lacquer. It amazed me that she played hockey and still

35

had unmarred nails. "Daddy," she said. Her face still hovered over the open notebook, a black spiral of hair at the strong nape of her neck as she wrote down the last figures. Now she looked up. "Can I borrow your sweater? The grayish blue one. Please. You never wear it anymore."

"That's a good sweater," I told her.

"Can I wear it tomorrow? I didn't spill anything on your jacket when I borrowed it, remember?"

"Don't get perfume on it."

"Thanks." She smiled quickly and swept up her books, cradling them in her arm, and left the kitchen. "And thanks for the help, too," she called back down the stairway.

And so the evening went. I don't know what time it had gotten to, but I was re-heating the coffee when Maeve came into the kitchen fresh from her bath. She likes a scalding tub at bedtime and her instep and toes showed tender pink beneath the hem of her nightrobe. "How late are you going to stay up?" she asked. We talked about the memo I was writing to the head of my department, talked about my chances of getting a promotion, or at least a raise. Maeve said not to worry about it. "They want to know what I've been doing for the last decade," I said. And we talked about Nina some more and I remembered to say that she would pick up her coat when she came home for Thanksgiving. "And I saw my father today,"

I said. "He was driving his old car and he passed me on Storrow Drive."

6

What can I tell you about Maeve? Maeve has green eyes, high cheekbones, and hair like a long black banner — hair glossy as a crow's wing, thanks to the walnut oil or whatever it is she uses. The morning I met her she sank into my heart like an axe. That evening she pillowed her bright cheek on my chest and murmured, "You splendid man," and I said, "Marry me!" and she said, "Yes. My mother is dead but you can meet my father." Her father was a huge jovial man with a zigzag crack of melancholy from the death of his young wife. "My Maeve is named after Maeve of Connacht, the Irish queen," he boomed out. "The queen was called Maeve of the Golden Hole because she could piss a hole so deep in a snowbank a cow would break a leg in it." He laughed and laughed, then he sighed and turned to his daughter. "You might as well marry him. I was thinking last week to turn off the heat in your old room. — And may you both live forever," he added.

Maeve weighs barely more than she did the day we married, needs glasses to see up close, had a small lump taken from her breast a few years ago, still has a narrow waist and a straight back, broad shoulders, all her teeth and a low laugh. In the early years a sharp edge on my voice would make her eyes brim, as if she had been slapped (a trait she passed on to our Nico), and she would stand there blinking while I hurried and stumbled to apologize, but all that is much changed and I don't say harsh words anymore, or else she had grown thicker skin, for there are no tears. Besides, she gives as good as she gets. As a mother, she's a loving, patient and fond woman who would change a diaper, jiggle her hand on the kid's privates and sing, "Pretty girl! Yes you are! Yes you are!" and who now massages their feet, sore from ballet or soccer, and recites their French vocabulary with them. She's thrifty at the market, clever in the kitchen and generous at the table. She's amorous. Her breasts are no longer full, but her flesh is still silken and warm and what was sometimes a tense passage is now luxurious. She will be regal, demand me on my knees, or at my beck and call come meekly to my feet, or roll us on the furs heaped on the study floor. She's faithful, too, at the end of things. Maybe the proper word is not faithful but fastidious; she doesn't crave a messy mess in her lap. On the other hand, I have seen her turn a young man's heart inside out and shake it till it was as light as a poor man's pocket. And she is forgiving, or fairly charitable, or she tries to be. But you would not want to see her standing in her nightrobe by the fire, listening to me explain about Grace Greentree, Maeve's eyes as calm as mirrors while one forgetful hand caresses the dog's ear, twisting it between her fingers till the poor hound yelps and creeps away. When I recall the hidden gardens in my own heart and know that Maeve is no better than I am, that's when I worry about us. I've never wanted to marry anyone else. My Maeve is no angel and her Nicolo is no saint, but in this world this is all we have. I love her and she says she loves me and I believe it, mostly, just as she believes me, or says she does, when I say it to her. If she should ever die — well, I cannot finish a sentence that begins that way.

7

The next day my mother looked a shade worse, but when I asked how she felt she said the pain wasn't as bad as yesterday. Then she added that she had eaten only a bit of lunch, because they had brought it to her cold and she had gotten angry and had thrown the metal dish cover onto the floor. "I can't get well if I don't eat and I can't eat cold soup and cold potatoes and cold string beans!" she said. I steered the conversation onto Nina and we talked about her and then about my aunt Regina, whom I should visit, yes, and after a while my mother told me she was tired, wanted to nap, so I kissed her and left.

I drove to the Square. After I had locked the car a light rain began to fall, but instead of ducking into the first restaurant I came to I decided to walk to Da Ponte's Café, as if Nina might be there. It was the same hour as yesterday and I sat at the same table where Nina and I had been, and again watched the rain falling beyond the window and breathed the faint odor of pastry dough. I supposed it was good that my mother had the spirit to throw the dish cover to the floor, but the episode oppressed me. Now a waitress brought me a menu, took my order and went off. I thought about my father and tried to recall if I had dreamed about him last night, and then I thought about Maeve's father and attempted to calculate how many years it had been since he had died — had blown his brains out, poor sick man. I looked at the people walking past, huddled against the rain, and someone in a yellow rain jacket came in toward my table and here was Nina's friend. "Hi," she said pleasantly. She had no air of surprise, but came forward as if we had agreed to meet here. I said hello and stood up, trying to recall her name. "Roxane," she said, shaking my hand.

"Will you join me for lunch?" I asked.

"Sure." She smiled and began — zip, zip, zip, zip, zip — to energetically unfasten her floppy yellow jacket. "Isn't this rain amazing?" She pulled the costume off over her head and ran a hand back through her drenched hair, looking at me. "Does rain depress you?" she asked.

"No. This is the way I look. It's my face."

She laughed. "No, no, no. That's not what I meant at all. And you have a handsome face. I meant, when it rains this much it begins to rain in my head. Today while I was walking in the rain I realized — he's not going to marry me, not ever. This is going nowhere. It's always been going nowhere."

"Are you sure?" That was a dumb remark but I didn't know what to say.

"Yes. I'm sure. What a fool I am," she said flatly.

"I'm sorry. I'm really sorry —"

"No, it was stupid of me to bring it up." She looked away, frowning.

The waitress had come over and I watched as Roxane bent her head to read the menu. Her hair stood up every which way, glistening like wet straw, and her eyelashes were matted with rainwater. She wore a green sweater with frayed cuffs, and while studying the menu she never raised her eyes, but her hand floated gently from the table and her middle finger caught a drop that had crept from her hairline and down her temple. The waitress took the order and went off. Roxane looked across to me as if to speak, but did not.

"What are you photographing today?" I asked.

"I'm typing letters. It's a really *small* business."

We talked about her workday, and when our lunch arrived Roxane announced that she had talked about herself much too much. "Now what about you? What have you been doing today?" she asked. Her eyes were large, or maybe they only seemed so because of the clear, straight way she looked at me.

"I've taught a couple of classes. I've been to visit my mother in the hospital," I began.

"Oh! I didn't know." She hesitated, then went on cautiously. "How is she?"

I told her my mother was improving. I explained that she had had a bit of bone removed from some vertebrae. As if to reassure me, Roxane told me about her own grandmother who had broken a hip a year ago, but was almost good as new. She used a cane to get around and said she was going to visit Roxane one of these days. "My grandmom writes to me practically every month — ever since my mother and father took off," she said.

"Took off? What do you mean? Where did they go?"

"They went to different parts of the country. My father lives up in Oregon and my mother stays down in Arizona. They're not divorced," she added. "They've been doing that since I was eighteen. It doesn't bother me."

"It must keep you busy writing letters."

"Not very," she said.

I asked about brothers and sisters. All she had was a younger sister who lived in Australia, married to an Australian. Something she had said or something in her voice had caused me an odd pang of loneliness, and I felt an awkward desire to comfort her. Roxane's straight gaze invited you to look directly at her, to frankly take in those gray-green eyes, the hard cheeks, the slight freckling across the bridge of her nose, and for a moment I lost what she was saying.

"— but I like it right here in Cambridge and Boston and I'm talking about myself again. Please tell me something about you," she said.

I told her that I couldn't think of anything to tell about me, told her that about me was boring.

"Nina told me lots about you and you didn't sound boring at all. On the contrary, you sounded very interesting. I used to wish I had a father like you. Nina used to —"

"Hey! I pushed your car once when it was stuck in a snowbank," I said abruptly. It had just come back to me, and I was happy.

She smiled, delighted that I had remembered. "That's right. That was me."

"That was the only time we met, I think."

"No. I opened the door for you once. I was on my way out from Nina's and you were just arriving."

So we talked along. We talked about her old car, the one in the snowbank, and how it had broken down so many times she finally had to shoot it, and about the classes I taught, and how she had taken five years to get through college because she had totally wrecked her sophomore year, how gymnastics had been her entire life until she sprained her back when she was eighteen, and how I ran only two miles a day and only three times a week and how even that was getting to be too much for me. We had a second cup of coffee and I watched her talking and studied the way her hair stood up like an old whitewash brush, the ends so pale, and I thought about how long she must have worked at it, and all to transform herself into something strange and beautiful, though so many people must laugh at it. And for a moment it seemed I could feel the blood moving painfully around my heart and I wondered why it was we are drawn to this person and not that one, and why it is we love now what we have never loved before. Then it was later than we thought and time to go.

"We had a fight," Roxane said outside. "No one writes to me anymore except my grandmom."

We were walking along the crowded curve of Brattle Street. The rain had grown finer and now hung weightless and gray in the air. I was flattered and excited by thinking she used to wish she had a father like me. We stayed close and kept our heads down and at every step I felt Roxane's shoulder brush against mine, the shock flaring again and again through the cloth and into the flesh.

"If you were my daughter I'd write to you all the time," I told her.

"It doesn't bother me. I'm not exactly a waif, you know. And I do make a pest of myself. I hope you didn't mind too much when I joined you and Nina at lunch yesterday."

I lied, of course, and told her I hadn't minded at all.

"Now I have to cut across to the subway," she said. She paused on the margin of the sidewalk, clutching those useless floppy lapels of the rain jacket shut against her chin. She looked at me and smiled, obviously happy.

I smiled back. She was a sturdy and good-looking young woman and I wanted to tell her so. "I enjoyed having lunch with you," was all I said.

We shook hands goodbye and she stepped off the curb into the street.

"I'm in the phone book," she said over her shoulder to me. "Look me up. Give me a call when, you know, when you happen to be around. Or whenever." Then she turned and ran with her shimmering reflection between the cars and trucks toward the subway entrance.

8

And now I drove around to visit my aunt Regina as I had promised. "Nicolo," she said at the door. "What are you doing out there in the drizzle?"

"Are you going to let me in?"

Gina's hair was thick and white and she had a habit of plowing her hand back through it, so it looked like one of those dazzling clouds that blossom up on a summer's day. She took my coat and gave it a toss that left it clinging like a drunkard to the newel post at the foot of the stairway. Then she lead me down the narrow hall toward the kitchen where the air had begun to pulse with *beach baby, beach baby, there on the sand* — I stumbled against a shadowy trunk, its dull brass corners slowly coming into visibility.

"*I haven't completely unpacked from Gloucester!*" she said, lifting her voice against the pounding music. "*Watch your step.*"

Gina had remodeled the kitchen some while ago, so that it was white formica and blond wood, illuminated from above by a cluster of plain white globes, and she had lowered an interior wall to waist height to make a white marble-topped counter which looked into the diningroom. Then, having established the blank modernity of this interior, she had destroyed the effect by hanging huge swaths of cloth on the walls, thick sprays and bouquets and whole orchards of color everywhere. At the marble counter now she scooped up her pen, the loose stamps, her cigarette pack, a half-eaten orange, the envelopes and the scattered sheets of stationery, looked around for an open place to put them, didn't find one, then set everything in a heap back on the counter again. She stepped around to the diningroom, turned off the music and came back, smiled. I've been crazy about Gina since I was five. Now she was wearing silver hoop earrings, dark pants and a tight gray sweater, and the sweater had a v neck which exposed her corded throat and sharp collarbone. But it was her voice, rich and deep as the ocean floor, that people always remembered best.

"You're looking well," I told her.

"Yes. I can imagine." She didn't look bad, actually. "And if you had phoned before you came over I'd be looking even better. Can I give you some coffee? Tea? *Un aperitivo?*"

"The drink sounds good."

She stood two thick-bottomed glasses side by side on the kitchen counter and dropped an ice cube in each. "How's my sister?" she asked, her back to me as she worked.

"She's fine. Yesterday she got mad and threw a dish cover on the floor because her food was cold, but today she's in a much better mood."

"She told me it was just bone they removed." Gina took a bottle of dark Cinzano from one of the cabinets. "Should I believe her?"

"Yes. It was just bone."

"It's not cancer?" she asked, still not turning to face me.

"No. Part of the vertebrae was growing against the spinal cord. Like a bone spur pressing against a nerve."

She turned and handed me my drink. "That's not cancer?" she asked, watching me.

"It's not cancer."

Gina studied me an instant more to make sure I was telling the truth, then raised her glass to touch mine. "Evviva," she said.

"Evviva." I hadn't had a drink of plain vermouth in a long time and it tasted pleasantly bitter.

"I guess you know about Mercurio," she said a moment later.

"Yeah. I know."

"He used to be so lucky. That was the thing about Mercurio, he always landed on his feet," she told me.

"Even when he fell out of the sky."

"And my sister Lucia with all her ailments. — Now it looks like Mercurio will go first."

"My father went first." I cut in more harshly than I had intended.

"I meant my brothers and sisters. Did you think I forgot your father? Your father was a lovable man. God, what a depressing conversation! We need a change of subject. Let's get comfortable in the other room."

The diningroom was also a sitting room and a temporary greenhouse where Gina had set out the jumbled profusion of flowers, ferns and herbs which she had brought back from Gloucester. The disheveled plants, some still in blossom, were arrayed on the floor in front of a pair of glass sliding doors that looked out onto a messy stone patio and a rickety gray board fence. Gina and Maeve and I had taken our coffee out onto the patio after dinner last spring, just before Gina left for Gloucester. Now an ancient café table stood there, round and white and alone, its liquid surface spotted with tiny locust leaves. The rain seemed to have stopped. I turned from the glass door and sat in the chair opposite Gina. She had just knotted a blue kerchief around her neck, or else I hadn't noticed it before.

"I saw your daughter last week," Gina said. She drew up her foot, tucked it under the other leg. "In the Square where they're laying all those bricks. We stopped and talked. She introduced me to the young man she had with her, but I can't recall his name."

"Felix Stout. His name is Felix Stout. — Did

Nina tell you her plans for the future? She has none. She's going to graduate with a big debt and no job," I said.

"Maybe the Japanese will lead her to something."

"Which Japanese?"

"She told me she was learning Japanese."

"Oh, that. That's nothing," I assured her. "When she was a kid she read a book about elves and learned elvish."

"She was talking about actually going to Japan. She seemed quite serious about it."

"Nina's always quite serious about something. I wish she'd get intense about a career or a job or money."

"She's bright and she's beautiful. And you worry too much." She brushed aside my worries with a wave of her arm that set her bracelets jingling. "Now tell me about Morgan Kathleen. What's she been up to? And Nico."

So we sipped our drinks and talked about my kids and I asked what news she had from her Arianne. Her daughter Arianne was one of my favorite cousins. Just now she was setting up obstetrical clinics in Third World countries and, Gina said, not even God knew what she would be doing next. Gina went to the counter, fetched back her cigarette pack and a silver ashtray shaped like a scallop shell. She told me that her granddaughter, Arianne's daughter, had gone to live with a boyfriend.

"Refresh my memory. Which young man did she move in with?"

"My granddaughter? She moved in with the carpenter, I mean shipwright. He builds ships. You remember him. He's the one with the gold beard, and he wears suspenders and those old fashioned shirts without collars like men used to wear a hundred years ago. His clothes have something to do with honest workmanship or personal integrity or natural living. My granddaughter explained it to me. I think young men are much more interesting than they used to be." Gina set the scallop ashtray in her lap and shook out a cigarette. "He lives in a cozy loft over his studio in Marblehead. Now they both live up there. I think they may get married. — Maybe I'll get married, too. What do you think?"

My aunt Regina had been going with the same man for thirty years and for a time they had even lived together. "Sure. Why not?" I said.

"He doesn't drink at all anymore. I wonder if I'd have to stop drinking," she said.

We talked about drinking and then she asked about Morgan Kathleen, was she seeing anybody, and our talk circled back to Nina once more.

"You do worry too much," Gina told me. "It's a sin, you know. Worry is a sin."

I told her she didn't know what she was talking about.

"Didn't the good nuns teach me?" she said. "Worry is one of the *seven deadly sins*. Don't smirk, Nicolo! I used to know the Latin name for it. *Gula*, I think it is. Yes, *gula*." She was so pleased.

"*Gula* is gluttony." I began to laugh. "And all your life you thought it was worry was a sin?"

She dropped the burnt match into the ashtray and leaned back to exhale a plume of milky blue smoke, letting her head loll even further back on the cushion, stretching her throat back till it was smooth and young again, smiling to herself. "Well, it's *gula* or *cura* or some damn thing like that," she said idly.

9

Now I have to tell you some things about my aunt Regina. As I said, my grandmother's nine children were Lucia and Marissa and Bianca and Candida and Dante and Sandro and Silvio and Mercurio and Regina. My mother was the second in this list, Regina was the last, and the arithmetic of our family made my aunt Regina only ten years older than I was. She grew up a wild girl. There were already four reckless brothers and four headstrong sisters, so her wildness was overlooked and what everyone remarked about was her voice. Her voice was strong and pure and could wake up a boulder or lull the fretful waves to sleep. But by the time she was fourteen they forgot about her voice and began to talk about her smoking in the choir loft, her rudeness to the nuns, her escapades with boys, and the autumn when she was sixteen she ran away — or was packed off — to live with her oldest married sister, my mother. I was in first grade and, because my brother Rafe's little room was already crowded with his crib and changing table, Gina shared my bedroom. She ate me up with kisses and played with me, let me ride horseback on her, would even stand up with me still clinging to her shoulders, my cheek in her hair and (here's the best part) let me slide luxuriously down her back onto my bed. I remember the bureau with her things on it: a blue hand-mirror, a brush and a big comb and some exquisitely tiny bottles, each with a different perfume which she would sometimes let me smell. I've been told that I used to run home from school and dash past my mother to show my papers to Gina. I remember the afternoon I climbed the stairs and found Gina face down on her bed, sobbing as she rolled from side to side and beat her pillow. I had never seen a grown-up in such a storm of tears and after watching her a while I crept down the stairs, my school papers still in my hand, to look for my mother. When I asked why Gina was crying, my mother told me not to worry. "No one ever died of a broken heart," she said crisply. "At least Gina never will." That summer my Cavallù grandparents sailed to Sicily to visit their daughter Lucia, taking Regina away with them, and I didn't know when I would see Regina again.

My grandparents left behind their huge empty home on the avenue and the roomy carriage house in back of it. A private school rented the big house and we rented the carriage house, a remodeled building whose rear windows overlooked an old burying ground. After three years my aunt Regina returned to this country and stayed with us a while, but it was a short visit and she never moved her belongings out of her suitcase and into her bureau. I recall her seated on a kitchen chair, one knee crossed upon the other, her brown high-heel shoes lying on the floor and her stockinged foot bobbing energetically as she talked. She spoke in Italian while my mother worked at the sink, laughing, her arms flecked with soapsuds. Gina's purse was open on the table, an empty cigarette pack beside it, so I sat there and played with the cigarette pack, first unfolding the paper and then carefully peeling away the fragile sheet of silver foil. I held the paper near my nose and secretly drank in the exciting scent of Gina's perfume mixed with the odor of tobacco. She saw me and smiled and I hurriedly crumpled the paper, dropped it in the ashtray, ashamed. "Come with me," she said briskly. In the bedroom she pulled her suitcase to the middle of the floor, flung it open and knelt to search among the tumbled sweaters, stockings, blouses. "Here," she said, handing me something like a large leather billfold. She asked did I like it and I said yes. "Your passport goes in here," she explained. "And this part holds your train tickets and baggage checks. And your money goes in here. — I got it for you," she added. I knew she hadn't gotten it for me, but I felt it was a more special present because she had decided just now to give it to me rather than to anyone else. "You have enormous eyes," she whispered to me. Then she scratched the back of my neck with her dangerously sharp red fingernails and went off to the kitchen. The scent of her perfume clung to the creases of the leather, making a dark secret odor which I longed to drink. While Gina stayed with us I kept the billfold on my bureau, but after she left I was afraid my mother would take it away, so I hid it in the bottom drawer under my sweaters, along side her blue hand-mirror.

In June of 1941 Gina married John Campagnia of Gloucester, owner and skipper of the fishing ship *Saint Andrew*, a ninety-foot dragger with a crew of five. He was older than any of her brothers, an amateur explorer, mountain climber, surveyor and map maker, a vigorous man with a quick smile. I recall him — or perhaps only a photograph Gina took of him — in a thick black sweater with a black captain's hat pushed back rakishly on his head, grinning. He was a favorite with us kids. Gina saved his life once when she stood on a shuddering wharf at Duncan's Point and sang into the black gale that was driving his ship to the rocks. At her singing the winds fell silent and her voice went over the plunging sea and calmed it long enough for John to slide into the harbor, though every window in the wheelhouse was stove in. When the United States entered the war he got himself into the Coast

Guard and two years later he was gone, swept from an icy deck into the flinty North Atlantic. "When that happens," John had told us, "you freeze before you drown."

We were living in the big front house (the war had put an end to the private school which had been renting it), so there was plenty of room for Gina and her baby to stay with us. Gina looked awful. She was thin, her flesh the color of old candle wax except under her eyes where it was brown. She had pulled her long black hair to the back of her head, held it loosely there in her hand as one would hold a heavy rope or hawser, and with the other hand she had scissored it off. I recall her sitting at the table, a cup of cold coffee and a full ashtray beside her while she breast-fed Arianne. Gina wore a black cardigan sweater, the left shoulder blotched and stiff where Arianne spit up milk. My mother cut vegetables into a pot on the stove, talking of this and that, but Gina was mostly silent. Every now and again she crushed out a half-smoked cigarette, took a sip of black coffee and said, "Nicolo, light me a match." I would strike the match while she leaned across the table holding a fresh cigarette to her lips, the tremor of her hand like an endless shiver.

10

After the loss of her husband, my aunt Regina stayed indoors with her child and did not go out except to walk the heights of Cape Ann or to stare for hours at the surf breaking over Norman's Woe. Then she grew restless, began to look around for a way to go on living and eventually she opened a bakery shop up hill from the harbor. That year I graduated from high school and went to Gloucester to work the summer for her. I was seventeen. My aunt was the most beautiful woman I had ever seen up close. She and her daughter Arianne lived in a small apartment over the bakery, and I slept on a mattress made up on the floor in Arianne's room. Arianne was six years old by then. She was a pretty kid with horribly tangled hair and she wore hand-me-down dresses from her older cousins which made her look like a badly wrapped parcel. I used to read to her at bedtime and wonder at the starry conjunctions that had put Gina in my room when I was six, and me in Arianne's room now that I was as old as Gina had been back then.

My job was to scour the pans after the

baker left in the morning, serve the customers, scrub the counter and sweep the floor. Later I learned I was there also to keep Gina company or to go away and take Arianne with me (tucked under my arm because I had mistaken her, shrieking and giggling, for a loaf of French bread) when Gina wanted to be alone. I made friends, swam every afternoon, sailed now and then. After dinner we played Monopoly, or Gina put on her dance records and we pieced together one of those huge puzzles that took us a week to complete, or I studied my calculus, because I was entering MIT that fall.

Once in a while Gina went out with one of her men friends. On those evenings she would sit at the kitchen table wrapped in a white towel and paint her toenails and fingernails bright red, chatting happily while Arianne and I ate dinner. After her nails had dried, after she had blown on them and shaken them as if they were on fire, she would go to her bedroom to dress. Arianne would slide the checkerboard onto the table and kneel up on her chair so we could play Chinese checkers. Then Gina would come clattering into the kitchen in her high-heel sandals, blouse, underpants, garter belt — her skirt in her hand — to set up the ironing board. I would try not to watch her, would try at least not to be caught watching her. Arianne did say something. "What?" I asked her. "It's *your* move," she repeated. I hastily moved one of my pieces. Now and again

I glanced sideways at Gina, who was attentively ironing the pleats in the pale blue skirt, her back to us. Her garter belt fascinated me — the tense straps, the glittering hooks, the frosty lace webbing like cake decoration. "It's *your* move, dummy," Arianne said.

And some hot nights, when there was nothing at all to do, the three of us would walk down hill to the harbor and buy ice cream cones and stroll along the wharf and then climb home again as the sky cooled and the stars came out. One sweaty night I was at the kitchen table trying to read H. B. Phillips' *Analytic Geometry And Calculus* when Gina sat down across from me in her white towel and began to make herself a drink. "It's a mint julep. Want one?" she asked. She swirled it with a spoon, then took a sip. I said no and went back to the book, the dullest thing ever written. "Don't they drink at the Massachusetts Institute of Technology?" she asked. I told her I hated drinking. "You would," she said flatly. She took up the glass and went to her bedroom and returned a while later clothed in a white sleeveless dress and white high-heel sandals. "You need to learn some new dance steps," she announced. I made a groan and slumped in my chair. She put the record player on the table and turned the volume down so as not to awaken Arianne. "I already know how to dance," I said.

"Good," she said, closing my *Analytic Geometry And Calculus*. "We can dance."

"It's too hot."

"Hurry up or the record will be over." She grasped my hand and pulled me to my feet and I breathed her spicy perfume. We began to dance. "Is this the way you hold somebody? Way out here?" She asked, her voice rising.

I held her somewhat closer.

"That's better," she said. A moment later she turned inside my arm so that we were dancing much closer. Now the only sounds were the soft music and the sweeping hush of our footsteps on the linoleum. "Isn't this better?" she asked.

"I guess so." Actually it felt strange to be dancing so close with Gina. In the bakery she was always giving me a pat here or as shove there, but now in her bare arms and in the haze of her perfume I was afraid I might get hard and embarrass myself. As soon as the record ended I went to the bathroom and washed my heated face and neck with cool water. Gina had made herself another mint julep, now she put a record on and we began to dance. "How come you're not out with that girl?" she asked me.

"What girl?"

"The one you go swimming with," she said.

"If you mean Judy, say Judy. That's her name, you know."

Gina smiled. "The one you write letters to isn't named Judy," she said.

"The one I write letters to is just an old high school friend."

"You have lots of girls," she said.

"I don't have lots of girls and you know it," I said hotly.

She looked at me. "You're a handsome boy. Did your mother ever tell you that?"

I didn't know what to answer. We just danced and listened to the music and I began to sweat where our cheeks touched.

"What's Judy like?" she asked.

"She's all right."

Gina took her cheek from mine so she could look at me. "I hope you're being careful," she said.

"What do you mean?"

"When you're out with her. At night, I mean. I hope you're careful when you, you know."

"Oh. We don't do *that*," I assured her, telling the truth.

"Ho, ho. I'll bet you don't."

"We don't. We really don't."

Whenever a record ended, Gina would play the other side or take a fresh one from the stack on the table, some Benny Goodman and Les Brown, but mostly Glenn Miller — "Moonlight Cocktail," "In The Mood," things like that. She made another drink and we played some of the records two or three times.

Then she stumbled, caught hold of me to keep from falling, kissed the side of my neck. I strove for a grown-up tone and asked her was she drunk. "I don't think so," she said. She seemed about to laugh, then kissed me, darting her tongue into my mouth. I pulled back but she grabbed my belt buckle. "What's in here?" she asked, smiling. She started to stroke my groin with her other hand and I broke away, frightened.

"What? Do you think I'm drunk?"

"I guess so." I didn't know what was going on.

She stood alone in the middle of the kitchen and glanced about with a frown, as if she had a headache. "I think I'll go to bed now," she said.

Next morning I was awakened by Arianne shrieking and sobbing as if she were being beaten in the kitchen. She was getting her hair brushed. I showered and pulled on a fresh pair of whites. The kitchen linoleum felt pleasantly cool to my bare feet. "Today is Sunday," Arianne explained. "And your hair looks beautiful, beautiful, beautiful," I told her. The sound of church bells came drifting from Our Lady of Good Voyage. Gina brought me a bowl of strawberries and a pitcher of cream and seated herself on the other side of the table, so I could no longer avoid facing her. "Are you mad at me or are we still friends forever?" she asked. "Friends forever," I said, shovelling in the strawberries. "Then why don't you smile? — Not *that* way, Nicolo. That's a smirk. — Now tell me all about calculus. Isn't today beautiful? Do you want to go see the blessing of the fleet?"

11

Now we can return from the past and pick this up at Thanksgiving. By then my mother was recuperating quite well and we were able to bring her out to our house for Thanksgiving. Morgan Kathleen, dark and sullen, refused to take part in childish festivities, so it was good Nina and sweet-tempered Nico who perched side by side on the kitchen bench, as they had every Thanksgiving morning since they were little, and to please their nana, who sat against a stack of pillows in a ladder-back chair, they strung cranberry necklaces for the turkey.

We had two guests to dinner. One was Felix Stout, Nina's jovial friend, and the other was Finley Fisher, Maeve's graphic artist. Both young men were in their thirties, Fisher being the thin, pencil-shaped artist, and Felix the wide one who pulled the cork from the wine bottle with his teeth and strolled around the table to pour each of us a glassful. My mother was seated at the end of the table, opposite me, two hard pillows at her back. Maeve had changed from her kitchen clothes and came to the table in a black jersey top and a long skirt made of velvet patches. Nina looked beautiful, flushed and serene all at once. Nico looked detached, amused, a cool thirteen. Morgan Kathleen, dark and pretty, came downstairs in one of her nana's 1925 dresses (thin white cloth, no hips, droopy sash) with her face made up like nana at eighteen in the brown photo that was pinned to her bulletin board. When our dishes were loaded and we were ready to eat, we looked to my mother. She took up her glass and in a raspy voice said, "Let's give thanks because the family, because all of us here —" She faltered, thinking about dad, and her gaze zigzagged across the faces watching her. "Because we are here, together," she began more strongly, then paused. "*La famiglia!*" she said confidently.

After dinner the cloth was stained with pale lemon Asti and littered with the torn hulls of roasted chestnuts and the silver foil from Italian candies. We lingered a long while over coffee, talking of this and that. There's a delicious Italian nougat, called *torrone*, that comes in miniature blocks about a half inch by one inch by two, jacketed in what we kids used to call paper ("Watch me eat paper!") though we knew it was only egg wafer, further wrapped in silver foil and packed into small cardboard boxes, each box decorated with a colored portrait of a notable Italian such as Verdi or Orlando Furioso or Pythagoras. These candies come only at Thanksgiving and Christmas, so that eating them brings to mind all those earlier Thanksgivings and Christmases that are lined up from here to childhood. That is why — as the table talk drifted and Morgan Kathleen phoned a friend, and while my mother talked to Fisher and Maeve poured him another coffee, and Nico watched Felix demonstrate how to crack walnuts in the crook of his arm and Nina laughed, distracting and bewitching him — I sat there with a dozen or more empty *torrone* boxes and worked on the miniature Stonehenge I had begun when I was six, listening to everyone around me now but hearing my father and my uncle Zitti argue about politics and the nature of truth. Still later in the day Mike Bruno and his wife Laurel came over. Mike and Felix and I ended up in the long room off the kitchen, watching football on TV, just the three of us, because Maeve had asked sweet Fisher to build a fire in the living room and he was at it for the rest of the afternoon.

12

I have a few things to say about Felix Stout and they might as well come here. I liked Felix. He wasn't quite my height but just a bit shorter, or maybe it only seemed that way because he was so much wider than I was. Don't get me wrong — he wasn't fat, he was muscular and broad. He presented the world a rumpled face, ginger hair and thick eyebrows, a comfortably big chest, a compact waist and — let's admit it — ridiculous spindle-like legs. He had grown up in Brooklyn but if he had any accent at all it was a slight Irish lilt, a rhythm and a way of talking that made him easy to listen to.

Nina said that Felix had been around and we all agreed about that. He was a gypsy scholar, one of those academics who have no permanent place at any institution, but must survive from season to season by getting a niggardly fellowship here, then a stingy teaching job there and a starvation research grant someplace else. The life suited Felix. He didn't want to stay anyplace. He had graduated from Brooklyn College with a BA and sometime later had taken an advanced degree from Trinity College in Dublin, or at least he had studied there or possibly had merely taken a tour of the place. You never knew with Felix. The biographical passages of his conversation always sounded fraudulent to me. One day he was complaining to us about his sore big toe and he went on to discuss the nature of medication, his belief in a healing touch — himself, he confided, had a certificate in midwifery from a college in Grenoble — the low character of doctors, and so on. Frankly, I didn't believe him when it came to midwifery. Then a month later I talked to an obstetrician who recalled meeting Felix Stout, yes, at a holistic health conference: she was certain the man had delivered babies, was convinced of his intelligence and delighted when I told her that he was writing a book.

Felix's book was about great scientific truths that had turned out to be not true after all, facts which had turned into fictions, into fabulous mythologies. According to him, Galileo's sea-drenched moon, beautiful with pearl-drop archipelagos and snowy mountains, or Lowell's sandy Mars with its broken network of canals and slowly withering cities, are not blunders or blurred observations of nature. They are visions. Yes, said Felix, they are visions which give meaning to our life and these visions are more truthful than the shifting, sliding facts. During that winter Felix scribbled his way through chapters on the peaceful Tasaday, a bogus tribe in the Philippines, and the harmoniously sexual Samoans, another fictitious bunch.

I liked his notions, because they fit so nicely with my own. Furthermore, shortly after we met, Felix exhumed and read my last three articles and my most recent book, out of print a decade, and he was obviously taken by the paper in which I argued that we had actually fabricated the grand contours of our landscape, that the rocky coast of New England had been composed by stony-souled Puritans, the misty Hudson Valley and the gentle Berkshire mountains invented by romantic Transcendentalists, and blah blah blah complete with footnotes. In short, I liked him. I liked him but I didn't like the idea of him liking young Nina. As with many of the people I am fond of, the light of God shone on him through the cracks in his head.

13

One cold gray afternoon I walked around a corner into Harvard Square and in the rush of people saw Roxane Beach who at that instant saw me. Her face lighted up, my heart gave a crazy lurch. I opened my arms. "It's good to see you —" I began.

"I've missed you," she said, giving me a hug.

We went down a side street and ducked into a coffee shop. Her cheeks were still bright from the cold and her hair looked better than I had remembered — still white at the tips, but now with a deep wheat color at the roots, and it stood in thick, electrified brushes that made my palm itch to touch it. "You look splendidly healthy," I said, setting down the tray.

"That's because I've moved into a new apartment." She took a sip of coffee, then cautiously touched the steaming mug to her cheek and the tip of her cold nose. She smiled. "Actually, it's an old apartment, much older than my old place. The last time you saw me I was living in one of those maximum security cells with a steel-jacketed door and steel walls. It was like living in a submarine, except it never went anywhere."

I asked about her new place.

"It's great. It has lots of windows. I think it was an Irish tenement a hundred years ago, but it's been fixed up since then. At least it *can* be fixed up. Anyway, *I* can fix it up."

I suppose I asked one question after another. I felt light headed with pleasure and was happy simply to listen to her talk, to watch her, to glance now and again into her eyes.

"And what brings you to Cambridge?" she said. She lifted her coffee mug in both hands and for a moment looked over the rim at me. "Did you have lunch with Nina?"

"No. I came here to pick up a book at Schoenhof's." I shifted in my chair, uncomfortable now about the friendship between her and Nina.

"I haven't seen Nina in ages," she said, as if to put me at my ease. "What's the big flat book?"

The big flat book was a remarkably dull monograph on Pierre Bonnard (1867-1947), happily illustrated by old sunstruck photos of his unclothed model under a tree in his backyard, and some lavish reproductions of his paintings.

"Didn't he do a woman in a bathtub?" she said, carefully lifting a heavy page. "Yes. Here she is." She paused to gaze at the lush painting, then began slowly to turn the pages. "And here's another. And another. And — Good God! How many women in bathtubs did he paint?"

"Lots and if you spill coffee on that overpriced book I'll break your arm."

"I won't spill a drop, but it must have been an obsession, all these bathtubs."

"Only if you don't like water or women. I love water and women."

She looked at me and smiled, then she closed the volume. "I've begun to wonder if I should keep on with photography. Sometimes it seems impossible. Or maybe I'm not good enough."

"But you're doing well and —"

"Oh, I can make a living at it, at commercial photography, and I do. But I wanted to be a good photographer, a great photographer."

"What's wrong with that?"

"I wanted to be an artist. I wanted my photos to be that good."

"And that's impossible?"

She came forward, opening her hand to me as if to disclose something. "A photograph — if it's any good — has a kind of accidental air about it. The trick is to achieve that accidental look. That's not easy. A good photographer is like one of those Impressionist painters who makes the painting look casual and maybe just the slightest bit hasty. You know what I mean? So the painting itself suggests that the artist dashed it off it while walking from the picnic blanket to the rowboat — and that gives us a lot of pleasure in the scene. I'm convinced we like those paintings because everyone in them seems to be having a good time, the people, the trees, the houses, and the painter. A good photograph is that way. And a good photo has certain everyday things in it, too." Then she interrupted herself and said, "Do you mind if I go on with this a whole lot longer? Because I have all sorts of ideas. And I really want to talk with you."

I didn't mind at all. In fact, I was amazed that I could feel such chaotic pleasure streaming through my arteries and still make any sense of what she was saying. She went on to tell me that a good photographer doesn't try to be timeless in photos. Quite the contrary, she insisted that a good photo has people and random things in it which are wholly caught up in the passing moment when the photo is taken. I was able to grasp that part of what she said, anyway. And somehow it was those little random things floating in time that made old photographs quite different from old paintings. There was more, of course, much more if you count Roxane's repertoire of gestures, for in an exuberant way her hands appeared to unlatch or pluck or fasten or pat whatever she spoke about. And all the while she spoke a small rhythmic shadow at the base of her throat showed where a pulse beat, and I forgot myself in contemplation of it, and of the warmth and scent I imagined rising from within the frayed neckline of her sweater, so that now she leaned forward and in a low voice asked me, "What's wrong? Is there food on my chin?"

"No, no, no."

"So what do you think?" she asked.

"I think you're going to be a great photographer."

Outside on the sidewalk I asked where she was parked. She wasn't parked, she said, zipping shut her collar. She told me how the front bumper had fallen off and now the car was in a body shop run by criminals in East Cambridge. I told her I'd give her a ride home. She said no, it's out of the way, it's not on the way to anyplace and, besides, she wanted to walk. I looked at her. "I take it back," she said. "I'd love a ride."

We slammed the car doors and abruptly felt the close, intimate silence. Roxane turned away and reached for the seat belt, the excessively busy rustle of her rain gear sounding unnaturally loud. I swung about and accidentally bumped her head with my book as I tossed it onto the back seat. The car, sensing our awkwardness, lurched nervously from the curb, stalled, shot along the street, slewed around the corner and at last took us smoothly away. We chatted with forced ease about the traffic and I went on and on about my friend Felix who had said he was coming to my office that afternoon, but by wonderful good luck dumb Felix had not turned up, giving me this free time, so it was providential that we had bumped into each other. "Turn right at the next street," Roxane told me. The car sailed wildly around the corner. "There it is. That one. My place is up in back," she added, out of breath as if she had run all the way. I pulled over to the line of parked cars and stopped, the motor still running. "Number 123 Dublin Street," she said. I cleared my throat, my mouth suddenly dry. "That's easy to remember," I croaked. Her gloved hand was on the door latch. I told her I was glad we had met again. She said she was glad, too. I looked at her. "Give us a kiss," she said. We gave us a kiss. Then she was gone and I was driving away, homeward, my head on fire.

When I got there Maeve told me that boisterous Felix Stout had stopped by in the middle of the afternoon.

"He was supposed to meet me in my office. He was going to drop off something he wanted me to read," I said.

Felix had realized his mistake, said Maeve, as soon as she told him I wasn't at home. The thing he wanted me to read was now on her desk, she added.

"What did he have to say about Nina?" I asked.

"He didn't talk about Nina. He talked mostly about himself. Did you know he was once a translator for the Vatican? How was your day?" she asked me.

I told her how I had bumped into that friend of Nina's, you know, Roxane Beach, and we had had a cup of coffee and I had bought this book with these stunning colors which she should take a look at.

14

I was careful to schedule nothing for the late afternoon exactly one week later, so I could see Roxane. I felt sly as a snake for doing it, but I hadn't been able to think of anything else for seven days and was going to go crazy if I didn't see her. I left my office, drove across the river to Cambridge and ground through the traffic near the Square, then I turned onto the dim side street where we had gone a week ago. Now I drove at a crawl, peering left and right at everyone on the sidewalks. I hadn't phoned Roxane, you understand. I planned to meet her by accident. Because I knew that sooner or later I would tell Maeve about this and I wanted to be able to tell her it happened by accident. And I knew it was twisted logic and knew I was a twisted man, but none of that made any difference to me. All I wanted was to run into Roxane. Traffic was jammed at the sunny end of the street and I came to a halt in the gloom behind a truck. I felt like an old fool for wanting to see her, for driving over here, for going in circles and for bringing myself to this dreary penumbral side street. I could see it was all for nothing. She wasn't here, wouldn't ever be here. Furthermore, I knew this Nicolo very well and knew he was not going to improve soon. The truck ahead of me moved a bit, then halted. I put the car in gear and began to inch forward. Somebody pounded on the passenger window and it was Roxane. The truck pulled away with its eclipse. Roxane slid in and slammed the door as we shot into the sunlight, banging up over the corner curb and down the avenue. "I hope you were looking for me" she said, out of breath.

"Yes, I was looking for you." My heart was hammering so hard I was out of breath, too.

"Wonderful. Why are you scowling?"

"Scowling? Am I scowling?"

"Yes," she said, grabbing the dashboard to steady herself. "And for God's sake slow down."

We bought some pastries at a French bakery run by a Vietnamese couple, then I cut over to Cambridgeport and parked at the first empty place on her street. I followed her up a zigzag stairway and down a hall and there, tacked across her door, was a ragged piece of paper with *Dont go away Ill be right back* in angular handwriting. She pulled down the note and unlocked the door. "In case you came when I was out," she explained, crumpling the paper. She led me inside where a faint tang of fresh paint hung in the air.

"Look around. Tell me what you think of

it," she said, moving behind me so as not to obscure my view. "Well, what do you think?"

It looked like what you might salvage from a dynamited house. There was a sofa, or at least an oak sofa frame with a lilac futon mattress on it, a couple of expensive bentwood chairs, a scruffy black coffee table, or more precisely a scruffy black table with the legs amputated at the knees, and a rug of woven raffia or sea grass or string or something like that. Two housebroken paint cans had made a mess on the newspaper on the floor between the windows, and a big oblong piece of sky, perhaps a tall mirror, leaned crazily in the corner.

"Of course, I haven't had time to put up any pictures," she began apologetically.

"It's nice. It's very nice." I turned and found her watching me, her face open with expectation. "I think it's great. Wonderful," I said. And it was, because this is where she lived.

She smiled broadly. "It's full of light, isn't it? The kitchen is squashed into the wall, but I don't mind. The shower, in there. And over here, my bedroom — come look."

She led me past a stack of open packing boxes. The little room had a shelf with five cameras, a cluttered bureau and a low bed with a heap of fresh unironed laundry resting on it. By the bed stood a square carton with hand slots, the kind of carton that milk bottles used to come in years ago, but this one held a collection of children's books, a doll, some other toys and a kid's big wind-up alarm clock. I picked up a friendly looking ruler and turned it over. *Surprise!* Here was my father's long lost Keuffel & Esser slide rule or its twin brother. It was a marvelous thing (Pat. June. 5. 1900) made of rose-colored mahogany inlaid with an ivory surface upon which rows of meticulously incised numerals marched out of step, jamming together and spreading apart in logarithmic periods. I moved the cursor cautiously a bit to the left, a bit to the right. A diagonal crack had ruptured the crystal long ago, but the hairline still read true. I was swept by a nostalgia born from the tattered coverlet on her low bed and the homey smell of fresh laundry and this antique slide rule. It had belonged to her father, Roxane told me, and he had left it behind when calculators came out. She asked did I know how to use it. I told her my last class at MIT had been a hundred years ago. "But, yes, I know how to use it," I said.

"Now give me your coat," she said. "Do you want espresso? I've got a little espresso machine."

While Roxane put together the coffee I pulled off my tie and walked up and down to take the view from the windows, looking this way and that through the wrought iron branches of a tree and past a yellow tenement, the two of us chatting with an edgy gaiety about nothing much. In my pacing I stumbled against a big galvanized zinc wash tub which contained a mess of audio cassettes, a couple of large notebooks, some phono records, a gymnastics trophy and other loose junk. Roxane picked out a framed photograph. "Here's me and my family," she said.

Sure enough: here was young Roxane Beach (parted lips, hair straight to her shoulders) with her arm around the neck of a younger girl (grin, braces on teeth), and behind the kid sister stood a good-looking woman with a brilliant smile. The man was standing on the other edge of the group, half behind Roxane, with a rugged outdoor face and eyes that seemed to strain past the camera to the horizon. I asked when it had been taken. "That was at Christmas, my freshman year." She stood beside me and studied the picture with deep curiosity a while. "He knows all about computers. I think he's working for a new company now," she told me. She balanced the picture on the narrow window sill where it teetered dangerously, then tried to establish it here or there on the low table beside our mugs and the cream pitcher, then took it with her when she went to turn off the coffee. She asked me did I see my father much. "My father's dead and, yes, I see him all the time," I said. She turned to look at me, to see if I were joking, but said nothing. When she brought the coffee to the table she was still carrying the framed photograph of her exploded family in her other hand.

We ate the pastries straight from the bag and agreed that they had just the right Vietnamese touch, and we talked about what she had been doing at the studio and what I had been up to at the university. When we got to talking about photography she told me about Alfred Stieglitz, whose work she admired, and Georgia O'Keefe, whose independence she admired, and then about Imogen Cunningham, apparently a wonderful photographer I had never heard of. I asked were there any works of Roxane Beach I could look at. "Sure," she said. She pulled one of the big flat notebooks from the galvanized washtub, flipped a few pages, put it back and pulled out another, peeped into that. "This has the most recent stuff," she said. "It's commercial junk," she added. And she was right. I started to ask about her non-commercial work, but as I turned to the very end of the album a handful of loose photographs slid out. They were studio shots of Roxane herself. She laughed. No, they weren't shots of *her* she informed me, but of the jewelry she was wearing. "Would you like my neck? My ear? How about my wrist?"

"This one's nice. I'd like this one," I told her. It was a throwaway shot, taken just as she had turned her head to remove an earring: she was looking sideways at us and just starting to smile.

She showed me an album of her non-commercial work and as I turned the pages she pointed out what she had done well in this photo and where she had failed in that one.

"You're very hard on yourself," I said. "These are fine."

"I had a whole bunch of photos I took of a friend, but I tossed them out a while ago." She spoke as if I knew all about the friend.

I turned to look at her, but she was studying one of the photos and refused to glance up. Anyway, the friend was gone and that was fine with me.

"Well, I like these," I told her.

She jumped up and took the album back to the zinc tub. "Want to hear some music?"

"Sure."

She knelt at the tub as if she were scrubbing clothes and began to shuffle through the cassettes. "How about — let's see — how about some opera?"

"Are you serious?"

"You don't love opera?"

"I love opera. But we're not ready for it. It might inflame us." I joined her at the tub. "Let me take a look."

"Wait a sec." She had grabbed my wrist, sending a wild jolt up my arm and across my chest. "How about — how about something more contemporary?"

"Contemporary, yes, contemporary," I said, massaging my arm.

She snapped a cassette into the player behind the sofa and some rock group began to scream *Oh, she's so fine!*

I don't recall what we talked about. In no time at all, the late afternoon had grown dark and now a solitary table lamp low on the floor gave us our only light, a bright circle on the stringy rug and a larger, dimmer one on the ceiling. I had pulled on my coat. "Have you got everything?" she asked. I said yes, no gloves, no hat. We looked at each other in the half light and silence by the door. She smiled, her fingers just touching mine. I put my hand to her cheek, to her neck, lifting and plowing through that mass of hair which was so soft it startled me. She had slipped her arms under my jacket when I clamped my arms around her. "I'm inside," she murmured. And I whispered to her, half hoping she would not hear, "Oh, kid, this is impossible."

"I don't care," is all she said.

I held her until she relaxed her grip, then I gave one last pat on the back and let her go. Outside her door she said, "I keep thinking there was something else —" I started to say again that I had everything, but she dashed back in and came out a moment later with the photo of herself. "It's the one you said you liked. Give us a —" I kissed her again and again, ate her mouth, her cheeks, jaw bone, throat, and ran out to the car. I paused at the wheel to look at the trembling photo in the glow of the dashboard, my breath making puffs of steam in the cold air. On the back she had written a quick, angular *NICOLO LOVE ROXANE.*

15

I hate sly people, hate liars and cheats and double-crossers, and so does Maeve. So we assume the best about each other, try to assume it even when things don't look that good. Maeve wants to know enough but not too much, and above all she doesn't want to be caught unawares. "Spare me the details," she says. "All I want is no surprises." Maybe I could carry on behind her back if I had the stomach for it, but I don't have the stomach for it, and sneaking around spoils whatever I'm sneaking around to do. Maeve knows this, of course, and plays her own game and more than once has turned her back, not to make it easier for me but to make it harder. It's true I wanted to fuck Roxane, to mount up and gallop, gallop, gallop till she had no breath left except to cry *Nicolo* and lie sobbing on my chest. But this is a fallen world and if I then told Maeve about Roxane she wouldn't see things in a golden light and love Roxane — no, not at all — she would rage and throw something at me or shout some spiteful secret I didn't want to hear, or weep or become majestic and cold.

Then here would be Nicolo and there would be Maeve and over there would be Roxane, not helped by Nicolo and despised by Maeve — everything blown apart. And I confess it crept into my vain head now and again that Roxane looked young and pretty, while ape-man Nicolo looked old and foolish and gross, particularly foolish and gross around a kid half his age, his daughter's friend. Leave it to an ugly man to be saved by vanity. Anyway, I didn't visit or write or call Roxane the next day, or the day after or the next day after that. Or the next, next, next one either. I felt criminal for wanting to get in touch with her and rotten for not doing it. By noon on the seventh day I had a stone the size of a fist in my chest.

I was standing dead in the line at the university cafeteria when somebody tapped my shoulder and here was old Slattery. "Save me a place and I'll make sparkling conversation," he said. As usual, he had mis-buttoned his vest and his chin had a patch of white stubble which he had forgotten while shaving, but I liked Slattery and knew he would talk enough for both of us. I found an empty table, swept away the clotted plastic forks and soggy tea bags, and he joined me with his lunch tray. "Today I met my ten-o'clock for the last time. I kept it down to fifty minutes. I hate long goodbyes," he said briskly. I told him he'd see them soon enough during exam period. "That's not the same. I won't get to talk," he said. We had begun to eat but now he paused to look at me. "Are you okay?" he asked. I told him I was fine, a little tired was all. He looked at me a moment longer and then said, "Sure. You look cheerful and brave, like a man about to face a firing squad."

He talked about one thing and another, about Celtics basketball (good), Notre Dame football (bad), the Church and the Council of Trent (1564). I didn't have much to say, but Slattery was writing an article on the Puritan New England Primer and the Catholic Catechism, so he made up for my silence by giving a restless monologue on the *Catechismus Romanus*, the Deharbe Catechism, the Maynooth Catechism, and the Baltimore Catechism. I was familiar with that last one: it had a blue paper cover and on the inside in heavy schoolhouse print were numbered questions and answers on church doctrine. It was one of the few books I had hated as a child.

"I can still recite it," I said. *"Why did God make you?* Do you remember?" I asked him.

"Sure. *God made me to know him and love him and serve him in this world and to be happy with him forever in the next.* Everybody knows that. Now let me ask you one. *What effects followed the sin of our first parents?"*

"Our nature was corrupted by the sin of our first parents, and —" I hesitated, trying to recall the lines. "No. Wait. Don't tell me. *Our*

nature was corrupted by the sin of our first parents and, and — I thought I had it."

"*Which,*" Slattery said. "*Which darkened our understanding, weakened our will and left in us a strong inclination to evil.*"

"I knew it was something like that," I said. "Especially the part about my weak will and my evil."

After lunch, Slattery went off to the bookstore and I trudged back to my office. I sat there a while, suddenly tired, then picked up my book and lecture notes and headed out to teach this last class. I liked this group and had enjoyed the semester. I shoved my gloomy self aside and jogged into the classroom a bit late, the students deep in a hubbub of conversation, and as I turned to close the door I spied my father in the hall. He had stepped from an unlighted classroom of empty desks, his long black winter coat over his arm and his fedora in hand, and he was looking around. I tried not to believe it was him, but when he turned fully my way I saw that he was my dad, for sure, and I knew he would explain what was going on and why he had pretended to die. My book had tumbled in the air and my file folder of notes spread out like a bird, each loose sheet wheeling and gliding. He saw me and smiled as if to say, *Ah, there you are!* and gave a little wave, the same as he had once from the crowded sidelines at my high school track meet. Some kid in the front corner seat crouched over and began scrabbling around to pick up my papers. I turned to the class and said, "Excuse me a minute," and ducked out the door. A round student huffed and puffed past me, her loose bootlaces whipping the floor, and a pair of lovers who had been strolling down the corridor now stopped to lean against the wall, huddling together beneath the radiance of the overhead lights. There was no one else. I walked all the way to the stairwell and peered up and down, then walked back up the hall. It was terribly lonely except for the couple leaning against the wall together. I went back to my classroom, thanked the kid who had gathered up the scattered papers, and got on with my teaching.

I can't recall what I said, exactly. I suppose I summed up the course and showed them how far they had come, told them I hoped they had enjoyed our meetings, told them I certainly had. I must have said the things that I usually say on the last day of class. I know that I told them I was sorry we had done our classwork so well and had spent so much time on the subject, because the subject we had studied wasn't the real subject at all but only a way to it, and I tried to explain that everything I had taught them was less important than the things that I had never quite gotten to further down the road. I went on talking, trying to catch up on what I had left out, trying to reach those important truths that lay just beyond or above the course itself. I knew that some of them had come to school on borrowed money and had pawned their future to pay for time here and now, and I knew that a lot of others had been working at minimum wage twenty or thirty hours a week to earn their keep and had been getting up groggy to come to class. I said that they were better than they thought they were. And that was about it. It was time to stop lecturing. They had trusted me to know what I was talking about, to be fair and charitable and to like each one of them, no matter what, and to keep their secrets. And they had trusted me to not lead them astray, but to give them a little wisdom and a hand up in the world. Why else are we old men here in the academy, this land of the unaging young?

After class I dragged myself back to my office to look through my mail. There was a memo from my chairman and another from the dean, there were two committee reports, plus the result of balloting at the last departmental meeting, a picture postcard from a former student, a couple of requests for letters of recommendation, a handsome and informative schedule of last week's cultural events, many pretty advertisements from text book publishers. I tacked the postcard up on my corkboard, laid the recommendation forms beside my typewriter, tore up the other junk and threw it into the wastebasket. The memo from my chairman had been about the dean, and the dean's memo had asked me for yet more information pursuant to a meeting to consider my promotion. I began to work on that. Some while later Michael Bruno stuck his white beard in the door and asked was I going to join him and Slattery at the Espresso before heading home. I said I hoped so. I worked for a couple of hours, then threw everything into my briefcase and went to the Espresso.

Mike and Slattery were at a tiny table with a load of stained cups and Mike was discoursing on reality and saying that orgasms take place in the head. I took their orders for coffee, then went to the counter and by the time I returned they had been joined by Cohen, and now Slattery was talking Irish politics. I once jotted on a paper napkin a list of things that came up in conversation with these same four friends over coffee one afternoon, and months later I found the napkin in a seed catalog where I had used it as a bookmark. It was a dumb list, but reading it over I remembered how happy we had been that day, so pleased with each other and the clever things we had said. Now I sat there silent as a gravestone. If I had been alone with Mike I might have rolled the boulder from my chest and told him one thing or another. Mike Bruno (three wives, two mistresses, seven children) would have understood how this aging ape, though in love with the sweaty goddess at home, still lusted for young and mortal Roxane. And Mike would have understood that it was more than lust. After a while I said I had to get home, said good-by to everyone and left.

16

But instead of going straight home I knocked on Roxane's door. "Hi, come on in. I'm putting up some pictures. Tell me what you think," she said. She had smiled and walked back across the room as if it were natural for me to be there, as if I had not been keeping away for the past week. My heart was banging and I felt fractured, all ajar. She paused at the futon sofa where a dozen or more huge photographs and posters lay this way and that. I shut the door. Roxane took one of the posters and held it against the wall with her fingertips, leaning back somewhat to get a more distant view. "I'm glad you came," she said, not turning to me.

"Why?" My voice came out harsher than I expected.

"You're old and wise," she said after a moment's hesitation. Now she turned and looked over her shoulder at me. "I value your opinion. And you."

"It looks fine. I'll take you out to the house for dinner," I told her. I didn't mean it to sound like an order, but it came out that way.

She laid the poster slowly and gently over

the back of the sofa, as if something might break. "What do you mean?"

"I mean, please come out to the house for dinner."

"Am I expected?" She sounded a lot like Nina being difficult.

"Do you have a phone?"

I phoned Maeve and said, "You remember Roxane Beach? I'm calling from her place. Is there enough for one more at dinner?" And Maeve said, *Yes. Pasta. How soon do you think you'll get here?* And I said, "We're leaving right now." I hung up and said to Roxane, "You're expected."

"You didn't give her much chance to say no," she told me. Her cheeks were flushed now.

"It happens all the time. If there's not enough food, she says no. Where's your coat?"

"I've got to change my clothes," she said, starting for the bedroom.

I caught her wrist. "You look fine."

"Let me comb my hai —"

"Your hair is beautiful."

"My teeth. Let me brush me teeth or something. You don't have to let go my arm if you don't want."

In the car I caught the scent of Roxane's bath soap and minty toothpaste. We drove from gaudy Cambridge to the highway and the car began to speed up, tearing blindly into the dark countryside because I felt so miserable and so wildly happy at the same time. I knew well enough that by taking Roxane out to the house, by bringing her and Maeve and me together, I was giving everything away. Because Maeve would know at a glance, and Roxane would see that Maeve knew, and everything would be over before it started. The clever married couple had danced this dance before, more than once before. And Roxane would see that, too — she was no dummy — and would be revolted, disgusted with me. I understood all this, but it didn't matter because I wanted so much to be driving homeward through the dark with Roxane and I was.

Patches of snow gleamed along the side of the road and across the fields you could see distant window lights. I led Roxane through the narrow room to the steamy kitchen. "Maeve, you remember — " I began. But Maeve was already saying, "Roxane, it's good to see you. The kids have already had dinner, so it's just us three now. Nicolo will take your coat. Brush Calico off the bench. She likes to nap in the warmest spot in the house." We ate pasta *conchiglie* (little sea shells) with tomato sauce plus mushrooms and drank a bottle of wine. Our table talk, which had been much too lively, relaxed a bit. Then Maeve washed the dishes and Roxane volunteered to wipe them, seemed relieved and happy to wipe them, moving with a responsive attentiveness to Maeve's slightest gesture. I made the coffee. I could see Roxane trying to please Maeve, and could see Maeve giving her just enough approval and just enough of herself to keep Roxane at her side. We had taken a tour of the house and were sitting around the kitchen table with our coffee when Rover came in with a constellation of snowflakes melting on his back. Roxane rubbed his patient old head, chafing his black fur. She sighed. "It's snowing. It's snowing and I should get back to my place. And I do *like* it here," she added. It was on the tip of Maeve's tongue to say something smart about Roxane's desire to stay a bit longer, but something changed her mind and she merely smiled and rinsed out a cup. "Right," I said. "I'll get our coats."

It was a soft, windless snowfall that melted flake by flake where it touched the dark roadway. I had to concentrate on driving and that may be why we talked so little, or perhaps we shared the same melancholy feelings or maybe Roxane was tired. "Oh, I would love to fall asleep now," she murmured. The car was humming drowsily along the highway. "I haven't done that since I was a kid," she said. "Sleep if you want. I'll wake you when we get there," I told her. She said no, she couldn't, she was too old. "But it's not too bad driving, is it?" she asked. The snow whirling in the headlights made it dizzy, but not too bad. We talked about whether snow was really deeper in the country than in the city or did it only look that way, and about her car which she was going to rescue from the body shop on Monday. The drive seemed much, much shorter than it had been and in no time we were making the turns that brought us into Cambridge and down the wet black side street to her apartment. I parked, cut the engine, the wiper blades. It was so quiet in the car. Up by the streetlamp you could see the big flakes drifting endlessly down into the dark, and along the curb each car had a thin blanket of snow on the roof. I turned and found her watching me. I must have looked a hundred years old. "Here we are," I said, my tongue like wood. "Yes," she said. We got out and walked down the street to her place without a word between us, and then stood in the falling snow while Roxane searched for her keys. "Found it," she said. Upstairs at her apartment door she asked in a diminished voice, "Did I say thank you for inviting me out to dinner?" And I said, "I think so, yes, many times." Everything was going to silence. I took off my glove and touched her hair, wet from the snow. I wanted to speak, to tell her how much I liked her and how impossible it was: she nodded her head, she understood. A quick kiss on the mouth and we said good-night.

On the way home I kept thinking of Roxane and wondering how long it would be, the getting over her, like a slice to the heart. It had stopped snowing at some point and I hadn't noticed and when I got out of the car the stars were small and bright. Some of the light from the hall came with me into the bedroom. Maeve was half asleep, her hair across the pillow like a spill of ink. "Is it still snowing?" she murmured. I whispered no, it had stopped. I undressed in the dim room, washed, went downstairs and rattled the doors, then up to bed where Maeve lay deep in slumber, like the wooded hills outside.

17

While this was going on, other things were going on too, and Morgan Kathleen who used to leave a note to say where she was going and who was driving and what hour she was coming back (and at the promised hour I would hear automobile tires crunch on our gravel drive and against the minor throb of the running motor hear a car door slam and the shouted, "Goodby! See ya!" then the hush and thud of our front door as Morgan stepped inside, and I would come stockingfooted from the study, a pen in my book holding my place, and ask if she had remembered to — "Yes, daddy. I locked it and turned out the lights. Kiss, kiss. Night, night." — and she would swing off to her bedroom, her door falling gently shut behind her) now left no notes when she went out and said nothing when she came in. Now there was the same scraping hush as our front door opened, then the creak of a stairway tread, but by the time I had padded out from my study, the upstairs hall was empty and dark, save for a line of light beneath her bedroom door. One Saturday she stumbled and crashed while mounting the stairs, then brushed past me, murmuring "Goodnight, daddy," with her face averted, her hair sour with smoke. Another night I was awakened by Maeve coming back to bed, for something had drawn her from sleep and she had risen to find Morgan sitting on the floor of the bathroom, pale and nauseated.

"She's drinking a lot, she's drinking too much," I said. Maeve stopped typing, shifted her eyeglasses to the crown of her head, looked at me. "I know," she said neutrally.

"I thought you talked to her about that."

"I did."

"I'll talk with her tonight."

"No, don't!" she cried. "I'll explain later. Don't say anything to her *now*."

I had started to turn away, but then I knew. "She's missed her goddamn period again."

"I was going to tell you later."

A day or so after that, Maeve told me the crises had passed, the tide was flowing. "Look at the good side," she added. "This one gave her a real scare. She'll be more careful in the future."

But Morgan was not more careful. One Friday night the front knocker went *thump thump thump* and I reached the hall as the big door swung in and Morgan Kathleen stumbled past me, falling. "Maeve —" I began. Out in the dark, an automobile scuttled across the gravel and rattled onto the road. Maeve caught her beneath the other arm and we steered her toward the stairway, this swift daughter so heavy now, sluggish, shambling, veering toward the newel post. Morgan groaned, as if awaking. Her boot struck the first rise, she pitched forward and threw up, splashing on the stair.

The next afternoon Morgan Kathleen sat on the old wooden chest in my study, sat with her shoulders hunched and her hands tucked under her thighs, her face half turned away, looking down. Maeve stood by the doorway, a shoulder against the jamb and her arms folded. "Why don't you just quit it, Morgan? Why don't you just give it a rest?" I said.

"Quit what?" she asked.

"Drinking! Drinking! For God's sake, what have we been talking about for the past half hour?"

"She thought you meant — " Maeve began. "Look, you can have all the romance you want. But you have to be a grown-up and take responsibility for what you do," Maeve told her. "You can't be responsible and drunk at the same time."

Morgan flushed and looked sideways at me.

"Romance?" I said. "I think you ought to slow down before you have a bad accident. Take one step at a time. That's all. Take one step at a time."

"You'll enjoy it a lot more, believe me," Maeve added.

"Okay. Okay," Morgan said, hurriedly. "No drinking." She lifted her head, the color still high in her cheeks, and her boot heels thumped softly against the chest as she began swinging her legs just a bit, rather like a young child. She sighed and blew the hair back from her forehead. "Okay."

18

I tried not to think of Roxane. I didn't bring her up in conversation and Maeve didn't say a word about her, and even after Nina got home and I kept expecting or maybe hoping that she would say, "Oh, I bumped into Roxane in the Square the other day and —" her name never came up, not even once. I've never much cared for limp and melancholy people, in fact I can't stand them, so whenever I caught myself brooding over Roxane I went out and split wood or looked for something else to do. At this season of the year there was plenty to do and I got around to enjoying it.

We put the tree up a few days before Christmas. My mother had phoned early that morning to say that she had made *strufoli* and *pizzelli* for us, and to announce that she had decided she was well enough to take a plane trip to Washington, DC, to spend a few days with my brother Rafe and his family. She was scrupulous about spending alternate Thanksgivings and Christmases with Rafe and with me, and was deeply satisfied now at being able to carry out this trip for which she had, apparently, bought a secret ticket a month ago. By the time I drove back from my mother's, Maeve had brought the boxes of lights and ornaments and cold air down from the attic. So I tramped out and sawed the lower branches from the tree and trimmed the butt end, then lugged it into the house and held it upright in the stand while Nico dived under and turned the screws to fix it in place. Fortunately, Maeve and the kids did all the rest. They strung the lights and draped the fancy garlands of silver and gold. They cautiously lifted each ornament from its frayed cardboard niche — "Oh, remember this?" — and hung it here or there — "Not *there*, dummy. We already have too many exactly like it over there" — until the tree was filled with apple-red globes and gold ones and green ones and translucent blue stars, and a little ceramic nest with three turquoise eggs in it, and a wizened seventy-five-year-old glass Santa Claus from Germany, and a jointed wooden bear (which no one liked), and a miniature trumpet that really worked when you blew through it, and a little wood seagull, and enough glass bells to furnish a glockenspiel, and — "Watch out! Watch out for the edge, it's sharp!" — dangerous sheetmetal roosters from Mexico, and an intricately painted Roumanian egg, and frosty globes with a window through which you could spy a snow-covered cabin and snow-covered pine tree, and in this blue one — "The Virgin Mary, herself. See?" — and more red balls and bells and at the very top of the tree an angel, shaped like the weather vane on our shed, blowing a trumpet. Maeve took the pine boughs I had cut from the tree and laid them along the fireplace mantel and on the big shelf in the hutch, so the next day when everyone (except for Morgan Kathleen who had left early to go skating with Kevin) was busy decorating the Christmas cookies we breathed the scent of fresh-cut pine.

It was good to have the proper number at dinner now that Nina was home. Other family tables had four, which is one to a side, square and all boxed in; or they had three, which is an only child — or none, which is worse. But we made five, which is never neat, though star-shaped and plenty. Of course, the Nina who dwelled at home was not precisely the same one I had lunch with in Cambridge. That one strode off to class at nine in the morning, devoured a bowl of salad for lunch, argued past midnight, then went places and did things I would never hear about. The Nina at home slept under a *mille fiore* quilt on which a lady with flowers in her hair greeted a white unicorn. Maeve, faithfully following Nina's design, had sewed it ages ago.

Our Nina's room was no ordinary room, but an enchanted chamber where some early cartographer had hung his maps of the Hobbit's Shire, of fabulous Narnia and distant Prydain. And as you looked around, you saw that it was also a haven for speckled fawns and snowy seabirds, playful dolphins and dreamy Botticellian women, a cozy room whose walls opened onto endless savannas and forests of golden bamboo. The long bookcase (one of my earliest constructions — I did better on the headboard) held her high-school yearbooks, private journals and a microscope. It held also her mother's broken old Oz books and Nina's own collection of novels about outgoing youngsters who venture to a distant realm — oh, you know, a land whose inhabitants live in tree tops and speak a musical and curiously written language, a faraway kingdom of encounters and swordplay, a world of hostile witches and wizards and friendly beasts, of ships and mirrors and rings, flight without wings, and other acts of magic. Her door still displayed the sign she had elaborately lettered when she was fourteen. *I will now swear by my gratitude for this fair new land, that here beneath this green and gentle sky, I shall not lift my hand to any other, except to offer love and joy.*

After Christmas we loafed around. I had no classes and Maeve put aside her editing and we visited Laurel and Mike Bruno and other friends, then Laurel and Mike visited us, and one blue-sky day Maeve and I trooped through the woods on snow shoes (watched by a patrol of white-tail deer), and on another all of us (except for Morgan Kathleen who went out to the Mall with Jenny) sprawled in front of the fireplace, reading or working on a jigsaw puzzle or playing with the cat. One Saturday, Maeve and I attended the wedding of Charlotte Aline Squires, my former student, and Thomas William Oesterman. We had an especially happy time at the reception and stayed longer than we had planned. And I don't know why, just as we drove away in the darkening afternoon, Roxane came to mind and it felt as if my heart were being squeezed in my chest.

One morning Finley Fisher stumbled through our door, hauling a big black portfolio, to show us an alphabet he had designed. He had drawn it up almost a year ago, but only yesterday had received a letter from *Visual*, the graphics journal, notifying him that his was one of six designs the magazine planned to reproduce in its next issue. I had never seen him so talkative. Nina said, "Oh, let's see!" and swept her text books from the kitchen table. Fisher unzipped his portfolio, explaining that he hadn't designed a whole type font, merely a decorative alphabet, something fluid like *art nouveau* but not too fancy, and, well, here it is. I didn't know what I thought of it, but Maeve said it was wonderful, and maybe it was.

And, of course, big Felix Stout stopped by one morning with his skis half out the window of his little car, a white VW that resembled a giant sugar-candy egg. He was on his way to ski the headwall at Mount Suicide, he said. He came in to admire passionately our tree in the livingroom and the creche in the kitchen, and we asked him did he want breakfast. Maeve was handing him a plate of scrambled eggs when Nina came downstairs with her drawing pad and colored pens and books. I was getting used to those damn books: the thin one was *A Modern Japanese Reader* and the fat one was *Obunsha's Essential Dictionary*. Felix began a discourse on Japanese calligraphy and hieroglyphics. "*Kanji,*" Nina told him. "The characters are called *kanji*. Remember?" She sat on the bench across the table from him, flipped open her reader and began turning the pages as if he weren't there.

"Like this," Felix said, stabbing at something on a page.

"No. That's *katakana*. And that's *hiragana*. You have a memory like a sieve, Felix." She opened her drawing pad. "Like this. This is the *kanji* for man," she said, making two little strokes with her pen.

"Simple. I could have guessed that. What's the *kanji* for woman?"

"Like this."

"It doesn't look much like a woman."

"I hope not. Look, here's the one for child." She swung the pad around so he could see. "It looks like a child, doesn't it? I mean, if you use your imagination."

"Do you ever go skiing?"

She laughed. "No."

"Draw me the *kanji* for *yes*."

"I like crosscountry skiing but not downhill," she told him.

"I meant crosscountry. I hate downhill. Macho madness."

"All right," she said briskly, scooping up her books and pens. "But I want to be back here for lunch."

They returned a few hours later and we all had lunch, and it seemed to me they were playing footsie under the table, but when lunch was over Felix left for Mount Ejaculation, or whatever it was, in New Hampshire.

19

I suppose the snow that fell that winter was no different from the snow that fell in winters before, whether it sifted down as if from a gently tapped flour sieve or came like crushed diamond driven at a slant or, what I liked most, floated here slowly in blossoms and loose petals, and I don't know why I liked it again after so many years of not liking it, welcomed it (Rover coming in from the dark afternoon with snowflakes on his back, Calico placing first this paw hesitantly and then that one down and this other up, shaking it) took pleasure in it with Nico and Morgan Kathleen, marveled at the way it broke the sky, which had seemed like iron, so there was nothing there, only this foreground of houses and black trees, barns, hills and around us a milky blue space, luminous and palpable, marveled at the way it filled the empty trees so that by morning there was a precarious fragile replica, a dazzling white tree within each black one, as if the two parts had fallen loose from each other, and not only here but down the road at Buttrick's Corner and Simonds' and throughout all of Hosmer's woods — each branch, each twig — from Wayland Marsh to the Merrimack, and I wondered at the snow itself, that common water should make these studious crystals to simplify the world to snow.

I had showed Maeve the photo that Roxane gave me. "Oh, yes, that's her," was all she said, glancing at it and handing it back at the same time. I knew she wouldn't turn it over and read the jagged note or say *Why did she give you this?* — that's not her style, thank God, not my Maeve. I put the photo on a bookshelf in my study, disguised it amid a jumble of innocent snapshots of friends and former students. Now in January I took it down and cautiously turned it over and, like a monk in a scriptorium, I read and re-read her lovely angular handwriting *NICOLO LOVE ROXANE*. I was humiliated by my own adolescent behavior and hid the photo in a box of old letters. Still, whenever the phone rang I had the lunatic notion that it was Roxane, wanting to talk with me.

Maeve has a theory about chance meetings, those lucky encounters that you secretly long for. She says you just head to where you think the other person might be and it doesn't matter when you get there — there's no such thing as early or late — you just go there and, if it's meant to be, the other person will turn up, will just happen to be passing through that precise spot at exactly that moment. I tried it. I drove to the university, ostensibly to pick up my accumulated mail, and on the way home I veered over to Cambridge. But when I got to the Square it was desolate and filthy and I knew at a glance Roxane was nowhere nearby. Of course, I turned down the narrow side street where we had spent an afternoon drinking coffee, then went to Cambridgeport and drove slowly along Dublin street, peering at the people on the sidewalks, and watched the blank door to her building as I went past, all the while feeling as if I had soot in my veins.

Maeve is one of the few people I know who actually believes in this kind of madness. She believes that on any day of the year you might step into the next room and meet someone who makes you feel you've been knocked down and have to catch your breath. "Afterward, if you're lucky, you smooth your skirt and comb your hair and say, *What stupidity!* But if you're not lucky, you sell the children and buy plane tickets to Montserrat. It happens all the time," she tells me. Maeve has never made fun of anyone's erotic mania, even when it made the sufferer really comic. In her view, such people are merely unfortunate, just as a woman who is rapt by a holy vision and goes ecstatically crazy is unfortunate, or a man knocked cuckoo by a lightning bolt. Passion obeys itself, she says, and goes wherever it wants to go. "You can't stop it. You can tell yourself he's too old or too young or too ugly or even too stupid, but it won't do any good."

So Maeve would have been fine to talk to, except that she's my wife. As it turned out, she was the one who bumped into Roxane at the evening rush hour outside the Atrium in Cambridge. They paused to say hello — Roxane's hair was longer and she was wearing it down — and ended up having a cup of coffee together. "She's an interesting person," was all Maeve said about it.

We spent a pleasant weekend with the Springwells at their ski house in Vermont, then argued in the car on the way home. "We were all so restrained and nailed down," Maeve said. "I mean, we were all close as ever, but so sedate and — heavy. Even lying on the pillows in front of the fire, drinking wine. In the old days we would have been looser by then and something would have happened."

"In the old days you were younger."

"Thanks, Nicolo."

"Anyway, you didn't always like what happened when we got loose."

"I never liked lolling around on a filthy mattress on the floor in a room full of pot with half a dozen people I didn't know trying to lay me, if that's what you mean!"

"That was nobody's fault," I said at last.

"I liked the way we used to be with our friends." Her voice was calm again. "I liked the way we used to fool around with Jason and Penny. Even the things we wore were prettier. I had a good time when we took off our clothes and swam in that pool. And I liked Penny playing the guitar, still naked. Things like that. We had a lightness in our lives."

"More than twenty years ago."

"I don't feel that old."

"I do."

"You think you're a hundred, Nicolo! You've *always* thought so. That's what drags us down. Our hearts don't have to be all crumpled up like a wad of dirty laundry!" she cried. "We could have more light and space in our lives."

"We're old and ugly! Have you looked in a mirror recently? We're not young and beautiful, Maeve. That's the drag."

When the new semester rolled around I stuck my head in Mike Bruno's office and asked would he have time for a drink after work. At the pub I told him I had a problem. "How long has it been since your last confession?" he asked. I told him it had been ages and ages, and that now I had a problem. He caught something in the tone of my voice and looked at me a long moment, a sad red crescent hanging under each eye. "The body or the soul?" he asked. I told him the soul. He sighed and said, "Well, that's a relief. I'm sure she's beautiful, talented and good. What's the problem?"

"I'm headed for the grave, Mike."

"I think not," he said. "Not yet."

"Then why do I feel like I'm dying. Why do I feel like I'm dying all the time?"

20

When I was a kid we lived for some years in a carriage house that had no backyard, but only a low stone wall with an old burying ground on the other side. We lived on the second floor, over the refashioned horse stalls and carriage bays, and from our back windows we could look into the graveyard and beyond it to a wide meadow and beyond that to the woods. Those woods stretched endlessly northward to a place where snow fell all day and all night, where the quiet water of Hudson Bay had snow falling into it, and across the bay there was a pale blue ice field and that was the North Pole. When Rafe and I looked down from our bedroom window the closest thing was the dull white obelisk erected to the memory of ISAAC HASTINGS ESQ. It stood with a few other gravestones inside a railing made of dark iron pipe, the upper pipe bearing a ridge of sawteeth. The stones kept to themselves in this quiet corner, their shoulders toward us, and I didn't like them. We could see a much nicer monument from our kitchen windows. It was a sturdy rectangular pillar crowned with a fancy stone urn encircled by stone drapery, and from the top of the urn sprouted a stone flame. It stood in the sun and faced our way and at breakfast or lunch or anytime at all we could read *In memory of DAVID FISK*, who died Feb. 14. 1710. aged 87 years. and his Descendants. The monument had been erected by one of his Descendants in 1856 and was surrounded by a family of smaller gravestones, all packed inside an elaborate cast-iron fence of leafy scrolls and points. Like the Hastings place, it had a gate so you could go inside and visit, and sometimes we did.

There were no other real monuments in the cemetery, nothing quite so big or so fancy. Most other gravestones were thick slabs of gray slate with one end jammed into the ground. They stood side by side in short rows, which had gaps here and there, and some rows faced this way and some faced another, and some slates leaned backward and others leaned forward or slumped to the side, so you had a ragged congregation to walk around on the way to the woods. One of the best parts of the burying ground was a big oval space of grass with no gravestones at all. Each spring a cold shallow sea appeared at the far end of it and there Rafe and I would tread cautiously in our rubber boots and float our toy ships, including a white ocean liner, designed to be pulled across a rug on submerged wheels, which listed badly in that miniature Atlantic. During the summer the open area became a playing field, especially good because the gravestones around the edge stopped a baseball from rolling too far when there were only four or five players and no one wanted to chase it.

The gravestones weren't cut straight across like a playing card. The tops were rounded up in a half circle with a smaller half circle on the left and right, like shoulders. The part enclosed by the half circle had a picture cut into it and the ones I liked most showed a weeping willow, the thin trunk standing to the side and the branches curving up and descending over an urn. If you took a sharp stone you could scratch along the old chiseled lines and make the picture show up brighter, white on the dark slate. The ones I didn't like were the ones with skulls cut into them. The very oldest slates were at our end of the burying ground and they all had skulls. I guessed that in the old days stonecutters were all right at carving numerals and letters, though even there they often misjudged the spacing and had to squeeze a letter in above a word, but they were no good at carving skulls. The drilled huge circular eye sockets that took up most of the cranium, then they cut a narrow triangular nose socket and rows of big square clenched teeth. And they gave the skull wings that swelled up left and right, so it looked like the wings sprouted from the neck, except there was no neck because the chin rested on an hourglass. The worst was by a stonecutter who had chiseled away at his slate until the face was only two side-by-side circles on a vertical stem that went down to an empty box. That was his idea of a death's head — two blank eyes, a long nose, mouth an empty slot — but to us it looked more like the key to an old clock. And I couldn't see why anyone had bothered to carve it, because it wasn't even a face but just barely the sign of a face, the way a name is the sign of a person.

At the bottom of the slate, down by the grass, they often put a rhyme, like this:

Stranger, thou who passeth by,
As thou art now, so once was I,
As I am now, so thou shalt be,
Prepare for death and follow me.

Sometimes you had to pull the gravestone up a bit to get at the last line. The underground part of the slate bore a dark moist sheen that quickly evaporated in the sun, and the bottom edge was as sharp as a blade. My cousin Renato switched a couple of slates once. But we never broke anything, at least we never broke a gravestone, never broke the part that had writing on it, anyway. Among the old slates there was a long, sandy stone slab laid flat on a brick base, like the lid on a huge brick box. The lid ran chest high and said, HERE LYETH JNTERRED YE REMAIN OF MR BENJAMIN

ESTABROOK and so on and so forth, and whenever we read it we wondered if the REMAIN were lying above ground in there, in the brick box. It wasn't hard for me and my cousin Melissa to pry out the crumbled bits of mortar at the corner, to wiggle the loosened brick, to remove it. We each took a turn peering into the void of death, then Melissa stood close at my side with her hand resting on mine while we inched our fingers inside. But there was nothing.

In all the graveyard, the stone we liked best was in the sunny middle of the place. It was only waist high, but it was very wide and had been carved to look like six slates joined together side by side: Sarah Childs, Eunice Childs, Abijah Childs, Abigail Childs, Benjn Childs, Moses Childs. They were brothers and sisters who had died about the same time. The slate had tilted back somewhat so you could view it better. It had no skulls or weeping willows, but in the blank above each inscription there was carved a face about as big as your hand. They were lined up, head and shoulders, so much alike as six bowling pins, except that the girls had plain collars and the boys had some button holes. We liked that stone and always gave it a friendly glance when we walked by, amused or maybe just satisfied by the thought that all the Childs had died as children.

As I grew up I played farther from home and the only time I went into the burying ground was on my way to someplace else, to the fields or more often to the woods beyond. I loved the woods and quickly learned how to find my way and how to glide from tree to tree without snapping a twig, so that Indians would call me Eagle, blood brother, the only white man they trusted. But the woods were not endless after all. One trail lead up through steep meadows dense with blueberry bushes and at the top was a bare stretch of gray rock, wrinkled with age. From up there you could look north to where the woods faded into fields, and that was where the Army was building an airbase. I played a lot of baseball in a nearby meadow where we had a real diamond and as many as six players to a side. The bombers would coast over us with their heavy rumbles and if you were any good you could tell a B-25 from a B-24 or a B-19 without looking up. After the war my parents no longer grew a Victory garden, so there was no reason to shortcut through the cemetery to get there and, besides, I was far too old to play among the gravestones.

21

The summer after I graduated from college I took the train to Gloucester to visit my aunt Regina. I had spent two years at MIT and two years at Harvard, had a beautiful diploma and was now twenty-one years old — a young man in a dazzling seersucker suit, white with blue stripes. The train stops on the hill above Gloucester and from there you plunge down any narrow street, catching hold of a gate post here or a fence rail there to keep from falling, till you level off at the wharves. From the crest above the town I could look over the roofs to the harbor, which was cerulean blue with flecks of zinc white for boats, and over the harbor to Eastern Point and over the Point to the horizon line, which had been painted very neatly that day. I pulled off my necktie, opened my shirt and jogged down to my aunt's place. I found her alone in the bakery kitchen, her back to me. The room was small — whitewashed walls with blue trim. I said, "Hi, Gina." She looked over her shoulder and began to smile. I had her by the buttock and breast when she wheeled and slapped my face.

"*Four years of college and you've learned absolutely nothing!*" Her eyes sparkled with tears, then she bit her trembling lip and slapped me across the face again with the other hand. I ran out the door and stumbled down to the harbor where the air stank of fish and diesel fumes.

The buildings along the waterfront were bleached gray as sea salt and half of them were falling down and I walked along feeling low. At the foot of Union Hill a small truck was parked by the curb with an old man seated on the running board reading a newspaper. He had set five rusty buckets of flowers in the narrow strip of shade along the sidewalk — carnations, irises, snapdragons, things like that. I bought a few of each and then climbed the hill to Gina's. My overnight bag was shoved against the kitchen wall where I had dropped it. I went out to the café terrace and when Gina saw me she smiled with relief and said, "Nicolo," and held out her hands. The people at the tables looked up and Gina stood there with my flowers in her arms, smiling at everyone. Then she told Rita, the waitress, to get a scissors and a pitcher of water, and we sat down. There was a steep view over the roofs downhill and out to the blue harbor. Gina trimmed the stems and began to arrange the flowers in the big glass pitcher, moving her head this way and that to see the effect of her work. "You shouldn't run away like that," she said, glancing at me. "I was afraid you weren't coming back."

"I won't do it again."

We agreed that I was going to stay all day today and tomorrow and not go home till Monday. My cousin Arianne, ten years old now, was off visiting her grandmother, Mrs. Campagnia, so I could sleep in her room and not on a mattress on the floor like I used to. Then Gina brought me a platter of food, which was just in time because I was starving. "Did you eat on the terrace when you visited Palermo?" she asked. She meant the old villa in Sicily where her mother was living. I said yes, we ate there every day. Gina grew pensive and sat in the sun not talking, but just looking across the roofs to the harbor, and I suppose she was remembering the old villa with the blue-flowered tiles on the back wall. You could sit on that terrace and look over the walled garden and see Monte Pellegrino, which is all one rock but tan like a loaf of well-baked bread, and you knew the harbor was down there at the side of it. Her father had died in Palermo two years ago, the plans for a cargo ship spread out before him on the table on the terrace. She looked sad. I touched her shoulder and said, "Where shall we go tonight?"

That evening Gina tossed me the keys to her big convertible and we drove north along the coast. The sun glinted on the hot chromium knobs and made the fake leather upholstery smell good. The steering wheel hummed in my hands and the wind lifted Gina's hair, blowing if forward — this was the way to live. Gina talked about her brother Mercurio, who was coming to Gloucester to see if he could make a zillion bucks freezing fish, and she asked was I going to get drafted, and I said I sure wasn't going to volunteer, and we talked about Korea and agreed it was a stupid war and a dumb way to get killed. She asked did I still keep in touch with that girl I had met in Gloucester four summers ago, and I said no. Then she asked about somebody in college and I said, "No. We went crazy for two years. That was enough. I'm trying to forget her."

"Oh. Well. I hope there were others," Gina said. "Better ones."

"Yeah, yeah, there were others."

But I didn't want to talk about any of that. We just cruised along, listening to the music and not saying much, and I wanted to drive that way forever. Down by Ipswich the road passed across an inlet of glossy black water where there was a shuttered boat house and a flock of small white sailboats sleeping at anchor, their masts bare.

"When you were in Sicily did you go to the beach at Mondello?" she asked me. "Did you go dancing at that place they built over the water? Lo Stabilimento?"

I said yes, and told her how I had been

there with a party of Sicilian relatives I didn't even know.

"If you and I had been there at the same time, we could have gone dancing together."

I laughed. "I still don't dance very well," I said.

"Come on!" she said, pushing my shoulder. "There are some places down the road."

When we had danced in her kitchen four summers ago it had been awkward enough, and the prospect of doing it in public made me sweat. But Gina said, "The one with the lights over the water. Stop when we get there." So I parked and pulled up my damned necktie and we went in to dance. It was a disused boathouse with some tables at one end and a four-piece band at the other. There were open windows with screens, but the inside air was warm and where our cheeks touched got damp. Gina was wearing the perfume from that other summer and the familiar spicy odor made me feel odd, as if I were melting and going tense at the same time. "How many women did you get to know over the past four years?" she asked. Before I could think about an answer, she laughed and said, "What's the matter? Are you still adding them up?"

To hide my embarrassment I said, "What about you? How many men?"

She looked at me and smiled slightly, then slid her arm over my shoulder and I heard her bracelets jingle behind my back, but she wouldn't answer. When the set was finished, Gina plucked at her blouse, slightly pumping the cloth between her breasts to create a breeze. "It's hot in here and I'm sweaty. Why don't we get going?" she said.

So we headed home. Now it had grown dark and I was concentrating on the road when Gina abruptly began to talk about some clown she had gotten involved with during the past winter. At first I couldn't follow her, then I realized she was telling me how rotten it was to be single and, no — she corrected herself — not rotten, but hard and lonely to be single while trying to raise Arianne properly and at the same time to run the bakery and the café, too. Then she told me about this bull carpenter who had done some hammer-and-nail work for her last summer, and how boorishly he behaved in a restaurant, in a bowling alley, in the front seat of a car. And recently she had met a lawyer who came from a fine old New England family with a drinking problem. "Et cetera, et cetera, et cetera," she said, as we arrived home.

Before going up to the apartment Gina walked onto the unlighted café terrace to take a final look around. The harbor below us was black. There were lights trembling across the water from Rocky Neck. The sky was immense. The iron railing around the edge of the terrace was cold now and a thin gleam of water had begun to condense on it. Gina shivered. "Take my jacket," I offered. "No. I'm fine. Really. Feel," she said, putting her warm hand on mine. I desperately wanted to say something, but it must have been unsayable because it never came. The wide constellations, the lights on the water and the scent of Gina's perfume were revolving in a cloud in my head. I broke out with, "Today was the longest day of the year. Did you know that?" I don't know what I expected her to say. She looked at me a moment and then smiled, I could see that much. "Then tonight's the shortest night and I need my sleep," she said.

22

Next morning I went to the kitchen and Gina was seated on a chair with a bowl of cream clamped between her knees, whipping it with an egg-beater. The air was full of sunlight. "Good morning," I said. She glanced up and smiled. Her arms and legs looked dark against the white sundress. "Good morning," she said. She put the bowl on the table and stood up, looking into my eyes. I kissed her mouth and she slid her arms under mine, her hands on my bare back. We kissed again and I tried to get all of her, to hold her, taste her, breathe her. "Oh, you angel," she said. "You angel." She had her hands on my tail, my flanks. "I like you so much," I confessed. "For years and years I've liked you," I said. She ran her hands over my chest, my shoulders, my arms. "That's all right," she said, laughing. We stumbled against the table, against the wall and one thing led to another. I started to unbuckle. "Wait a sec," she said. "Wait. Let me go get —" But I caught her again and we staggered, fumbled and ended up kneeling face to face on the kitchen floor, my pants down on my ankles.

She had her hands on my face and was kissing me and suddenly I felt it coming, tried to wrench away. I came in a mess. "Oh, you're beautiful," she said soothingly. "Yes, you are. Yes, you are." No, I was an animal on my hands and knees, and Gina was kneeling beside me, stroking my neck, my back.

She vanished down the hall and I hobbled to the sink, washed off my hands and pulled up my pants. Then I turned on the cold water and stuck my head into the stream. "What are you *doing*?" Gina cried, coming in. I banged my head on the faucet as I turned around. "Cooling off," I said.

"Sit down. Dry your hair. I'll finish making the whipped cream and we'll have breakfast."

It was Sunday, so the terrace was vacant and we ate out there. The sun was hot. The awning was furled against the house and now when you looked up there was an empty rectangle of zinc pipe-lines against the sky, a blueprint showing where to tie the canvas roof. "Eat," Gina told me. The whipped cream was sweet, silken and heavy, like an exotic perfume, and within the cream the crushed strawberries were pleasingly tart, their tiny pores rasping against my tongue, flooding my mouth. Gina smiled but didn't say anything. The harbor was blue and there was a broad path in the middle that glittered like beaten silver. Everything looked extraordinarily bright, like the way home from the ophthamologist after he had put drops in my eyes. "Want to go in now?" Gina asked. My heart jumped as if in panic and I knew it would be impossible to sound natural, so I just nodded *yes*. Inside, she pulled the twisted linens from her bed, threw them in a corner and took a fresh sheet from the closet shelf. The big glass pitcher with the flowers I had had given her was on the bedside table. She handed me an edge of cloth. I stood on one side of the bed and she stood on the other, the white sheet billowing up between us like a fairweather cloud and then sinking, expiring gently to the mattress. Her tanned arm swept away the wrinkles. I began to tuck in the sheet. She came around to this side of the bed and stood in front of me, waiting. My heart was banging so fast it was hard to breathe. There was a light sheen of sweat on her upper lip and under her eyes and she was trembling. I was almost faint with desire or power or happiness. Gina lifted her hair to show me the nape of her neck and the knot which held her sundress. "Undo me," she said.

How much do you want to know? Gina was thirty-one years old, the most beautiful woman in Essex County, my aunt. At the moment of our embrace I discovered everything I had ever craved was embodied in her and now instead of eluding my grasp it was rising toward me, desiring me as well. She called me her angel and said, "Yes that again do that again do that —" The scalding brush stroke of her thigh upon my hip, the flecks of gold in the iris of her eye, the lemon scent of her hair, the flowers shaking their pollen to the bedside table, the sound of church bells in this window and the sea shining in that one — all broke upon me like a foaming wave. I had not known that I could be so frightened and awkward, brutish, happy and grateful all at once. I lay drenched. Later Gina kissed my ear and murmured, "Get my cigarettes, will you? They're in the kitchen." I stumbled off and when I looked down hill at the placid harbor and the idle fishing boats I thought how odd that the scene out there had stayed the same when everything else in the world had changed. Gina steadied my hand while I lit her cigarette, then she drew her legs up beside her on the bed and sat, exhaling a sigh of smoke. The roll of her belly glistened with sweat and I looked away, confused and embarrassed, as if she were more naked now. "Are you all right?" she asked.

"Me? I'm fine!"

She smiled, knowing more than I did. "So am I. I'm fine, too. I hope you can keep a secret."

"Of course I can."

"Because, you know, we have a big one. And if my sister ever finds out she'll kill me."

"I won't tell if you won't," I promised.

She had put her cigarette in the clam shell on the bedside table and now she turned to me, laughing. "You make me so happy," she cried, opening her arms.

I threw myself on her. I was immensely pleased with myself that morning, but the idea that I was making my aunt happy had never entered my head. I was crazy about her, couldn't get enough of her. That evening I phoned home and told my mother that I was going to stay in Gloucester an extra day, maybe a day or two, actually, to help Regina in the café.

23

The next days were crazy. About mid-morning Gina would leave the café and run upstairs to pull me from bed. I'd go down to the terrace, eat the scrambled eggs or French toast or whatever she had made for me, then I'd go to the kitchen and begin scrubbing pots. After the noon rush, I'd load up a plate and carry it out to the terrace to eat with Gina or Rita or Dominic under the yellow canvas awning. Gina was proud of the terrace and you could see why. The buildings and roofs down hill blocked out messy Rogers Street and the rotting wharves, but the rest of the world was open to view. The light that all morning long had filtered through the canvas seemed to have gotten trapped and to have accumulated there, and by mid-afternoon the air was so thick with light you could touch it, could see it on your hands like pollen or pale yellow paint. After lunch, Gina would go upstairs and a minute or two later I'd follow her. I'd shave and shower, come to the bedroom with a towel around my waist and my hair dripping, because she said she wanted me that way. She would kiss me here and there, all over, as if she were drinking little sips of water. I tried to keep it quiet but could never hold back for long and I'd lunge, making her laugh, then she would begin whispering and her breath on my ear would send me into a frenzy. What I remember most is the yeasty odor of freshly pounded dough that came from her flesh after we made love. Later we would drink espresso at the window right above the yellow awning. This was the lull in the afternoon and almost no one was down there except Rita, who was not visible unless she was watering flowers along the edge of the terrace.

Sometimes Gina would leave Rita in charge of things and we would take off for an hour or two. We drove over to Rockport a few times and strolled around on the jetty with the tourists, and once we bought a pair of identical jerseys, white with red stripes, which we thought was marvelous because they made us look like twins, or at least brother and sister. Another day we visited a museum of some sort because Gina wanted to look at their collection of silver tea pots, I think, and for the first time I saw the old paintings by Fitz Hugh Lane, views of tranquil New England harbors that made you want to weep they were so sad. But most afternoons we drove to Good Harbor beach and played around in the icy surf, then lay on the hot sand and let the sun thaw our bones. "Ah, this is the best part," Gina used to say, closing her eyes. I would watch her as she stood wringing the sea water from her hair, or as she knelt on the towel beside me smoothing oil on her arms, and I'd feel such delight amid all these men and women, because we were half naked and still no one could guess what we had been doing.

Gina's hair was black black black and I had always thought black was night and cool, but when she came indoors from the sun and you put your hands into it and lifted, you could feel the heavy silken heat of the day. I thought she was big — I mean, I believed and remembered her body larger than it actually was. Maybe I did this because she was ten years older than I was or because she was a mother or maybe because I was out of my mind and thought she was a goddess, but it always surprised me to discover Gina was a shade shorter than I. One afternoon she had to pull on her skirt and run downstairs to take care of something, and she forgot her belt on the floor. It was just a narrow strip of white leather and you could see the worn place where it had been cinched again and again. When I closed it to the worn mark I was amazed at how small a circle it made. I was sitting on the edge of the bed studying it, wondering how so much could be inside, when she returned out of breath, stepped from her skirt and stood in front of me with her hand in my hair, filling my vision and becoming the whole world again. Her skin looked pale coffee color by day and cinnamon by lamplight, and the aureoles of her breasts were dark in a fashion I had never seen before. Gina's flesh had a hidden scent, the way honey has a scent — you can begin to smell it but you can't get at it unless the honey is on your tongue — the same with her flesh, her warm skin, which I would begin to breath and then lick and swallow while she put her fingertips on my shoulders, laughing and whispering *Oh angel, I'm melting look at it I'm melting.* We looked very much alike and Gina once went so far as to tell a sales clerk that I was her brother. Genes cascading from generation to generation had given us similar faces, and that was no wonder, but in addition we each had a scar over the left eye — hers from falling on ice, mine from skiing — and we took this as a sign our lives were convergent and linked by predestination. And it was curious, in the idle studies after making love, to recognize a similar curve of eyelid here, or an identical sweep of whorled hair down there.

We lived in the sun, made love in the sun, so that love making hung in the air like sunlight, like the warm scent of Gina's flesh, like her voice singing along with the old opera records. The only times we made love in the dark was when Arianne was in the apartment. Arianne was fetched back from her grandmother's place every three or four days as she shifted alliances among her playmates. On those afternoons the three of us would go for a quick swim, or Gina would take her shopping for sunglasses or some such item, and in the evening we would all play Monopoly until it was time for her to go to bed. As soon as Arianne was asleep, Gina would step out of her underpants and still dressed we would sneak downstairs to the terrace with a blanket to spread on the tiles. We always meant to get down on the blanket, but on the first night Gina was standing at the rail looking down over the black roofs to where lights shimmered in the water and I was standing behind her, my arms around her, and she put my hands over her breasts and we began. After that it was always that way in the dark, me behind her while she gripped the cold iron rail, my hands on her breasts, on her flanks, our mouths open, wordless. It was odd with no sun, queer not to see her face and to do it blind in the dark.

One day I answered the phone and it was my mother. I said I was fine and Gina needed me to work in the shop and I liked Gloucester, everything was fine. She asked to speak to her sister. Gina told her, "Don't be silly," and "No, not at all," and "I don't know. As long as he wants," and "Of course," and "Bye, Marissa." Then she lit a cigarette, sat morosely on the window sill with the phone in her lap. I washed the espresso cups and rinsed out the sink. Gina phoned old Mrs Campagnia and asked how was she and how was Arianne. Then Arianne must have come on the phone, because Gina's voice changed and she asked about riding a bicycle someplace. After she hung up, she lit another cigarette. "What do you think of me?" she asked abruptly. She gave me a half angry, searching look and at the same time she seemed almost afraid. I said, "I haven't been thinking. But I like you so much. I like you more than anyone I know." She sat on the sill a moment longer, watching me. Then she jumped up and crushed her cigarette in the sink and said briskly, "Let's go out for a drive! Where shall we go?" We didn't know where to go, so we drove up hill and roared past the railroad station and kept on as if we were going to the mainland. But, instead, we decided to go down the Dogtown Road to see how far it would go, and when the road broke up we parked the car and walked along the stony ruts to Dogtown Common. Now we were in the middle of Cape Ann and there wasn't a sound, not even the chirp of a cricket. There were bramble hills and dells and huge boulders that rested this way and that, as if God had dumped them here after making the rest of the world, and there were those ancient cellar holes bordered by stunted juniper and apple trees planted in olden days. "Why did anyone ever live here? You can't even see the ocean," Gina said. The ocean was two miles away in any direction, but in this absent village the air was silent and hot and windless. It was interesting to poke around, but the place was so lonesome that I was relieved to get back to the café and to work up a sweat mopping the terrace.

Gina loved flowers, so once at the end of the day I ran down to the old guy with the flower truck while he was putting away his pails and I bought dozens of daisies, carnations, chrysanthemums, irises, everything, and bought them back to her. I took my shower, pulled on my pants and found Gina on the empty terrace. She was in a white sleeveless dress and was seated with her arm full of flowers and was arranging them in two big glass vases. She smiled at me when I sat down. I watched her sorting and choosing, watched her hand and listened to the little jingling of her bracelets. It was the bracelets that started me, because she often wore them naked on the bed and their rhythmic jingling had become an accompaniment to those frenzies. Now on the terrace, when I touched the inside of her knee she opened her legs to my hand and went on arranging flowers, with only a faint sheen of sweat beneath her eyes to show her mind. I felt a dizzy lift, as though in a wave just when it curls over, and I couldn't tell you if it was the hot satin feel of her thigh or the odor of the flowers, for she never let go of the armful even when I knelt and pushed her dress up, knocked over a chair and backed her to the wall. Afterward, when I stepped away, she opened her eyes and we watched as her dress slowly unfurled and all the flower petals drifted down from the wrinkles.

But mostly it was on the bed with the sun in the window. Afterward, Gina would lean back against the heaped pillows, the wisps of hair in her armpits curled now from the damp, and a valley of sweat glistening between her breasts. And in the faint warm aroma of fresh dough that came from her, she would light a cigarette and take the clam shell ashtray from the bedtable and set it on her stomach, right over her deep sweat-filled belly button. Then she would tell me some bit of gossip she had heard from Rita or some wild story about herself. "*Caro*," she said. "You have beautiful legs. Strong legs. Handsome legs. You know about those legs?" she asked one day.

"What are you talking about?"

"Your legs. You inherited them from one of your ancestors. Let me tell you about those legs." She paused to pluck a flake of tobacco from the tip of her tongue. "Your grandfather married his bride on the dock in Boston," she began.

"I know the story," I said.

"I'm going to tell you some things you don't know."

Then Gina told me the story of my grandfather Pacifico Cavallù and how he married my grandmother Marianna and so on.

24

Pacifico Cavallù married Marianna Morelli on the dock in Boston in 1904. In those days, there was a large shed built along the wharf and inside there was a green fence, and on the other side of the fence were the customs men and the immigration men, and beyond those officials was another fence, and on the far side of that were the ragged lines of people coming from the ship. On the morning the *Canopic* came in, Pacifico went to the dock and waited for Marianna to walk down the gangplank and make her way through the long zigzag of fences and baggage to the place where he paced back and forth. As for Marianna, she stepped from the gangplank and wondered for the first time if Pacifico would be there. Not all the young women who disembarked with marriage plans were greeted by their betrothed. Sometimes a man had changed his mind and had left town — or worse, he had already married, had been married for months or even years, but had never found the courage to write home about it — or worst of all, he was already married but to do his duty he married once again, and only a week later would his new wife learn about the other one and her three babies. But Pacifico and Marianna kept their promise and found one another in that labyrinth of desks and fences and gates, and there on the cold dock they signed the certificate of marriage and were legally joined.

Yes, it was only a civil wedding. But that was enough for Pacifico, since he was a rationalist and free thinker who enjoyed calling a priest Mister instead of Father. And it was enough for Marianna, too, because she didn't want to wait weeks and weeks just for a church ceremony conducted by one of those mistrustful Irish priests who, she had heard, hated beautiful women. They took a hack from the dock directly to Hanover street and had a festive five-hour dinner at the crowded table of a family who were friends of her father's, and after that they were put at the head of a parade of guests, steamer trunks and suitcases, and marched around the corner to Pacifico's rooms on Prince Street. They were eager to be alone. The courtship had been difficult, because the Cavallù family came from Palermo on the island of Sicily, where everyone lived like animals, and the Morelli came from Reggio on the Italian mainland, where everyone lived like thieves. They had gone through a year of formal visits, secret meetings, letters, and smuggled notes, and had endured another year and more separated by the Atlantic Ocean.

Now they stood alone in the cold bed-sitting room that overlooked Prince Street. They listened to the clatter of footsteps diminish down the stairway, the voices vanish in the street. In the silence they threw their arms around each other and held tight without a word. "You're here. You're real," Pacifico said at last, almost crushing her in his grip. "Yes. A miracle," Marianna said. She started to laugh, then broke into sobs, then laughed again and began wiping her eyes. "Here. Sit down. Here," he said, pulling up a chair. Then he knelt by the fireplace grate, struck a match and started to ignite the spils of paper and wood that underlay the coal. "I'm lighting the fire," he explained, jumping up to go down the corridor. He returned a minute later with an armful of bottles, a corkscrew and two plain water glasses. Marianna was kneeling at the grate to work the bellows. Pacifico poured the brandy. "For the heart," he announced. She stood up and took the heavy glass. They sipped the cordial and looked straight at each other, but his wide-set eyes appeared to see so much that Marianna glanced away and said, "So. This is your — our — room."

"Do you like it?" he asked.

She looked around. "It's handsome," she began. It was a plain square room, except for where the narrow fireplace cut off one of the corners, and it was not big enough to accommodate two simple wood chairs and a small round table with a fringed shawl, a bookcase, a three-panel folding screen, two steamer trunks, five suitcases, a wooden chest, and a matrimonial bed. "And I love it."

"Would you like to sit down?"

"No."

"Oh."

Marianna abruptly finished her brandy with a huge gulp. Then her eyes brimmed, she gasped as if her throat were on fire and held the glass out to him. But when he set it on the table she said, "No. No. Fill it again." Pacifico laughed and was about to say something, but after taking in her defiant expression he made a straight face and poured her glass more than half full. They talked about the dinner guests for a time, and laughed over the pompous official who had stamped their marriage certificate that afternoon, and Marianna told stories about the crossing. It got to be late. "Now would you like to sit down?" Pacifico asked her.

"No."

"Oh."

"I think I should open my trunk."

"Now?"

"My night clothes —"

"Oh! Yes. Of course. Certainly."

Pacifico crowded her trunks and suitcases against the wooden chest and stood the folding screen in front of them. He went down the hall and washed his face in cold water, then came back and began studiously to poke the fire. At the rustle of cloth behind him he turned and saw Marianna's blue wrapper billow into the hall, the momentary gleam of her naked instep and heel lingering behind like a fading footprint. He pulled out his necktie, put his collar button on the fireplace shelf, poured himself another brandy. Then he stepped behind the screen, stripped off his clothes and put on his robe. He returned to the fireplace, took up his glass and drained it. He went to the small table and pulled the cork from another bottle. And here was Marianna. "What's that?" she asked, holding out her empty glass.

"Asti," he answered, pouring. "For the soul."

"I like Asti," she said. Her hair was piled in a loose black rampart above her brow and her cheeks were flushed. She smiled at him and lifted the glass to her lips. Her head tilted back further and further and you could see her throat work as she swallowed gulp after gulp until the glass was empty. She took a deep breath. "You know, I can still feel the ocean. I can still feel the movement of the ship. All that time we were on the dock, I could still feel it moving up and down. Then it went away. But now I can feel it again, as if the ocean were under the floor, as if the whole room was tilting like this, this way and that way." She held out her glass to be filled.

"Listen," he said. He set their glasses aside on the table and took her hand. "Let's sit down."

He sat her on the edge of the bed, then he crashed to his knees and rolled his head in her lap. Pacifico felt his head become suddenly monstrous, heavy and huge — God, yes, his head was the head of a bull and his brains a tightened muscle, and he groaned for shame. He sat beside her. When he put his arm around her shoulders, she turned her hot face to his and they kissed. Little by little and they were lying wrapped close on the bed with their robes in a tangle and Marianna's embroidered nightdress all bunched and twisted, and they continued to do one thing and another until they were quite disheveled, damp, exhausted, excited, half dizzy and a wee bit sick. Yet the moment never came to do the final thing. Of course, they both understood that they had not seen each other for a year and six months. They understood that possibly Marianna needed a few days to reacquaint herself with him before she could open up to him, understood that if Pacifico did not push ahead and maybe tear something in her, then something delicate might rupture in him, causing his parts to wither, understood that if he rushed her against her will, she might panic and freeze forever. Now Pacifico stacked one pillow on top of the other and leaned back with Marianna in his arms. They began to talk. They talked about the same things they had written about, for as if to know him in that interval when they had been apart, Marianna asked to hear again about his first days in Boston, how he had joined a work crew and been transported to the pine forests of Maine. So he told her about building the road for the lumber men, about swinging the pick and what it did to his hands and arms and shoulders. And he went on to tell how six months later he had returned to the city having taught himself enough English to call himself a contractor, and how he had rounded up Italian work gangs of his own which, for a good price, he delivered by train to his former boss in those same Maine woods, rattling back and forth by rail week after week until the ground froze so hard no one could heave a pick into it, and how by then he had taught himself to read and write English so well he got himself a job in a general store, writing up orders and bills of sale for the Neapolitan proprietor who had no language at all. And Marianna told him again about the intrigues at home, about her eight older sisters and their husbands and children, about parcels of land the size of your foot, about the oranges groves and silk, about her father (the mathematician) and her mother (who never aged), and about herself. "But tell me again about the Irishman. You left that out," she said. So they spoke the old letters back and forth, the sound of their voices weaving finer and finer detail, until at length it was morning, Marianna lay asleep on his chest and the fire was dead in the grate.

The day after their wedding, Pacifico gave Marianna a tour of Boston. They rode the subway from North Station to Arlington Street, walked through the leafless Boston Gardens, looked into the store windows on Boylston and returned to the North End to shop for food. At dinner they discussed everything they had done together. It's true, they didn't talk about what had not happened last night, but now in the bed-sitting room they agreed not to drink brandy or Asti but simply coffee. "Because tonight we want to begin, to stay —" Pacifico hesitated.

"Awake and alert. Of course," Marianna said, flushing slightly. "And we can have a drop of Asti or brandy, later on, in case, well, just to —" she trailed off.

"Relax and keep us warm. Of course," he said, nodding.

When Marianna stepped behind the screen to change into her nightdress, Pacifico picked up the round table and set it down by the fireplace. He scooped more coal onto the grate. And when she went to boil the coffee, he stripped off his trousers and pulled on his robe. The table was just big enough to hold the kerosene lamp, the two cups of coffee and the plate of sweet biscuits. That plate, by the way, was decorated at its center with the Trinacria, the three-legged beast which is wholly three legs and which is Sicily — it's still here, chipped but not broken. They talked of one thing and another and in a while the biscuits were gone and their cups were almost empty. Still, they lingered at the table. Pacifico enjoyed watching her as she spoke — her flushed cheeks, her gestures. He was still amazed that she was so lovely and yet so tangible, amazed that she had left her family and sailed across the Atlantic to be with him forever. All his life he would remember how beautiful, frightened and bold she was. Now she was telling him about when she was a girl and how she used to daydream about the babies she would have, how many, what their names would be, what they would do as they grew up. When she stopped and looked full at him, he lowered his cup so gently to its saucer that it made no sound at all. He put his large hands over hers on the table for the reliable pleasure of assuring himself that she was actually here in his room. She smiled and looked into his eyes and when she pressed her pointed nails ever so slowly but deeply into his palms, he smiled back. He sensed that this talk about babies was her oblique way of suggesting that they leave the table for the bed. Now Pacifico had a better idea. He took the coffee pot from the grate and filled her cup, then he lit one of his little cigars and waved aside the cloudlet of blue smoke. He laughed, because he was so happy.

"Let me tell you something about my mother and father," he said. "After all, our children are going to be half Sicilian and you don't really know what that means. No. No. Let me go on. I'll tell you a secret about myself, about my father, something that's been in my father's family for a long time — forever, I think."

Then Pacifico told her about his father, Angelo Cavallù, and his mother, Ava, and their wedding night.

25

The first time Ava saw Angelo naked was on their wedding night (11 May 1860) when he strode into their bedroom, accidentally revealing to her startled eyes that from the waist down he had the hindquarters of a horse. Now Angelo was no brute. He was a miller and this was in his house in Carco, Sicily. He had knocked gently and he had thought he heard her whisper *Come in*, but when he opened the door the room was ablaze with candles and Ava was still on her knees in prayer at the bedside. She lifted her head and saw — Angelo was wearing only the fancy shirt he had married in — saw those supreme flanks, hocks, fetlocks and horny soled feet. The blood drained from her face. For a moment she wavered and flickered, then she murmured the last words of her Hail Mary, blessed herself and stood up. "Amen," Angelo said, taking her cool hand in his. "I have something to tell you."

"Your legs —" she began.

"Remember," Angelo broke in. "God created horses, too. In fact, horses are among the most noble of God's creatures. Horses aren't soaked in blood. They don't have fangs or claws. They don't kill and they don't eat other horses. Horses are peaceful, more peaceful than men, not cowardly like sheep or stupid like oxen, but serene and powerful. God created horses just to show us what He could do in the way of power and beauty, and when He finished, He admired His handiwork. He admires horses. Horses have strength and grace and intelligence, horses have courage and endurance, horses have fidelity. Besides, I'm not wholly, not —"

"Your bottom half —" she began again.

"There've been other unions, but they were horrible mismatches and produced mongrel beasts. Harpies, manticores, bull-headed minotaurs. Only Chiron, the centaur, was a scholar and teacher. Besides, as I said —"

"Your *thing* —" she began once more.

"Don't let the great size frighten you." His voice was gentle, almost complacent.

"A *horse?*" she asked, astounded.

"A stallion," he said. He was quite frank about it. Sicily was a beautiful land where strange and terrible things happened every day of the week.

"I will not bed down with a horse!" Ava snatched her hand from his and ran around to the far side of the bed and stood there, watching him.

"It's been a long day and we're both tired,"

Angelo said, keeping quite still so as not to frighten her.

"So?"

"And when we're tired we should go to sleep."

"I'm never going to sleep. Certainly not with you," she said, her voice trembling.

"You look so fierce," Angelo remarked, simply to make her feel better. He had begun to stroll very slowly down the room on his side of the bed. "You look —"

"*Not tonight, not tomorrow night, not ever!*"

"Wild" he continued. "Like an animal. I like that, of course. An animal." He paused at the foot of the bed and smiled at her. "You are a magnificent woman."

Ava had almost started to say something but now she hesitated, her lips still parted, distracted by what he had just said.

"A splendid woman," he continued. "It's hard to believe that when I first saw you your legs were so thin I thought they would snap in two. You were always running after your aunt and everywhere she went you would follow her, trotting after her like a foal."

"Because I was ten years old," she protested.

"And now you are a woman of seventeen with beautiful teeth and strong round arms. And, I suppose, sturdy legs. We will be *superb* at making love."

Ava clapped her hands over her ears.

Angelo laughed. He praised her hair — told her it shimmered like a river at midnight — then spoke quietly about her luminous eyes, her gleaming shoulders something, her something breasts, and so on downward, dropping his voice softer and softer, so that Ava who had opened her fingers just a bit to hear him had to open them more and still more until, straining to catch his last words, she forgot herself and said, "What? What flower? — Stop! Don't come any closer!"

"Calm yourself," Angelo said. He seated himself on the low chest which stood against the wall by the foot of the bed. "How long do you plan to stand over there?" he asked.

"As long as I want to."

"Of course. But why not sit on the bed? Filomena scented the sheets with lavender, just for us."

Ava seated herself guardedly on the edge of the bed, watching him all the time.

"This is a pretty room, isn't it?" he said, looking around. "I whitewashed it myself a week ago." In fact, it was a pretty room. In addition to the bed there was a low dresser, a rush-bottomed chair, and in the space between two shuttered windows there was a washstand with an oval mirror hung above it. Angelo said, "The candles look nice, too. I didn't expect you to light them all at once, but they do look nice. Like a church at High Mass. Maybe that's why

I'm so sleepy. Church always makes me sleepy," he confessed. "Or maybe it's my age. I'm no child and at my age —"

"What are you doing?" Ava cried, jumping up.

"I'm unbuttoning my shirt. I'm going to bed."

"Bed? What bed? Stop!"

But Angelo was already on his feet, rampant, and now he threw off his shirt, letting it billow onto the chair, and there he stood naked while a dozen shadows of him reared and plunged on the whitewashed wall at his back. Ava had started to cover her eyes but it was too late. Now she simply looked at him and the candle flames grew calm again and the shadows grew still. His flesh was a rich chestnut color and his hair was black — black on his head, black in his beard, black everywhere. His shoulders gleamed, at the base of his throat there was a little hollow filled with golden shadow and on his chest the pattern of hair spread like the wings of a crow. His navel was deep and dark, his legs — ah, those splendid stallion legs — his flanks so smoothly muscled that as he walked the flesh shimmered, and the short downy hairs on his rump, the curling hairs on his thighs, the tassel-like hairs on his fetlocks, all sparkled like coal, and in the center, of course, as if the darkness of night had taken beastly shape — But Angelo was blowing out the candles one by one and it was becoming harder to see. He stopped when there was only the solitary chamberstick burning on the chest of drawers. Then he leapt into bed, stacked two pillows behind his back and sat with the sheets pulled to his chest. He looked at Ava. "I'm going to sleep," he said.

"I'm not sleepy."

"Would you like to rest on the top of the covers?"

She came and sat on the edge of the bed, her back to him.

"Give me your hand," he said.

"What are you going to do?" she asked, half turning.

"I'm going to sit here like we used to sit on the bench in your aunt's garden. What did we ever do there? Now give me your hand."

"All right," she said. She lay back on the covers against him and got comfortable. "But don't try to reason with me," she added.

"Of course not." He put his arms about her and took her hands. "Now that we're married, there's a secret I can tell you."

"I already know your secret," she said.

"Now listen. This is what you don't know. When a man of my kind, a man of my nature — when a man who is part stallion makes love to a woman, she inherits three gifts."

"Everything I ever inherited is in that ugly chest."

"These gifts come because he makes love to her. They come with his lovemaking, with his —" Angelo hesitated, hunting for the proper word.

"What three gifts?"

"Her childbirths will be easy, her milk will be sweet, and she will be beautiful forever."

"Angelo, you liar." She laughed.

"These talents will be yours by nature," he continued, undeflected. "And they'll be passed on to our daughters and their daughters, too, if we make love often enough."

"And the boys? What would they inherit?"

"My sons will be like me, of course." His breath was soft behind her ear. He went on talking in a voice gentle and resonant and even dreamy, speaking of his father and mother and the village where they lay, which was deep in the heart of Sicily, and in the hour or so that followed he told about those spirits hidden in the hills and fields around the village, told about the patron saints and beasts and, while his voice grew even sleepier, he talked about his relatives, not all of whom were horse, for one was a famous tree and another was a rock and there was an aunt —"

"Yes?" Ava said, turning to him. "Go on. I'm listening."

But Angelo was asleep. She turned all the way around and crept cautiously over the covers to study his face: his beard, his lips, the hard wrinkles at the corner of his eyes. *A handsome man*, she thought. His breathing was deep and slow, for he was fast asleep, but the guttering candle made the shadows on his face waver as if he were stirring and about to wake up. So Ava lay on the covers and listened to his soft, slow breathing and watched the candle flicker out and strove to keep awake.

Angelo awoke early and found Ava sleeping like a statue at his side atop the bed covers. He gazed at her in the milky light, at her flushed cheeks and parted lips — how young she was! — cautiously lifted his hand to caress her, but changed his mind and slipped softly out of bed. In the dim hall he pulled on his workpants and boots, then groped his way down the dark stairs to wash in the courtyard. He hoped that a brisk walk on the hills would relieve the painful energy compressed in his legs, his thighs. He pulled on his shirt and flung open the gate and abruptly a horse and rider materialized out of the gray air. "He has landed," the rider told him.

"Ah!" Angelo said.

"Yesterday at Marsala."

Angelo wheeled and ran back into the courtyard, pounded once on the stable door, once on the kitchen door, then clattered up the stairway to his bedroom. "Garibaldi has landed at Marsala and I'm going to join him!" he cried, throwing off his shirt. Ava reached for the latch on the window shutters, staring at him. Angelo sat on the bed to pull off his boots and pants, then flung on his wedding shirt and strode out to the hall. He returned clothed in the fancy shirt and his best pair of velveteen pants. "I have waited all my life for this," he said, pulling on his boots. He crossed the room to Ava who stood by the open window, still staring at him. "You're crazy," she said soberly. Angelo took both her hands in his and kissed her lips. "Remember that I love you," he told her.

"Garibaldi is an animal, a beast," she said, her voice rising.

He laughed. "Then he has come to the right place."

"We will die," she wailed.

"We have always died. But today you should be singing."

Ava wrenched her hands from his and began to beat her fists on his chest, shouting "Go, go, go, go, go —" She had broken into sobs.

"I have never been so happy," he said, putting his arms around this sturdy young woman who wept for him.

Angelo kissed the crown of her head and rushed down the stairway to the dining room. There he tossed back the lid of a black oak chest, peeled away the linens and flannels and came up with an antique bird gun, then he strode into the yard, pulling a heavy pistol from under the big flower pot by the door, and was shouting *Filomena* as he crossed to the stable where the boy had saddled the gelding. He mounted, took the bundle of food which Filomena handed up to him — leftovers from the wedding wrapped in oilcloth — and went out through the gate at a canter, leaving the boy at the stable door, Filomena in the middle of the yard, his uncles and half-brothers asleep indoors, and his virgin bride face down on her bed, beating her pillow.

Garibaldi had landed on the western shore of Sicily and everyone knew what he had come to do. He was a simple man with a simple desire. He would drive the King's troops first from that great island and then from the Kingdom of Naples and the forlorn southern peninsula, so that these lands could join with those in the north and become one Italy, a single nation as it had been ages ago. The King had 24,864 well-equipped troops waiting in Sicily. Garibaldi had come ashore with only 1,000 volunteers, some in red shirts and others in street clothes, and for guns they had junk — antique smooth-bore muskets, 100 Enfield rifles and five ancient cannons without gun carriages. At dawn the next morning he walked his patched-together army inland through seas of green corn and beans to Rampagallo, and the following day he trudged with them past silvery groves of olive trees up to the sun-baked highlands of Salemi. They spent the night in Salemi, some in houses and others in monasteries and still others under tents in the orchards outside. The next day their numbers increased a bit as volunteer *squadre* came up from the countryside, armed with flintlocks or pruning hooks, and somewhere among them was Angelo, Angelo Cavallù, *our* Angelo. He was dusty, for his horse had collapsed of exhaustion and Angelo had trotted over the hills and into town on his own two feet. That afternoon he saw Garibaldi dismount, stroll across a corner of the piazza and pass through a doorway: a pleasant-looking man with a rich honey-color beard, clothed in a loose red shirt — a man who moved with the effortless grace of an animal. Garibaldi was content at that moment, for he had just ridden in from a survey of the ground along the road to Palermo and now he was going to study a big map of Sicily which one of his officers had found. Until then he had not had a good map. That night, when he folded the map and went to bed, rain had begun to fall, but when he awoke at three the next morning the rain had ceased and it was beautiful. He pulled on his pants, drank a cup of coffee, called in his officers, told them what he planned to do and sent them to rouse his little army. He had been walking up and down the room and now he burst into song. Here was a fifty-three-year-old man about to attack an army of vastly superior numbers in a battle in which defeat meant death and he sang like a lover going to meet his mistress, because he was about to have his heart's desire.

That morning Angelo marched with the *squadre* down the road and through a valley where everyone bought oranges and lemons, then they left the road and trudged up a stony hillside. From the top of their bald hill they looked across a shallow alley to a steeper, terraced hill on top of which brightly uniformed troops were gathered in squares — there and there and there and there and over there. They were too many. Angelo's disheartened *squadre*, which had never been in a battle before, drifted quietly off to the side to watch how it was done. Over there, General Sforza ordered his trumpets to sound and ranks of identical soldiers began to step down the hill, to wade across the stream at the bottom and mount toward the volunteers, firing as they came. Over here, a bugler blew that fancy musical reveille which Garibaldi loved so much and a handful of his skirmishers began to fire at the oncoming troops. Of their own accord, the rest of Garibaldi's men, who had been sitting on the stony rubbish high on the hill, stood up — men in red shirts, men in street jackets, some even in top hats — and now they were running down at the troops in a burst of musketry. Angelo galloped after them. The Garibaldini drove the army back across the stream and part way up the terraced hillside. Then everything slowed. The afternoon grew slack and there was only the irregular clatter of gunfire, or once in a while the top of the enemy hill blossomed into white puffs of smoke and cannonballs shrieked past, and the sun roamed aimlessly overhead. It grew hot, terribly hot. Every so often Garibaldi's redshirts were driven down, or they climbed further up, but their numbers always diminished and now there were not so many — in fact, there were only a few hundred crouched on the steep hillside, pressed together here and there beneath the ragged terraces. Angelo sat with his shoulder against his own bit of loose stone wall, sucking the juice from his last orange, and he peered higher up the hill to where Garibaldi huddled with his bare sword and a crowd of his outlandinsh army. The terrace wall they clung to was nearest the summit and royalist troops were firing volley after volley down on them, even throwing rocks. *He is a lion*, thought Angelo, *but I am only part of a horse and maybe not the best part at that. What do we do now?* A rock hit Garibaldi on the back and he stood up, his sword flashing. His men stood up beside him. Now Garibaldi was climbing the terrace, his men were climbing the terrace. They were rising up everywhere on the hillside, rising and climbing through the ragged noise, crawling higher and higher, clawing up over the last heap of stones into a hazy white smoke filled with crackling gunfire and screams. Then there was the long hilltop slanting off and royalist troops running away, streaming down and away to the far valley, fleeing.

Angelo marched here and there and elsewhere with Garibaldi for two weeks while the old fox outwitted the King's generals and drove the royal army from Sicily, then Angelo walked home. He wore a stained slouch hat and such tattered velveteen that when he turned in at the gate only his dog, Micu, recognized who it was, circling him and barking excitedly and leaping while Filomena and the boy stared. His bride cried, "Angelo!" from an upstairs window, "Angelo!" from the doorway, "Angelo!" as she threw her arms around his neck. He kissed her forehead and each cheek and said, "Tell Filomena to start heating water because I am going to take a long, long bath."

In the house they poured pots of steaming water into the copper tub which Angelo had dragged to the side of the bed. Ava laid out the towels, brush and soap on the table between the windows and turned to go, but Angelo took her wrist in one hand and gently closed the door with his other. Without a word he shed his shirt, pulled off his boots and stepped out of his pants. Ava stood at the window, staring out, and heard his gasp as he lowered himself into the scalding water.

"I cannot wash my own back," he said in a reasonable voice.

Ava turned hesitantly, a light flush on her cheeks, and took the soap and brush from the table and knelt behind his back. She lifted a cupped handful of water and let it trickle onto his shoulder, then another handful and another and one more. She dipped the soap into the water and slid it tenderly all the way across his back from the tip of one shoulder to the tip of the other. "Ah, that's good," Angelo murmured. Ava pressed her wet palm to his warm back and rubbed in a circle, making suds. "The first time I saw Garibaldi I was so close I could have reached out and touched him," he told her. "He's an old man, older than I am, but he moves very lightly, like an animal. — Would you like me to tell you what I've been doing for two weeks?" Ava dipped the soap into the water and swept it up and down his marvelous, silken back, enjoying herself. "Yes. Tell me," she said absently.

Later, when he had finished with his stories and his bath, Angelo stepped from the tub, letting the water sluice from him in streams as if he were a mountain, then he toweled himself dry and fell asleep in his bed for a day and a night. He dreamed. Maybe the dreams came from his aching muscles or the marrow of his bones or maybe they came from his blood, which was, after all, the mingled blood of men and beasts, of Siculi and Greeks, Romans, Carthaginians, Byzantines, Arabs, Jews, Normans, Spaniards — in other words, pure Sicilian blood. Occasionally his magnificent legs twitched and he gave a deep resonant groan, because he was dreaming not only his own story but the cruel three-thousand-year history of all Sicily. He was having a nightmare. At last he awoke and in the pale blue dawn he found Ava sleeping at his side, on top of the covers, an arm flung over her head and her hair spread loose upon the pillow.

He kissed her lips. Before she could rub the sleep from her eyes, Angelo said, "Come with me. I'll show you the world in the morning." He began to open the shutters. Ava stood there in her white chemise and watched him as the room filled up with light. She wanted to look at those equine hindquarters, those powerful flanks and long shins, wanted to see the dark whorls of hair on his chest, the satin nap on his underbelly, his black pouch and stallion thing. His flesh was the color of bronze and smooth beneath her fingertips as a chestnut fresh from its hull. Suddenly he knelt and scooped up the hem of her chemise, standing and lifting it so rapidly that she barely had time to raise her arms before the garment was unfurling in air, falling into a shadowy corner of the room. He put a warm hand on her haunch and when she lowered her eyes he kissed the nape of her neck. Now he whispered a few words in her ear and she tossed her head back, laughing. Who knows what happened next? Her births were always easy, her milk was always sweet, and she remained beautiful into old age. Their daughters inherited these traits. Their sons had legs like their father.

26

It snowed in Boston all that day in 1904. The large flakes had come falling soundlessly out of the dark before anyone was awake, melting into the flinty waters of the inner harbor, settling down on Paul Revere's clapboard house and the Old North Church and Copp's Hill Burying Ground, blotting out the paving stones and filling up the streets, such as Prince Street, so that by dawn the rooms where Pacifico and Marianna lived were freezing. It snowed and snowed. By mid morning gangs of ragged men were clearing the sidewalks and roadways, the ringing *clink* and *plank* of a dozen shovels making a crazy musical sound below the windows, and in the middle of the afternoon Pacifico was able to take Marianna out for a look at the North End. It was a crowded scramble of crooked street — "Like Reggio, except for the snow," he claimed — and when you stood here in the middle, the sea was only a quarter mile away, that way or that way or that way. And if you went the other way you travelled deeper into Boston, to the State House with the gold dome, to the Common and the fancy shops which they had looked at yesterday. But this street in the North End is where they would be living. "The Irish up there, the Jews over there, and the Italians right here," he explained. Later the wind began to blow, passing through Marianna's coat as if it were a sieve. She clung to his arm and they headed back, pausing at the corner of Hanover and Prince Street to marvel at a dray horse shaggy with icicles, its breath steaming the air.

Once in their rooms, Marianna removed her soaked shoes, jammed a kerchief into each toe and stood the shoes by the fireplace to dry, while Pacifico stuffed newspaper into the cracks around the windows. Near bedtime they sat down in their nightrobes at the small table to drink a glass of wine and eat the chestnuts which Marianna had been roasting in a flat tin pan on the grate. She held the pan with a dish towel and tipped the chestnuts into the plate on the table. Pacifico watched and tried to make out any change in her face or her gestures, any telltale sign about last night. But it was impossible to tell. She was a woman just one finger shorter than he was and only three months younger: she was no little girl. Marianna placed the empty tin pan on the floor, sat down, and catching his gaze, smiled at him. Her face was a luminous amber above the kerosene lamp and her freshly brushed hair hung about her head and shoulders in loose black coils with a fiery glint here and there.

Pacifico stood up, pulled the top blanket from the bed and tucked it around her in the chair. He kissed the nape of her neck. "So," he said softly. "Do you think our sons will have legs like a stallion?"

Marianna laughed and turned her head to kiss his cheek. "You mean like that poor horse we saw pulling the wagon full of snow? I certainly hope not. And maybe all our children will be girls. Did you ever think of that?"

"No. Never."

"Neither did papà. Now he has eight daughters and no sons." She put a hot chestnut into his hand.

"Your father is an admirable man. I've always said so." This was not the direction he wanted the conversation to go. He returned to his chair and began picking at the chestnut hull. "But maybe he lacked passion."

"What do you mean?"

"Perhaps, you know, when it came to making babies —" He broke off.

"Mamà had girls because she wanted girls. It's as simple as that. And I'm sure papà was passionate. Why not? Why wouldn't he be?" Marianna examined the chestnut in her hand, then thrust her thumbnail into the slit and tore the hull away with a twist of her wrist. She let it steam in the cool air for a moment, then popped it into her mouth.

"Passion turns a man into an animal," he said. "It transforms him into a beast and that frightens a woman. Sometimes. Maybe he was afraid of frightening your mother."

Marianna tilted her head back, gulped down her wine and set the empty glass slowly and ever so gently on the table. She smiled. "I have a secret to tell you about mamà. She's not frightened of the cat or anything else. But everybody knows it and it's no secret. Now let me tell you this other thing which is the secret."

Then Marianna told him about her mother, Stella, and her father, Franco, and how they first met.

27

The first time Franco watched Stella undress (20 August 1860) in her room at the bordello Conca d'Oro, her freshness and beauty struck him so hard that he fell to his knees, opened his arms and asked her to marry him. "I've never seen anyone so beautiful and I love you," he said. Stella looked at him, her face as serene as polished marble, and began slowly to unpin her hair. The room was filled with dusky golden light which filtered through the shuttered windows. "Marry me," he whispered. "Marry me," She held the pin in her teeth and calmly watched him while her hands searched in the coiled mass of her hair and when she had found the last one she laid all the pins in a sea shell on the bed table. She had worked a few years and was no longer surprised at the way men behaved in her room. "What do I say?" she asked distantly.

"Say yes."

"Yes," she recited, her loosened hair turning languidly about her breast and arm, unrolling over her wrist, across her thigh.

"Diva," the young man murmured. "Goddess."

"Yes. I am a goddess." She was matter-of-fact about it. Of course, the people of southern Italy never made much of a difference between mortals and gods, and you never knew when a man might become a god, or a goddess become a woman, or vice versa.

Franco knelt slowly forward and kissed her feet, embraced her legs as if gathering an armful of long-stemmed flowers, and plunged his face into her dark —

"But first you must wash," Stella told him, firmly turning his hot cheek aside so that he might see the big white pitcher and bowl on the low table. "Over there," she said. Franco staggered to his feet, his head filled with the odor of lemon flowers and brine. He poured the water into the bowl, set the pitcher down with a hollow clink on the marble, and began to scrub his face. "Not your *face*! Not in *that*!" Stella cried.

Franco straightened up and turned, water streaming from his bare shoulders and chest onto his trousers. "What?"

"Not your face, *caro*. Wash —" Stella sighed and took up the towel that lay folded on the table and began to dry his chin. "You're new here?" she asked.

Franco was distracted by her nakedness so near to him, by the way her long hair fell upon her breasts, turned about her arm and uncoiled heavily to her knees. "Yes!" he said, getting his wits together. He told her he came from a village in the Calabrian mountains, but that he had travelled around and picked up an education and, as a matter of fact, in a short time he was going off to teach mathematics. He said he believed in mathematics and he thought he would like teaching it. Just now he was down here in Reggio — "the home of Pythagoras," he noted — merely to stroll around and enjoy the cafés and views of the sea. This Reggio was a city of vistas and he had discovered he was crazy about looking at the sea. Then he unbuckled and, because he was shy, turned his back to her before he stepped out of his pants.

"Maybe you'll see the Fata Morgana," Stella said, coming around to watch him. "The castles float in the air far above the water. It's famous."

"An optical illusion, a mirage," Franco said, hurriedly soaping himself.

"Of course it's an illusion. Morgana conjures the castles out of thin air. That's why it's called Fata Morgana, because she's the one who creates it."

"I'm a rationalist," he informed her. "I'm a freethinker and a mathematician and I don't believe in — What are you looking at?" he asked, covering his drenched privates with his hand.

"Don't worry. It won't fly away. Here's a towel." She walked idly to the shuttered window and peered between the slats at the balcony and at the sunny strip of street below. "I don't know anything about rationalists or freethinkers, but the Royalists don't like them. Have you seen all the soldiers?"

"They don't frighten me."

"They say Garibaldi has come over from Sicily."

"They've been saying that for weeks."

"How long have you been here in Reggio?" she asked, peeping again through the shutters to the sunny balcony.

"Three days," he said. "How long have you been at the Conca d'Oro?"

For a while she did not answer. "Forever, I think."

"That's not true."

Stella turned to him as if she were weary, the golden light spreading up like a fan behind her. "All my life, this life, I've been here."

Franco studied her face to see what she meant, but in that topaz shadow he could never make it out. She seemed made of honey-colored marble and so remote he felt half afraid of her. "You are the most beautiful woman I've ever seen," he whispered.

Stella smiled. "Yes. I'm a goddess. And you are a very young man — a rationalist, a freethinker and a mathematician." And taking Franco's hand she led him to her bed, drew up her long legs and sank back upon the white pillows as if bedded in clouds.

Franco was young and enthusiastic and they made love for a long, long time, but even with a goddess it comes to an end. Stella arose and went to the big mirror that stood by the bed and Franco, leaning up on his elbow, watched her draw on her blue silk robe.

"If you were my wife —" he began.

"I wouldn't respect you. How could I respect anyone foolish enough to marry a whore?" She was brushing her hair in long slow strokes.

"I believe in the future, not the past. I don't *care* what you've done."

"Because you don't *know* what I've done. If you want to marry me you must come back tonight and watch me at work."

"Are you serious?" he asked.

"You can hide on the balcony and watch through the shutters." She took a pin from the fluted sea shell on her bedtable and began to coil her hair upon her head.

"And then —"

"Afterward, you must tell me everything you saw," she said.

"Why?"

"So I'll know that you really watched. And then —"

"Then I'll ask you to marry me," said Franco, swinging himself from the bed.

"Then you won't ask," said Stella.

Franco returned early that night. The room looked just the same as it had that afternoon, but now there was an oil lamp burning on the low table beside the wash basin and Stella had her hair up in a large braided knot.

"Did you think I'd come back?" he asked cheerfully.

"Yes," she said.

Stella set a bottle of brandy and two glasses on the low table. She was wearing a white dress which left her golden shoulders and arms bare to the hazy lamplight. She poured out the brandy and they each took up a glass.

"My name is Franco Morelli and I live in our house in the town of Morano in Cosenza," he announced.

Stella looked at him in surprise. "My name is Stella Maria DiMare and I live in the bordello Conca d'Oro in Reggio, Calabria." She smiled.

They touched glasses and drank.

"You're a handsome young man. Did your mother ever tell you that?" she asked.

"I don't know. My mother died when I was a child."

"Oh. I'm sorry. My own mother died when I was born," she added.

"My father is a carpenter and cabinet maker."

"And my father was a fisherman," she said. Stella smiled, remembering him. "He used to tell me that he found me at sea. Other children were found under cabbages, but he used to say that he pulled in his nets one morning and there I was, swimming with all the fishes. I loved that story. He used to carry me on his shoulders. He died in 1848. I think it was during the bombardment. He sailed out and never came back."

Stella sat on the foot of her bed, Franco sat in a stiff chair, and they talked and talked, getting to know each other. Actually, Stella did most of the talking, for no one had ever asked her about herself and now she discovered that she liked to converse on that subject with this young man. In fact, she talked so much that she forgot where she was and remembered only at the last minute. "Oh! the time! I've got to tell mother superior you ran down the back stairs," she cried.

Franco jumped up and met himself in the tall mirror that stood by the bed — a flushed young man in a whore's bedroom. *How odd that a flat mirror reflects so little of the truth*, he thought.

"Hurry!" Stella said, unlatching the shuttered doors to the balcony. "This way. And be careful of the bird cages out there. Whatever you do, don't make any noise. After my last customer leaves I'll open the doors and let you in. Watch out for my doves!"

Stella shut the doors and adjusted the louvers so that Franco, out on the dark balcony, could peer in and see all that went on in the lighted room. Franco crouched among the bamboo bird cages and wondered how he could watch and not watch at the same time, for on the one hand he felt it was dishonorable to spy on the woman he loved and on the other hand he had given her his promise to spy in order to win her. He was turning this round and round in his mind when he heard the bedroom door open. He peeked between the slats and began to watch.

Well, what can I tell you? Stella's first customer was a cranky Neapolitan businessman whose limp thing wouldn't get hard no matter how she handled it, until he gave her an order to do thus and so with this and this. Next came the elegant son of a local landowner, a youth with a long nose who confused top with bottom, front with back, and one thing with another. And after him there came two Royalist officers, big men who tossed off their uniforms and shoved each other around like playful athletes before they set to work on Stella. It grew to be a very long night.

When her last customer had gone, Stella unlatched the doors to the balcony and whispered to Franco, *Come in*. He arose slowly and unsteadily from the lattice of shadows amid the bamboo bird cages. She poured two brimming glasses of brandy, drank one straight down and handed the other to him. But Franco stood wordless in the balcony doorway, his face white as a sheet of paper, his eyes dead as stones.

"Ah," Stella said gently. "I can see you've had a hard night."

Franco stared straight ahead, as if he were deaf, dumb and blind.

"I like you." She looked at him, then sighed and drank down his brandy. "Actually, I love you and I'm sorry I didn't tell you before."

He walked uncertainly into the room.

"Listen," she told him. "Garibaldi has landed and there's going to be a big battle tonight. You've got to get home."

"That's what I want, a good fight." He seemed to awaken.

"Did you hear me? Garibaldi has landed. When the troops find out they'll be shooting at anything that moves. You've got to get home"

"I'd like to kill a few troops myself," he said. "A few Neapolitans. Some landowners. A couple of officers." He laughed and his eyes brightened.

"*Carissimo*," she said, putting her hand to his cheek. "Garibaldi is immortal but you are not. Stay out of it. Go someplace safe."

But Franco had already crossed the room and now he threw open the chamber door and vaulted down the stairway, strode through a maroon parlor of gilded chairs, torn playing cards and overturned wineglasses, and burst into the street. He ran, turned away from the bordello and ran down whatever avenue opened for him, ran through a city of crumbling masonry and stucco and shuttered windows with no sound anywhere except his own clattering footfall. He ran where the streets themselves led, rushing now down a cobbled alley to a yet narrower passage that hurled him headlong into the Cathedral Square which abruptly swirled into a crackling chaos of gunfire, screams and plunging horses.

Garibaldi had landed. Everyone in Reggio had know he was coming, the only question was when. Italy is separated from Sicily by the Straits of Messina, and the northern end of the Straits is so narrow that anyone on the Italian side could climb a hill and look over the water to Garibaldi's camp and watch his men hammering together supply rafts, or inspect his make-shift flotilla of steamboats, fishing boats, rowboats and barges pulled up on the sand. The desolate King knew he was coming. He had ordered his warships to patrol the Straits, and he had packed 16,000 handsomely dressed troops into that part of Italy. The old general at the castle in Reggio certainly knew he was coming. He calculated that Garibaldi would cross the Straits and rush up from the shore to the streets of the city. That's why he positioned his colonel and the men of the 14th Line out front, had ordered them to bivouac in the large Square before the Cathedral. He figured that Garibaldi was an ordinary mortal.

On the morning of August 19 Garibaldi did appear, but not on the shore opposite his camp and not at the narrow northern end of the Straits at all, but on an empty stretch of beach thirty miles to the south. The Royal Navy never saw him. He simply appeared, materializing quietly out of the limpid dawn air with his men on a patch of sand that sloped gently up to a wilderness of cactuses and aloes. Eventually Neopolitan warships came up over the horizon and drew near and since not even Garibaldi could hide a steamboat on an open beach he and his crazy quilt army were discovered. The warships blew apart the grounded steamboat, but by then the entire army on the beach had vanished. Garibaldi had a simple plan. First he would march north to rendezvous with partisans already in the countryside, then he would transform all his men into substanceless shadows. The next night some would slip past the soldiers who guarded the city gates and once inside would glide noiselessly toward the Cathedral Square. He and the others would condense out of the black night air on the hills behind Reggio. When the redshirts and the Royalists were in blind battle in front of the Cathedral, Garibaldi and the rest of his army would sweep down upon the city and it would be theirs. The plan worked like a miracle. And Franco just happened to rush into the Square the moment the fight began.

The morning after the battle was quiet in the bordello Conca d'Oro. Stella sat in the half-shuttered light of her room with her forgotten sewing in her lap and gazed blankly at the dirty wall. She tried not to think of Franco, because whenever she did her heart felt hollow and heavy at the same time. She sighed and wondered what the next thousand years would bring and she was trying not to think at all when there was a BOOM and one of the shutters burst into splinters above her head. It took her a moment to realize that somebody had fired a shotgun at her balcony doors. "Stella DiMare!" he cried. She jumped up and put her cheek to the margin of the shutter, peering into the narrow street below. "Stella DiMare!" Of course it was Franco standing there, a pistol in his belt and a shotgun in his hand, shouting up at her. She pressed her back against the wall. "Yes!" she cried.

"My name is Franco Morelli from the town of Morano in Cosenza!" There was another BOOM as the top of the other door to the balcony exploded, filling the air with wood chips.

"I remember you," Stella shouted, her eyes shut against the soft patter of bird shot and plaster falling from the ceiling.

"Thank you," he cried. "I've come back to tell you what I saw in your room last night."

She opened her eyes. "And what did you see?"

"A jackass, a dog, and two pigs!" he shouted.

"Very clever! You're the cleverest young man I know."

"And *you*," he called up to her. "I saw *you*, diva."

Stella opened the shredded balcony shutters and stood there a moment, looking down on him. His necktie was gone, his shirt was open, his jaw was dark with a day's stubble — a handsome young man. She said nothing. Her face was as calm as the sea when night is over and morning about to begin and her eyes shimmered with sadness.

"Oh, yes. Everyone looked at you but I'm the only one who saw you. I know you for what you are. Diva. Goddess. I keep trying but I haven't shot anybody yet," he cried. "Will you marry me!"

Stella looked into Franco's face and smiled, then she turned and unlatched the door to one of the bamboo cages and withdrew one dove and another. She tossed them into the air where they blossomed in a flurry of white wings, then beat their way in a soaring helical sweep skyward, circle upon circle, one following the other like melody in a round. She smiled because she loved Franco. Now she flung open the other cages and as the doves shot up around her like rockets she leaned over the rail to say, "Yes, I will marry you." But by then the street was empty and Franco gone.

Franco had run off before Stella had answered, because he was afraid she might say no. In all other ways he was brave. The next day he hiked out of the city and up the hills northward, climbing to join the Garibaldini camped on the slopes high above the Striats. Franco chose a patch of ground slovenly with broken mudbanks, cactuses, tangled vineyards and orchards, chose it because the view was splendid. Below him on the lower terraces of the mountain were the Royalist troops, and way down below the Royalists flowed the blue waters of the Straits, and on the other side stood the lilac headlands of Sicily with smoky Mongibello to the south and the great Tyrrhenian Sea like azure enamel to the north horizon. Franco sat back against a crooked olive tree, his shotgun across his knees, but the call to advance and fire never came. Instead, the men of both armies — the redshirts in the balcony, the Royalists in the lower tiers — watched an artillary duel between the distant cannoneers on the Sicilian point and the warships of the Royal Navy. The following day Garibaldi gave the order to advance without firing. The men stood up, stretched and began to descend step by step upon the Royalist troops. Franco couldn't believe what was happening. Now and again cotton puffs of smoke appeared below and cannonballs shrieked up at them, thudding into the mountainside, and every so often he heard the crack of enemy rifle fire, but everyone continued to step carefully downward with their weapons silent. At one point word was passed along that they were to halt, so they halted. Franco sat on the ground and stared glumly at the town below, knowing that if the fight continued in this fashion he would never get to shoot anybody. Then he saw Garibaldi close at hand on the brown hillside where he stood talking with three of his officers. He had a full beard, wore a loose red shirt stained with sweat and he carried a long sword, was using it just now to make a sweeping orchestral gesture toward the gray mountains further north. Two of the men broke off and headed up the hill while Garibaldi and the remaining officer began to walk down toward the enemy. His voice was strange, more like music than speech, and Franco remembered it for the rest of his life. Word came again to advance without firing, so they did, and in a little while the King's soldiers threw down their rifles and surrendered. In a few days Garibaldi was to gallop north to Naples, disarming and sending home ten thousand Royalist troops on the way, and when he rode through the mountain provinces of Calabria, Basilicata and Campania, men would come forward to touch his hand, women would hold babies aloft to receive his blessing, and he was greeted as a god.

Now Franco trudged down the last hillock, crossed a dirt road and walked onto the empty shore. He broke open his shotgun, unloaded his pistol and laid them on the dry pebbles. Nearer the water he saw something like a discarded banner lying on the sand and when he looked more closely he saw that it was a forgotten pile of laundry, a woman's white dress and blue robe folded loosely and anchored there by the handful of sea shells heaped upon it. He tried not to think of Stella, but everything reminded him of her. He sighed. He pulled off his shoes, threw off his shirt and waded into the water. He washed his face, his scorched neck, his arms. The scent of brine and lemon blossoms, the swaying of the sea anemones, the convoluted drifting braids of tawny seaweed — everything reminded him of Stella. He gazed at the waves that came forever forward to meet him, waves that still rise and curl and curling fall like scalloped shells upon that beach, and as he watched a wave broke into foam and it was Stella who stood before him, wringing the seawater from her hair while she waded ashore. "Franco," she called to him. "You are a rationalist, a freethinker and a mathematician and I am the goddess who says yes." They had many children, each one as beautiful as her mother.

28

The snowfall ceased that night in 1904 and the air grew still and clear and there was no sound anywhere, as if the city of Boston slept enchanted in a block of ice. Certainly the rooms on Prince Street where Pacifico and Marianna lay under heaps of blankets were as cold as ice. Pacifico was stretched on his back and Marianna lay within his arm, her hand upon his chest. It was uncomfortable, but that's the way they had come to rest after making love and neither one had wanted to shift away for fear of seeming rude or indifferent. Marianna was half asleep. She was thinking about the ocean she had crossed to get here, or perhaps she was dreaming, for the ocean was calm and bright blue and at the edge where she walked the water brimmed and sparkled and fell warm against her ankles. The naked baby who was squatting and splashing in the water stood up with seaweed in her hair and walked beside Marianna on the beach, because she was Marianna's daughter. As for Pacifico, he had thought he was asleep but then he saw the gray margin beyond the edge of the window shade and recognized the pale rose tint cast on the ceiling by the coals in the grate. The day before yesterday he had been pleased with his furnishings but now he wished he had a bigger table and a bigger bed and a chest of drawers. He thought about getting them. He saw clearly that if he counted his knowledge of English as capital, he could offer it in exchange for part ownership of a business here in the North End, and then he could use his business as collateral for a loan to purchase a building, an apartment building or a mansion with many rooms, one for each child. Lying here he felt relaxed and invigorated at the same time, as if he had just finished swimming. Then he fell asleep, too.

29

Gina said that her brother Mercurio planned to make a zillion bucks in frozen fish. "When he gets here he'll ask me to invest in this business, whatever it is, and I'll say no, no, a thousand times no! He always wants to be bigger than papà."

"When is he coming?" I asked, thinking of us.

She shrugged, pulled his letter from the old mail she kept between the sugar bowl and the pepper shaker, and studied it. "Blah, blah, blah... *I'll be seeing you in a while around the end of the month.*"

"That's soon," I said.

Gina looked at me a moment. "*Caro*, he wrote this thing in May. The end of May has come and gone. You don't know your uncle Mercurio like I do. He's full of *plans*." She smiled. "Anyway, he's not going to sleep here. He likes to spend money. He'll go to a hotel."

So I forgot about my uncle Mercurio. Then a postcard arrived, saying, *Had a change of plans. See you soon. Con affetto, Mercurio.*

"What does soon mean?" I asked her.

She shrugged. "Who knows?" It was past the noon rush and we were with Rita at a terrace table under the yellow awning. As soon as she read the card to me I had stopped eating.

"Is he the one in the frozen fish business?" Rita asked, looking up from her salad.

"That's the business he wants to be in. It used to be shipping. Maybe *change of plans* means he wants to get into something else," Gina said. "Or maybe Coral is giving him problems again." Coral was his wife.

"No. It means he was delayed and now he's coming," I said, alarmed.

"You think so?" Gina's voice was light.

"Yes. *Soon.*"

"Oh, well. It doesn't matter," she said airily.

Rita glanced at her and then at me and was obviously interested. She had figured out what was going on between us some days ago, I realized.

"Arianne is coming home today," Gina said a moment later. "She's had enough of her grandmother, I think. And her grandmother has had enough of her, too."

"Her grandmother *adores* her," Rita said.

"Yes. Her grandmother spoils her," Gina said mildly.

I went back to eating while Gina and Rita talked about Arianne and her grandmother and how nice it was that Mrs Campagnia had made over a bedroom for her and so on. After Rita left we didn't talk and there was only the snapping sound of the canvas above our heads, like a sail luffing in the breeze. "Mercurio could arrive at any moment," Gina said at last.

"When did you decide about Arianne?"

"As soon as I got that damn postcard," she said.

"I better lay out the old mattress."

Gina continued to stare glumly across the roofs and down to the harbor where the chafed water was sparkling in the sun. Dominic stepped out the kitchen door with a towel draped around his neck as if he had just come from a gym. Usually he had lunch at this table with me or Rita or Gina, but today he seated himself on an upended milk crate by the wall. He knew what was going on, too, and had decided to keep clear of us.

"Aren't you eating today?" Gina called over to him.

He shambled to our table and sat down.

"My brother Mercurio is coming sometime but we don't know when," she said, knowing that Rita had already told him this.

Dominic nodded thoughtfully a moment, to show that he was getting the news for the first time. "I remember him. He always drives a nice car," he said at last.

"Right. You remember him."

Rita set Dom's lunch in front of him and went off to wash the tables. We sat and talked for a bit, then Gina crushed out her cigarette and marched upstairs to the apartment. I got out the mop and pail and began to swab the terrace, even though it needed only a sweeping. I felt queasy about using Arianne as a prop to show Mercurio that our household was just ordinary folks and that nothing crazy was going on. But I didn't want any trouble, either. I had thought we were fooling the world, but Rita and Dom had figured us out and I worried that Mercurio would, too. When I finished the terrace I went down and emptied the pail in the gutter and Gina came by with the car keys jingling in her hand. "I'm going to get Arianne," she said, crisply. She looked older. I put the mop and pail away and went upstairs. I hauled the mattress and bedclothes from Arianne's closet and flopped everything on the kitchen floor against the wall to make it look regular.

About an hour later I heard Arianne tramping slowly up the stairway and knew she was not happy about being taken from her grandmother's house and the kids who lived around there. She walked past me through the kitchen — "Hi, Arianne" — directly to her room without saying hello and jerked shut the droopy curtain which served as her door, making the brass curtain rings hiss and rattle. A moment later there was a *thump* as she bounced a tennis ball off her bedroom wall *thump* again and *thump* again. I asked her did she want to go for a walk. She told me there was no *thump* place to walk to *thump thump thump*. The ball had escaped and now rolled idly in the hall. I walked over and gently kicked it back under the curtain into her room. I asked did she want to play catch outside in the alley. "I'm never ever allowed to do anything I want to do!" she called back.

"Like what?"

"Like getting my ears pierced," she said.

"I don't know how to pierce ears."

"You use a needle and a potato, only my mother won't let me, of course!"

"Are you kidding me? How can you possibly use a needle and a potato to pierce ears?" Later we walked down to Silva's for ice cream cones and she explained how to pierce ears and that evening she won big at Monopoly and went to bed somewhat mollified. Afterward Gina and I put together a jigsaw puzzle on the kitchen table and played some old opera records and didn't go down to the terrace, but Mercurio didn't show up.

He didn't show up the next morning either. Late that afternoon Arianne and I walked down to Silva's for ice cream cones, and on the way back we wandered over to the flower-man's truck to look at his stuff and I bought Arianne a white rose which she had much admired. After dinner Gina and I took our coffee onto the terrace. Gloucester is just a fishing town, so all the shops close at five and the stillness spreads, and in the summer evening you can hear people calling and footsteps and after a while there is only empty silence and the gulls crying now and again. We were sitting there, looking down to the harbor, and everything was flooded with sun and silence, just like those terribly sad paintings by Fitz Hugh Lane. I turned to ask Gina if Lane had ever lived in Gloucester, but she looked so remote — she was staring at the horizon and her bare arm was on the table, a cigarette between her fingers — anyway, I didn't ask her. Then we heard *beep beep beep beep beep*, and we knew it was Mercurio out front in his car.

30

Mercurio had pulled up in a red British runabout. It had a leather padded cockpit, long sweeping mudguards, a chrome radiator and, as if that weren't enough, it also displayed five pairs of headlamps, foglights and signals on the bumper and around the hood. He climbed out laughing, apparently at the excesses of the automobile, threw the little red door shut behind him and gave Gina a hug. When I was a kid he had been in the Army Air Force, a waist gunner on a B-24, and though I could not now expect to find him standing in the harsh black-and-white sunshine of an old photograph (a grin on his face, his parachute like a flat pillow slung beneath his seat) still I was a bit disappointed to see him in civilian clothes. "This is for you. And you," he said, giving us each a small wrapped box. "Where's Arianne? I have something for her, too." Arianne received a charm bracelet with four sterling silver charms, Gina a silver hand mirror, and I got a silver pen-and-pencil set. "For the college graduate. I knew you were here because I visited with your mother yesterday," he told me. Later the four of us sat out on the terrace and ate the spumoni that Gina had bought especially for this occasion. Shortly before it got dark, Mercurio asked if I would come with him now and help find the buildings he planned to visit. He wanted to be able to drive directly to the addresses tomorrow morning. "And don't wait up for him," he told Gina as we left. "We're going out afterward. Right, Nicolo?"

"Oh. Well. Sure," I said, surprised and flattered.

We found the addresses, which were down by the harbor, and as darkness came up Mercurio said he wanted a change of scene, so we shot across Cape Ann and headed up the coast. For an hour he had been talking about refrigeration equipment, but I still couldn't figure out if he was working for someone else or had his own company. Now he talked about the shipping business he had been in earlier, but advised me that sea transport was a thing of the past and that air freight was the future. We made good time up the coast and soon entered that stretch where the ocean creeps in flat and brimming and where tall sea grass grows by the side of the road. We shot over a small bridge and went racing along. "That looks like a good place, the one with the lights over the water," he said. A moment later he wrenched the wheel and we veered off the road, skidded across the gravel parking lot and nosed up against the whitewashed rocks beside the door. It was the same old boat-house where Gina and I had gone dancing. "What do you think?" he asked me.

"Looks all right to me," I said, trying to echo his brisk way of talking.

We sat in a booth across the floor from where Gina and I had sat, and now I ordered a gin-and-tonic, a drink which I had never tasted but which I believed appropriate for hot weather. We were talking about the relatives, one thing and another, when Mercurio remarked that my mother was wondering why I wasn't at home. "And your father is probably wondering when you'll get a real job," he said, smiling.

"Did he say anything?"

"Your dad? No! Of course not. He loves you too much to say anything like that. Besides, they're both very proud of you. You had scholarships and jobs and so on."

I felt uncomfortable at this, so I looked into my glass, stirred the drink with my finger and drank it down.

"So. What are you going to do for a living?" he asked me.

"I don't know. I haven't figured that out yet."

"Four years of college and you haven't figured that out? What did you learn in college? How to stir your drink with your finger? You're becoming an intellectual. You're going to wind up like your uncle Zitti, discussing verbs and Socialism at the dinner table."

I laughed. "My father's an intellectual, after all," I reminded him.

"No, your father's an aeronautical engineer. And let me tell you, he's a wizard with that slide rule. He's very proud of you," he added.

I thought I heard a rebuke in Mercurio's last remark. I had another gin-and-tonic. "What did you do to get the Air Medal?" I asked.

"What?"

"You got an Air Medal in the war, right?" I said.

"With three bronze clusters, two silver. Flying Cross. Why?"

"What did you do?"

He didn't answer right away and for the first time all evening he looked somewhat tired. "All I did was, I did whatever I had to do. Mostly I was lucky." He shrugged. "You want medals, the man you want to talk to is my brother Silvio. He was in the lousy infantry, remember. New Guinea, the Philippines, and a lot of rotten little islands. He has a Silver Star or something. You ought to talk with him."

"He said it was a piece of tin and threw it in with the forks and spoons in our dining room drawer. I saw him do it."

Mercurio laughed. "That's Silvio. He had malaria back then. Remember how green he looked? That was the malaria."

"And there's Sandro and Dante. I forget what they got."

"Let's talk about you," he said. We spent the next few hours talking about my future, President Eisenhower, the Korean Police Action, the Air Force, and what I didn't learn in college. "Well," he said briskly. "Sooner or later it's time to grow up."

"I think we had this part of the conservation before," I said. "I mean conversation."

Mercurio smiled at me a moment. "Everybody makes mistakes," he said. "We're all human. The important thing is to not keep making the same mistake over and over again, no matter how it got started."

"I'm not feeling so good."

"That's all right. Can you hear me? Don't get caught making the same mistake over and over again. Now you take your aunt Gina. She's never going to straighten out."

"What?"

"I think you know what I mean. But let's talk about you."

"Me?"

"The world won't wait forever. Sooner or later you've got to quit fooling around or there'll be hell to pay. Can you hear me? Nicolo?"

"I think I've had enough. Maybe too much."

He smiled and sat back, relaxed. "We're all human. Get out and enjoy it."

"What a strange thing to say," I told him. "I'm just not feeling so good."

"Now I'll tell you what happened on my way back to base in Africa when I fell out of the sky."

I recall getting into the car and then feeling dizzy and sick as he spun us around the lot, scattering gravel before we catapulted onto the road. And I recall getting out of the car in front of Gina's café, seemingly only a moment later. "Wait a second, I'll go up with you. You look kind of wobbly," he said. I said no, not at all, I'm fine. Then I unlocked the bolt and pitched forward through the doorway. Mercurio had already hopped from car and now he kept his hand clamped to my arm as I stumbled up the stairway. The apartment door flew open and there was Gina in a pale nightdress, her hair in a wild tangle. "*What did you do to him, Mercurio? What did you do?*" she cried. Mercurio said, "Go back to bed, he's fine. You'll wake Arianne." I slipped past Gina and went to the bathroom and shut the door. Mercurio and Gina were talking in low voices. I pissed and washed up, then put my head under the faucet and washed again and after that I heard Mercurio revving the engine down in the street. I walked into the kitchen and Gina was seated at the table with her face in her hands. "What happened?" I asked. We could hear Mercurio's sportscar drive through the empty street, the noise getting smaller as he made the turn downhill to Rogers Street, and still smaller and smaller as he headed out along the Bass Rocks Road. I was so tired I thought I might fall down. "Don't cry, Gina. Please don't cry." I began to stroke her hair. She turned and her cheek scalded my chest.

"But now it's ruined," she said. "Now it's finished between you and me." Her eyes were brimming.

"What do you mean? He didn't say anything to me. Did he say anything to you?"

"No," she said. She sighed, but because she had been crying it came out like a long shudder. "But everything will change now." Then she wiped her eyes with the back of her hand and went to the bathroom to blow her nose on a piece of tissue. She said good-night from down the hall. I undressed to my shorts, turned out the kitchen light and felt my way to the mattress on the floor.

The next morning, shortly before the noon rush began, Mercurio came into the café kitchen. He had been out on the terrace with Gina and Arianne for half an hour. He smiled, but he didn't look really happy. "I just finished talking to your aunt and she doesn't want to invest in frozen fish. I've come to say goodby to you," he added, patting my shoulder.

"Wait up," I said. I dried my hands and pulled on a jersey and we walked out to the street together. The red runabout was parked at the curb in the sun.

"I'd like to let you drive around in this thing, but I have to get back to the city," he explained. "I'm sorry. I'm really sorry."

"That's all right," I said. "I enjoyed last night."

"You should think twice about drinking gin." He squinted in the hard sunlight and leaned back against the mudguard, and I saw him just the way he was in the old black-and-white photo, lounging beside the flank of his B-24 in the glare of the African sun. I liked standing there with him. "By the way —" he began and then broke off.

"What?"

"Be careful around Arianne. She has a crush on you."

"Me?" I thought he was out of his mind.

"So don't hang around naked in front of her. Know what I mean?"

"Why would I hang around naked?"

He had already seated himself in the leather cockpit and now he started the engine. "Why not?" He had to raise his voice against the throbbing roar. "We're all human."

"The important thing is to get out and enjoy it," I said.

He laughed, gunned the engine a couple of times and angled the car slowly into the street. He raised his hand and cried, "*Ciao, Nicolo!*" Then I shouted, "*Ciao, Mercurio!*" and he hurtled away.

31

Now at the age of fifty-three I went to Croissants, Ltd. and sat outdoors in the afternoon, with a cup of coffee and a roll, to read my office mail. Maeve was coming at five to hitch a ride home (the Reliant was out for repairs yet again) and until then I would read a book or watch the people going to and fro. The last envelope I opened contained a blue message slip that said, *While you were out you received a phone call from: Ms. Roseanne Beech.* I crammed the note into my breast pocket, threw everything else into the briefcase, jumped to an outdoor phone and called her. There was no answer. The sky was blue as a robin's egg, the air was mild and you could see the tree tops in a thin wash of green above Cambridge Common — all this convinced me she was nearby. I drove over to Dublin Street, parked in the first space I came to. The neighborhood smelled clean and damp, as if it had been rinsed and wrung out, and the trashy strip of soil in front of the tenements gave a sweet earthy odor. The sidewalks were empty except for a runner who had appeared from nowhere, coming my way. She was in a pale green sweatsuit and was Roxane who waved and called my name. I shouted, "Roxane!" and waved. The pigeons circling upward waved, the sparrows on the curbstone waved, the bare lilac bush poking through the fence slats — it waved, too. "I'm out. Of breath. And sweaty," she cried.

"You look great!" I said. "You look wonderful." I flung my arms around her.

"Oh, God. So do you." She started to laugh and gasped for breath. "Oh, God. No wind. Shower. Have hot water this week."

While Roxane was taking her shower I wandered around the room, delighted to see again the sawed-off table, the galvanized zinc washtub filled with audio tapes and records. She had added a bookcase which now held a few works on Zen, several volumes on photography and a bottom shelf dismal with psychiatry books. The cork bulletin board beside the refrigerator looked more interesting. I read the parking summons from the Cambridge Police Department, a telephone bill, and a recipe for banana bread, peered at the snapshots, checked the list of things to do (appt for glasses, pay mastercard, Susan brunch, buy bra and radial tires) and examined a blank postcard of Pierre Bonnard's *The Bathtub*.

"Almost done," she said, going into her bedroom. She came out barefoot in a lilac tank top and white denim jeans, a towel in her hand. I knew it was ridiculous to think how beautiful she looked in those cheap common clothes but I kept thinking *how beautiful, so beautiful*. She put her head down and began briskly to rub her hair in a the towel, saying, "I kept hoping I'd bump into you but it never happened. So I called." She flung her head back to settle her hair and then paused.

"I'm wild about you. You know that," I said.

She smiled. "What I knew for sure was that you would never phone or come by."

"I'm too old."

Roxane went on as if she hadn't heard me. "The reason I called —" She broke off and began again. "I have to tell you —" She hesitated, looking right at me.

Now the horrible thought crept into mind that I had misunderstood everything, that she had phoned not to bring us together again but to inform me about some change of fortune in her life, to announce that she had met somebody, some young man who made the world whole at last. I began to speak, but my mouth was too dry. "What?" I whispered.

"I want to see you. More. Always," she said.

I was frightened that I hadn't heard right.

"I know, I know," she rushed on. "It's impossible. That's why we stopped. I can tell by your face that you —."

"Roxane —" I started to reach for her.

But she had stepped past me and now banged two mugs onto the little counter, snatched two spoons from the drawer and slammed it shut with her hip in a sliding crash of tinware. "You think I'm crazy," she said, her back to me.

"Yes. You're crazy. All my friends are crazy." I put my hand on her bare shoulder and she turned inside my arm and we kissed. I don't understand how anyone as muscular as she was could be so light and yielding, as if we were meeting in water. Then I breathed that haze of lemon-scented shampoo and closed my fist slowly in her damp hair, and when I felt her hands on my flanks I pulled her head back, pressing my teeth into her cheek, her jaw, her neck — she lunged free and bit my mouth.

"Oh!" she cried. "Sorry. Are you okay?" Her cheeks were flushed.

"Yes, yes." I barked out a laugh, dabbed at my lip, looked at my finger tips to see if there was blood. "I'm fine."

"I'll make us coffee." She plowed her hands up through her hair and held them there a moment, as if confused. Her hair, held up in spikes and clumps, looked almost the way it had when I first met her. "Would you like coffee?"

"Actually, I don't have much time. I'm going to meet Maeve at five." I touched inside my lower lip and now my finger came away bloody. "Do you have any ice?"

Roxane opened the refrigerator door and

began working loose the ice tray. "How is Maeve?" she asked, conversationally.

"Maeve's fine. The doctor says her thyroid is a little low, but other than that she's fine. Why are we talking about Maeve?"

"She's so young-looking," Roxane said, handing me an ice cube. "Is this all right?"

"Yes. Maeve's beautiful. But if I should ever stop loving her she'd turn into an ugly old hag. It's a curse put on us by the faeries in Ireland. So I have to be careful."

Roxane smiled briefly. "I don't think you'll stop loving her. Are you staying or going? I can't tell when you keep walking around that way." Now there was an edge to her voice.

"Staying," I said. I gave up on the ice and dropped it into the sink.

"I'm never sure of anything around you."

"I'm crazy about you. You can be sure of that."

"Sometimes I want —. Oh, sometimes I want —" She broke off.

"You can have whatever you want."

"What do you mean? Are you some mythic figure who grants wishes?" She smiled.

"I care for you more than you know."

"There are some parts of my life I'd like to remake or do over again."

"That's not impossible," I told her.

Roxane studied my eyes a moment, trying to decide whether or not to believe me, then opened her mouth to speak but said nothing.

She went to the zinc washtub and pulled out her portfolio. "Let me show you my new work," she said. We went to the window and Roxane stood at my elbow, turning the pages — her lemon scented hair almost brushing my cheek, her fingers almost touching mine — while I looked at the photos and said I liked this one or that one, and so on. "Yes, of course, yes, I want to see you. More. Always," I told her. Then I had to go and I kissed her mouth, pressing hard, and when we broke away I could taste the blood again.

"Hey, wait! Will I call you or will you call me?" she asked.

"Either way," I said. Then I ran down the stairs, jumped into the car and drove off to meet Maeve, happy to have an orchestra tuning up inside my chest.

If you stand at the coffee bar at Croissants, Ltd. you can look through the plate glass at the tables outside. So I stood there filled with happiness and watched Maeve arrive, her raincoat and zippered carrying case in the crook of her arm. She looked unfamiliar and handsome, striding along between the tables, a rather tall woman raised even taller by those heels which she never wore except, now and then, for a flashy display of power. She was in her tan suit and had put her hair in a French roll and that was new, too. She saw me through the window and we waved. She came in smiling and let her tired carrying case and weary raincoat slump onto the counter. I asked her how it had gone. "It went well. Exhausting but well." She drew a fallen strand of hair from her cheek and tucked it behind her ear. "They seemed to like my work."

"They ought to. You're the best they'll ever see." I felt a surge of loyalty for Maeve's work.

"They went along with my suggestions, most of my suggestions, anyway. And they took three of Fisher's designs. Which is good, because he's been acting odd lately. This will make him happy."

"Finley Fisher is odd by nature. Much too gentle. What's he doing now?"

"Oh, nothing," she said, briskly. "Are you buying?"

"Sure. What'll you have?"

We took our coffee and rolls to an outdoor table. At that hour the place was populated with typists and clerks who had stopped for a coffee before taking the bus home, elderly business men with newspapers, talkative graduate students, women (with babies in strollers) who had come to buy pastries, brooding chess players, and parochial school girls in plaid jumpers, leaning their heads together to giggle.

"You look relaxed, no jacket or tie," Maeve said. "How long have you been here?"

"Not long."

"You look so happy. What's your secret? Where's your briefcase? I thought you were going to come early and drink coffee and read or watch women or something. — Hey, don't button up *now*. God knows, I like chest hair."

"What's the story on Fisher?" I said, to change the subject.

Maeve had turned her head and, biting her lip but not lowering her chin, she tried to peer at her feet while casting off her high-heel shoes. "Ah! Bliss! — I wish I knew. Maybe it's just me, but he seems —" She broke off.

"What?"

"I don't know. Maybe he doesn't want to know me. He seems to be backing away all the time, as if he thought I might bite."

"You like him," I said. "And maybe, just maybe, you've been coming on too strong."

"Me? Coming on to Finley?"

"You."

"You've got to be joking. Or daft," she said. "Anyway, he's going back to Scotland. Apparently he means it this time." Something had bumped my shin and now I felt her stockinged foot deliberately rub up my ankle and down. "What happened to your lip?" she asked. Her foot continued to rub annoyingly against my ankle.

"What do you mean?"

"It looks like you hurt it. It looks a little swollen." Her voice had become tender.

"Does it?" I touched my lip. It hurt all right. "By the way, I saw Roxane Beach this afternoon."

Her foot withdrew. "Oh! I forgot to tell

you! She phoned this morning. I told her to try your office and gave her the number. So how was Roxane?"

"She was fine." I wanted to rave about Roxane, wanted to say how wonderful she was and how insane I was about her. But before I got to that madness, Maeve had turned her face resolutely toward the Avenue to forestall me.

"Yup, she sounded fine," Maeve said.

32

A couple of days later, Roxane phoned me at my office. She was going to be doing a job in Boston and, she said, we could meet at this fancy new pub off Copley Square. The sky was uneven gray with shreds of torn cloud hanging down, but with rifts of blue here and there, so you couldn't tell if it was going to rain or shine. I was about to step into the pub when I saw her in the stream of people coming along the sidewalk. She threw an arm up and waved broadly — good God, what a wave! — my heart whacked against my ribs. She was in a pale coffee-color shirt with the sleeves rolled up to her elbows and she had a purse, or maybe it was a camera bag, slung over her shoulder. She dodged around the man in front of her and hit her stride, came up. "Great timing!" she said, much as my Nina would. I asked did she want to go inside for a drink, but she said she was hoping we could go for a walk. "You think it will rain?" she asked.

"Let's take a walk. This used to be one of the good places, Copley Square. But they've improved it so much it's inhuman. I liked it better the way it used to be."

We crossed to old Newbury, where the buildings were still within human scale, and turned down the long perspective toward the distant Gardens.

"Want to tell me about Newbury Street and what it was like fifty years ago?" she asked, looking sideways at me.

I told her I'd pinch her arm if she didn't show me more respect. We talked about her work and how it had gone that day, and she asked something about the rituals of academic promotion. When I told her my department had recommended me for promotion, she said she was *certain* the university would follow suit. We looked into boutique windows and remarked on this or that gaudy little item, inspected some splashy watercolors in a gallery, passed comments on the innocent patrons of each café, and stopped in an antique shop to ask the price of this checker board and that tintype, neither of which we intended to buy.

It was simply an hour such as I might spend with Maeve or Nina except, of course, she was not my Maeve or my Nina and I began to feel uncomfortable. Back in December I had thought that we were doing the right thing when we broke it off, when we had stood outside her door and wordlessly agreed that to continue to see each other was impossible, was wrong. And through the dreary winter I had savored the bleak satisfaction of knowing I had done right by Maeve, whose life was braided with mine, and by Roxane, who had a life of her own and some other man to find. The other day when Roxane had said she wanted to see me, see me more, see me always, I had said yes because that's the way I felt. I still felt that way in every bone and drop of blood. But if I had done the right thing back in December, I had to wonder what the hell I was doing now, walking down Newbury Street with Roxane at my side. "Where are we going?" I asked.

"That's the Public Gardens," Roxane said, looking ahead to the hazy green end of the street. Then small drops of rain began to fall. We looked around for shelter, dashed to a small coffee shop and ducked under the umbrella at one of the outdoor tables. "The chairs are dry. We can sit," Roxane said, opening her purse.

Not that Maeve had benefited from my faithfulness and my wonderful chastity. No, she hadn't, because during those gray winter weeks instead of feeling loyalty toward Maeve I felt only that I had betrayed myself and abandoned Roxane. Anyway, I wasn't worried about Maeve and me. I knew that when Maeve ran out of patience she would slam the closet door at bedtime and if I should ask *What's wrong with you?* she would say *You, you bastard, you!* then she would ostentatiously cram her amorous garments of satin and lace into a busted packing box, or she would wrench my gold chain from her naked waist and fling it in my face, and begin to have long lunches with one of those men who materialize whenever she wants — probably Fisher, this time. I wasn't even thinking of Maeve and me. The one I was worrying about was Roxane.

"Hey, Nicolo," Roxane said, taking my hand. "Wake up."

"What do you mean?"

"You looked so sad and far away just now. Where do you go when you go off like that?"

She had laced her fingers through mine and squeezed. God knows, I wanted to keep her. Yes, sure, I wanted to throw myself on her and gallop till she shook her frenzied head and sobbed in an agony of pleasure, but as much as that I ached to give her the solace she craved. It didn't come first and it didn't come last. It was mixed with all the other desires (Crush her bones! Take a drop of her sweat on my tongue!), this longing to give her whatever that exploded family had never given her, whatever her heart desired and not some quick, guilty lay and a lot of empty talk. "If you could have whatever you wanted —" I began.

"I'd get the hot water fixed in my apartment," she said.

"I mean for your future."

"Hot running water."

"Don't you want to meet a nice young man just about now?"

"God *damn* you, Nicolo!"

"Listen. I'm wild about you. You know that. — Are you listening? I like you. I like you more than you know. I think the world of you. — Oh, *shit*." Rain had begun to blow in.

"I thought you said we could get together!" she said, her voice rising.

"I did say that. I did! I did!"

"And I could have whatever I wanted. Not that I believed you for a minute."

"Yes, yes, yes. You *can* have whatever you want. That's what I've been trying to tell you."

"No! You've been trying to tell me to hunt up some handsome young cock my own age!"

The rain was falling more thickly now. I pulled my chair in closer to the table, trying to shelter under the canvas umbrella. Roxane, stiff in her chair, had not shifted at all and dark rain spots had begun to blossom on the shoulders of her tan shirt. She was still watching me.

"I don't want anything to happen to you," I said at last. "I *care* for you, Roxane."

"Roxane can take care of herself." Her voice was hard and her eyes gray, steady and direct. It was on the tip of my tongue to tell her that no, we can't take care of ourselves, that no heart can take care of itself, but I knew there was no use in my saying that. "All right," I said, tired, feeling my age.

"All I thought was, we could take a walk," she told me.

"Yes."

"And I could give you this." She smiled briefly and took from her bag a longish parcel swathed in white tissue.

"Oh," I said stupidly. "Thank you."

She relaxed and smiled more easily. "Go ahead, open it."

"It's not a necktie," I said confidently, unfolding the paper. "It's. It's. It's —" As a matter of fact, it was that old banged-up slide rule with the cracked cursor, one of those mementoes which Roxane had been hauling around in a crate ever since her family had fallen apart.

"You said you had one and lost it, so I thought — My father tried to teach me how to use it, but I never learned and I don't know why I've been keeping it. You seemed to like it so much. Do you want it?"

I worked the slide and moved the cursor here and there, trying to find a polite way not to accept it, trying to find a way to hand it back, this beautiful instrument of rosewood and ivory, identical to my own father's.

"From me to you, free for nothing, a gift," she said. She watched and waited.

"It's a wonderful gift," I said.

She smiled. The rain was softly blowing in on her side of the table and she was getting soaked. I asked where had she parked her car.

"It's got a flat. I took the T," she said.

"I'm parked down by Copley. Want to run for it?"

The rain was steady but light and gentle, so I bundled the slide rule in its blanket of tissue paper and we jogged to the parking lot. I unlocked the car door, she ducked in and immediately stretched across the seat to unlock my door. I dove in. "Dry at last," she said, kissing my cheek.

"You're not dry at all," I said. I twisted this way and that way and managed to pull off my jacket. "Here. Put it on."

"I'll ruin the lining," she said.

"Don't worry about it."

Roxane had drawn my jacket over her shoulders like a cape and held the lapels loosely shut at her throat. I had only glanced at her, but the warmth from seeing her sheltered in my jacket began to flow through my arteries like the heat of brandy. The buildings vanished behind us and we came onto the low bridge, the gray sky expanding upward and outward and the slate river spreading wide downstream. A blurred pencil sketch on the horizon resolved itself into the oblongs and dome of MIT. "My father used to teach there," I told her.

She watched the buildings loom out of the rain. "What was he like?" she asked a few moments later.

"He was a sweet-tempered man. My son gets it from him, I guess. My father taught aeronautical engineering. He was debonair when he was young. Stoic when he was old. He died a few years ago." I made the turn off the bridge and onto the Drive. "I saw him here on a rainy day last fall. He drove right past me."

"How do you know it was your dad you saw and not just somebody who looked like him?"

"He not only looked like my father, he drove like him and he was driving our old Ford."

"Doesn't that bother you, seeing him?"

"No. I miss my father. I don't know why he's around, but I like it. I miss him. But it's always a surprise when I actually see him," I said.

"It would bother me. I don't want any dead people haunting me."

I laughed. "He doesn't haunt me. It's not that way at all. It's more like going back. — I grew up with an old burying ground for a backyard and we used to play in it when we were kids."

"Morbid." She sank down inside the jacket.

"No, no, no. I'll take you there some time. I keep meaning to go back, but I never do."

The traffic was flowing smoothly and in less time than I wanted I made the turn toward Dublin Street.

"I do wish we could drive a little longer," she said. "I like the rain on the windshield and the way everything is so hazy out there." She gazed absently ahead, rubbing her cheek ever so slowly against the jacket lapel. "Your jacket smells good," she murmured.

I stopped at the curb across from her tenement house. Abruptly the rain ceased blurring the windshield and you could see that it was hardly raining at all, only the driving had made it seem that way. I reached for the oblong of tissue paper on the back seat — the slide rule — and turned to Roxane, but she had already stepped out and was handing me my jacket with a quick smile, saying, "See you soon, I hope." Then she ran across the shimmering black street and up the steps, turned, waved and slipped inside.

When I stepped out of the car I heard music throbbing from the house and knew that the kids were out and Maeve was dancing by herself in front of the stereo. She might have seen my car pull in or maybe she heard the heavy *wump* of the outside door, because by the time I entered the kitchen the musical clamor had dropped somewhat and here was Maeve coiling up her hair — the bone hairclip in her teeth, a great sweat stain under each arm — coming barefoot across the stone floor to greet me. There was a light flush on her cheeks and she was almost out of breath. "Welcome home," she said, smiling. Sgt. Pepper's Lonely Hearts Club Band thumped along behind her.

"You look like you've worked up an appetite," I said.

"I had a drink. Now I'm trying to work off the calories."

"Roxane gave me this," I said, cradling the rule in my hands. The band marched around us.

Maeve studied the ivory-covered slide and idly pushed it in and out while singing along with the band. *"What do I do when my love is away?"* Sweat had beaded on her upper lip.

"Does it worry you to be alone?" asked Ringo.

"Does this recording sound better than our old album?" she asked, handing me back the gift. "Felix, the stout, came by this afternoon. Brought the record. Never been played before."

"It's for Nina?"

"He said it's for all of us, actually."

"Did you tell him we have the original?"

"He knows that. This is for old times. Did you know he played in a rock band when he was younger? It was twenty years ago today — and all that. That's a lovely old engineering ruler," she added vaguely. Then a while later the kids came in and we had dinner as usual.

33

I'd never met a young woman who wanted to talk and talk and talk as much as Roxane. We talked in the car. We talked in the street. We talked across a café table. She told me about her job, her hometown, her friends, her grandmother, her theories of photography, her opinions on certain politicians and feminists, her doubts about God. She talked not from a desire to persuade me about this or that, nor even to inform me, but talked for the plain pleasure of being listened to, as if no one had ever listened to her before. As for me, I liked listening to Roxane. Of course, even though we talked a lot we came to a point where we began to do a few things, too.

"Ever been in Sadie's Shop?" she asked me. Sadie's store window held an array of belts and buckles, studded leather wrist bands, sunglasses, and chains. In the window corner stood a chipped female dummy wearing a rhinestone choker, a dusty black leather bra, red panties, black garter belt and fishnet stockings, one of them with a short rip. Through the glass door I spied a kid with whisk-broom hair, big red pimples on the back of his neck, drinking from a styrofoam cup. I started to say that I hadn't been down this way for a long time. "They have some nice things," Roxane said, going in.

The little hole was so crammed with loud music there was barely room for two racks of clothes and a display case. The fat woman behind the counter was bent over a sewing machine, her back to us. Roxane said something I couldn't catch, because of the racket, then began to look through the row of skirts. I examined the collection in the display case: riveted wrist bands, crotchless panties, black stockings, and some lethal looking cock rings. The kid (Grateful Dead t-shirt: skull and lightening bolt) put his styrofoam cup on the counter and reached across to tap the woman on her shoulder. "Hey, I'm going now. And you got customers." He nodded a greeting to me as he left. She glanced up, a round face with green eyes and the beginning of a smile. "If you want help, let me know," she told us, turning back to her machine. I had put on a polite face and tried to show a detached interest in all the nice things that Roxane had said were in here. Actually, the flimsy undergarments, the glittering array of chains and the heavy animal scent of leather — these things speaking of sexual power and enslavement had already begun to waken the hibernating beast in my black heart. That it was Roxane who brought us here was a little knife, stabbing and stabbing again, rousing.

Now she held up a blouse composed entirely of red and black squares for me to look at. "What do you think?" she asked over the noise. I told her it looked too much like a checkerboard. She turned back to the rack. On the wall above her was a display of eye masks, gorgeously ornate devices made of stiffened cloth and turkey feathers, in some of which the eyes were owlish rings and in others were almond shapes with sweeping peacock points. And one mask in particular, a crow-black crescent moon with iridescent horns, would have caught Maeve's attention. In all our fooling around, Maeve and I never entered a shop like this one. When we were first married I was ablaze to take her in white cotton underpants, nothing but that purity would do, and later when we did begin to play games it was always out of doors, under the innocent sun, like the time after skinny-dipping with the Springwells. I wondered if she would be indifferent to this stuff, or interested and furious at my being here without her.

"You like those?" Roxane asked me. "I've got some like that at home. Now tell me what you think of this." She held out a shimmering black blouse slashed here and there by a score of dazzling chrome zippers — a metamorphosis of that rain garment she had been wearing on the day I met her.

I laughed. "I like it. How do you feel about it?"

"I'll go try it on."

Roxane swung around the counter with the blouse and the woman looked up from the sewing machine. "Remember to watch your head, dear!" she cried. Roxane pulled open the slatted door and stooped into the back room.

"Lovely spring day, isn't it?" the woman shouted, lifting her cheerful voice over the pounding music.

"Lovely," I said.

She turned back to her sewing and I began to sort through a box of bondage postcards. The music halted, a disk jockey's voice came on for a minute or more, then The Rolling Stones began to play. The louvered door swung ajar and Roxane said, "Come and take a look." I crouched through the door, banged the back of my head on a pipe. The changing room was a white shower curtain drawn into a circle with a blazing floodlight where a shower head could have been. "What do you think?" Roxane asked. She had thrown off her jersey dress and pulled on the blouse and was standing there with her hands on her hips, seemingly naked from the waist down. "Christ!" I said. I could feel myself stirring loose, getting hard.

"Does it look comic?"

"No," I said, trying to breath evenly. The garment stretched over her torso like a tight

230

black leather glove, the chrome zipper teeth sparkling and winking against the black shimmer. The zipper chains shook ever so slightly and I knew she was breathing raggedly. "What happens if I pull this?" I asked, putting a finger through the zipper ring at her throat.

"Try it and find out." Her voice was hoarse, uneven.

I slashed it down and the blouse sprang open, the chrome teeth flashing. She had thrown off her bra, too, and her breasts shone white, stiffening. We stood motionless while the music of the Stones came blasting through the door, stood so close I felt her breath on my cheek. I put my hand on her flank. "You're beautiful. Let's get out of here," I said.

"You didn't tell me if you liked it."

"Yes. I like it."

"Then I'll get it for me."

That was all that happened. I had felt a compressed surge in my thighs and was about to rush her against a wall then and there, but there was no wall, only this flimsy white shower curtain in the glare of the floodlight, and all around us a mess of broken clothes racks, empty boxes, hangers and other junk. By the time we got back to Roxane's place I had cooled down just enough to think I should understand what I was about to do, no matter if it was blind or immoral or foolish or whatever. I had no hope of stopping, only the vanity to believe that I could understand anything at all at that point. But before I could begin, Roxane said, "I want to take a shower."

She had tugged open the bottom drawer of her bureau and was rummaging through a tangled nest of sweaters, sweat shirts and jerseys. "Just a sec," she said. She was tossing sweat shirts onto her bed — a green one, a blue one with a schooner that said GLOUCESTER, and one that was a Union Jack. "Which one do you like best?" she asked. I said I liked them all.

"Pick one."

I picked the green one because it was closest to me.

"Wear it, will you?" she told me.

"What do you mean?"

"Just put it on while I take my shower. It's clean. I washed it. Put it on."

"Why?"

"Will you put it on for me or not?"

I began to pull it on.

"No, no. Take off your shirt first."

I looked at her.

"Should I shut my eyes? Just put it on," she said.

I began to unbutton my shirt, tightening my stomach muscles so that when I took it off I'd look better than I was. I chucked it on the bed.

"You don't wear undershirts?" she asked.

I stretched up, keeping as hard as I could,

and pulled the sweat shirt on. "Some one told me it's sexier this way."

"Maeve told you that. Why do I keep seeing you when there's no future in it?"

"Who says there's no future in it? We get along fine, you and me."

So I sat on the sofa with my feet propped on the sawed-off coffee table and began to read *The Keepers of Light: A History & Working Guide to Early Photographic Processes*. When I next looked up, Roxane was in a black leather skirt and that black blouse with chrome zippers and she was rubbing her hair in a towel. "Come home with me to dinner," I said. I wasn't thinking, I just didn't want to leave without her.

"The last time we did that we ended up not seeing each other for a long time." She had ducked her head into the towel and was rubbing her hair, avoiding me.

"We won't stop seeing each other this time. We know better."

She continued to rub her hair for a while, thinking about it. "Okay," she said at last. I asked if I could get into my shirt now. She smiled and said yes. I yanked her into my lap and we crashed off the sofa onto the stringy carpet, rolling this way and that while she whipped and thrashed about, her teeth clenched and her lips drawn back, utterly silent as she scrambled to get the upper hand. We came to rest in a grove of chair legs with Roxane sprawled half on or half off me, her cheek on my chest. I lifted my hand through her damp hair again and again, breathing the scent of her lemon shampoo while she lay quite still, listening to my heart beat. Then we got up and brushed off our clothes and just before we left she tossed the green sweat shirt into her bedroom, saying, "It's ours and I get to wear it whenever I want."

34

I made the turn into our driveway and there was Stout's rusted wreck like a monstrous speckled egg about to hatch. Then Roxane's car swung onto the gravel and rolled up beside me. So here we were — Roxane in her tight black shirt with the chrome zippers, her hair like an exploding sun, and me with no necktie and half unbuttoned, lugging a briefcase heavy with paper into the kitchen. And there's Maeve looking much too surprised (even her glasses staring wide-eyed from the dark of her hair) her feet bare on the cool stone floor and her famous high cheeks red as apples. And at home at my table with a bottle in one hand, a mug in the other and the cork in his teeth, sits himself, Felix Stout.

"I stopped by —" he began to say, while the cork bounced and rolled on the table top.

"He stopped by at four," cut in Maeve. "I invited him to dinner at five, you said you'd be home by six and now it's seven. What delayed you? The water's boiling, I'll put in the pasta. Hi, Roxane."

"Hullo, Maeve," said Roxane.

"What about the kids?" I asked.

"Morgan Kathleen ate and went over to Lisa's. Nico is at soccer."

Felix had been agog at Roxane, looking as if I had made a spectacular mistake by bringing her home. "Would you like some before it's all gone?" he asked her, holding up the bottle.

Roxane smiled at him and said, "No, thank you."

"His name is Felix Stout," I told her.

And Maeve said, "Felix, that's Roxane Beach."

Felix got half way up, stretched his arm across the table. They shook hands. "Great shirt," he said. "What happens if someone pulls one of those zippers."

"Don't try it," she told him.

I trotted upstairs, dropped my briefcase in the study, threw my shirt into the bedroom, then stepped into the bathroom and opened both faucets full blast to the wash bowl. Of course, I had not known that Felix was going to be here and now I was annoyed at him, this man I liked so much, and ashamed at being annoyed and angry at being ashamed. I scrubbed my head and face, pulled the plug from the wash bowl, went to the bedroom to get myself a fresh shirt. When I walked into the kitchen, Roxane was setting the table and Felix was amusing her with a discourse on Sigmund Freud, that prude, that secret agent of repression, that witless literary critic (according to Felix) who thought our sexual life was some kind of evil allegory. Maeve was at the stove in a cloud of steam with a tumbler of whiskey in her hand and a pinched line at the corner of her mouth that showed she was not pleased at the way the evening was turning out. During the day she had changed her clothes and now wore a blue swimtop and a long wrap-around skirt, white with a Greek scroll design in blue along the bottom — a dress she liked to wear only when she was feeling free and open. She frowned as I came up. "What's the problem?" I asked, lifting the glasses off her head.

"Felix," she called, looking past me, raising her voice to him. "Fetch a bottle of wine from the box outside the door, will you? — There's *no* problem and where are you going with my glasses?" she asked me.

"You look better without them in your hair. On your desk. I'm putting them on your desk."

Roxane had come up. "I love the fragrance of that sauce. What do you put in it?"

"You probably smell the basil," Maeve said, distractedly.

"That's a beautiful skirt," Roxane said.

Maeve started to lift her chin, the way she does when she believe she's been slighted, but then tossed her head and smiled and said, "Nina gave it to me. Nicolo likes it because it opens to show a lot of leg," she added.

"What's that? What opens to show a lot of

leg?" Felix asked, coming up with a bottle of dark wine.

"This dress. Like this —" Maeve began to demonstrate.

"What have you got there?" I said.

"Your Chianti classico," he said.

"Great," I said, taking the bottle. "Let's go open it."

"Felix," said Maeve, calling him back. "There's a block of Romano in the refrigerator. Fetch it here, will you?"

We sat at the bare wood kitchen table and filled our glasses with Chianti, except for Maeve who brought her tumbler of Jameson whiskey with her. Then Roxane made a toast to all of us and I made a toast to the dinner and Maeve made one to our good appetites and Felix made another to all our appetites, the good and the wicked. Then we refilled our glasses and whatever spilled on the table was for the gods, as my grandfather used to say. Dinner was *fusilli* — "Corkscrews!" cried Felix — and tomato sauce. "I remember this sauce. I love it," said Roxane. I told her she should come visit in late August or September when Maeve gathers the Roma tomatoes and begins the long boiling down that renders them to raw sauce. "It goes on for days and the house is filled from morning till night with the odor of simmering tomatoes. You breathe it and have culinary visions," I said. Now Felix began to talk about visions and that led to one thing and another and when it came out that Roxane was a photographer Felix asked her what was the difference between nude photos and pornographic photos. Roxane began a little dissertation on form and content, but Felix was hungry for something more specific. "What do we see when we look at a nude photo that we don't see in a pornographic photo?" he asked her. "Or is it the other way around?" And before Roxane could answer, Maeve had smoothly interrupted to refill Felix's glass, distracting him from Roxane, and then we were talking about sex and morality and what it had been like back in the middle of the century. "I suppose that means the nineteen fifties," Maeve said, pleased to have Felix's attention again. "It was better then. I don't mean morality was better, I mean sex was better. You could sleep around and not worry about some sly virus taking up residence in your nerve ends or sabotaging all your white blood cells." But Felix said the fifties were a terrible time of sexual repression. "That's what everybody says," Maeve told him. "But I was there and it wasn't that way at all. Not for me, it wasn't." And Roxane laughed and said she didn't know anything about the fifties and ran her hand back through her hair, laughing, and I saw high beneath her bare arm where the sharp zipper teeth around the arm hole had pinched her tender flesh, leaving a pink welt, as if a maddened lover had bitten there.

The kitchen phone rang and it was Nina. I took it around the corner into the dining room so I could hear better. Nina might be calling to inform us that she had a fever of a hundred and three but wasn't going to the infirmary because all they did was hand out aspirin, or that she was coming home this weekend with two friends, or that she had just read this great page in Karl Marx or Emily Bronte and could she read it over the phone, it would only take a minute. Now she said, *Hi, dad. Listen. I called to tell you guys I'm going away for the weekend with Fisher and I won't be back until Monday or Tuesday. I didn't want you to call and not find me and wonder what had happened. We're driving up the coast or maybe through Maine and New Hampshire and Vermont. Say hi to mom.*

"Wait, wait, wait. Who are you going with?"

Finley.

"Finley?"

Yes, yes, yes. Finley Fisher! I'm going with Fin! It's no surprise, is it? We're just going to drive around New England for a few days. I've got to go now. Say hi to mom.

"You're going with Fin Fisher?"

Dad, please!

I suppose I said oh, or well, or be careful, and Nina said *Always am. Bye, dad*, and I guess I said have a good time or words like that. Then I returned to the kitchen and hung up the phone. They were busy talking and I saw beneath the table how Maeve had clamped a big bare foot on Felix's shoe, her toes on his ankle. It felt like a punch in the face. I sat down, stunned.

"Everything all right?" Roxane asked me, puzzled. "You look —"

I said yes, everything was all right, that was Nina.

"What did she say?" Maeve asked.

I told them that Nina was going away for the weekend.

"Oh. That's nice. Did she say where?" Maeve asked.

"Just a drive around New England," I said. "Pass the wine, will you?"

I filled my glass, then tilted my head back and kept gulping until the glass was empty. Maeve's face looked red to me and sweat glistened beneath her eyes when she laughed at whatever Felix said. Felix had loosened his tie and unbuttoned his shirt, letting his chest hair boil over — Maeve loves chest hair — and now he undid his cuffs and folded them back, revealing his big square wrists and bronze forearms. I didn't need to refill his glass because he was drunk enough on his own words, informing us on blah and blah and blah blah blah. As for Roxane, her cheeks glowed and she laughed or said this and that, glancing my way only when it was proper. I didn't have much to say but listened to the others and watched them — watched us all, actually —

and after a while I was laughing, too. I laughed at smug and stupid me, which wasn't much fun, but then I began to laugh at all of us for being so high-minded and round-about when it would be so much better to roll on the floor and do what we wanted to do, and I laughed to think that if we drank enough we'd get there but by then we'd be too drunk to do anything at all. Or maybe I was laughing because the wine had finally taken hold. Now Roxane ran her hands back through her hair, or slid open the zipper at the side of her shirt, saying she was hot, or lifted the hair from the nape of her neck and held it there a moment, did these and other small things because she knew I was taking pleasure in watching her, and because she wanted me to. After the pasta and wine, the four of us tore apart a basketful of grapes, apples and oranges. I discovered I had a lot to say. We never left the kitchen table but sat nailed to our chairs, talking and drinking espresso and cracking walnuts while the kids came home and made themselves sandwiches and went upstairs to shower and to bed. At midnight we staggered out onto the gravel drive, looked up and discovered the constellations. I was looking for Leo but Felix assured us that Leo was long gone. "Virgo. That's Virgo up there. Yup. Someplace," he said, bumping into Maeve and then putting his arm around her. And now he was filling her ear with some nonsense about Virgo. Roxane got into her car and rolled open the window. I leaned in, kissed her, felt her hand on my cheek and wanted to sob, because she and Maeve were floating together in my head and I was so confused I couldn't tell if I was joyful or miserable. Then we all said good-night and Roxane's car circled out and shot off, and a moment later Felix's VW wheeled around, crawled onto the road and scuttled away.

35

The next day I didn't want to think about anything or anybody — especially not about Roxane or Maeve or me — and since it was Saturday I asked Nico did he want to come down to the playing field to try throwing the boomerang. He said he didn't know.

"You don't know what?" I asked him.

"I don't know if that's what I want to do this morning."

"Come on," I said. He's a sweet kid, but sometimes he needs to be coaxed.

"Which playing field?"

"The high school."

"Everyone will see us."

"No one will be there. Your friends won't find out."

"There's always people there, dad."

"It's a big field. They won't be able to make out your face. You won't have to be ashamed that your father is trying to throw a boomerang. Quit being difficult and if you don't want to come, say so."

So I drove us to the high school parking lot. We walked past the tennis courts, each one in use, and then across the empty soccer fields and over the scruffy patch which became the middle of the football grid in the fall, and on toward the no-man's land that lay this side of the baseball outfield. "Okay, no one can see us here," I told him.

All those months my father was dying and I could do nothing about it, I would go outside and toss a tennis ball to Nico and he would chuck it back to me, so it would sail back and forth in soothing rhythm, back and forth and back and forth, until I was able to go back into the house again. And sometimes I would take one of the kites from the wall by our kitchen and we would come to this same field, play the string out and let the breeze take the kite up. Then it would be just the two of us here and the kite up there, the kite tugging at the string, trying to fly away, and the two of us standing here in the wide empty field, taking turns at the string, both of us looking up at the kite and talking about the air currents, quite the way my father used to, or not talking much at all. Those hours with Nico were the only restful times in all that spring and summer and fall.

"Here," I said, handing him the boomerang. "You try it." Nico threw and it went out and up a bit, making a slow turn as it windmilled down to the ground. We walked over to it and I picked it up, threw it. This time it went out too low, swept along a gentle curve and headed back to us, scuffing and then tumbling along the ground fifteen feet away. "I'm going to flex that thing. Give it more airfoil," I said.

"Yeah. Well. If you wait and throw it into the breeze at the right angle, it will come back right."

"Show me," I said.

We worked our way across the field — throwing and then walking forward the three or fifteen feet to where it had landed — until we were up against the scrub woods. Then we turned and began to work our way back. The high school looked small from out there and you could barely make clear the tennis courts, the tiny figures in white shorts and jerseys, or the road with the cars going noiselessly by. It was peaceful out there: just the two of us, me and my son.

36

Maeve stood straight as a post in her black satin nightrobe and looked down at the fireplace. "If I had known you had a fire I would have come down earlier," she said, watching the flames. She had risen from a scalding bath, put on the robe and those gold high-heel sandals and come down to the living room. Ordinarily she wore those garments prior to making love, but since that dinner Friday night there was a secret distance between us. She continued to stare at the fire and gave me no more than her shoulder.

"It got cold down here. I thought I'd burn the rest of this wood," I said.

"It's colder upstairs." She turned up the huge collar so it stood behind her head like a scallop shell. The shimmering black cloth fit tightly down to her waist, then hung heavy and loose. She held her big red hands out to the fire, spreading her fingers. "I think I'll have a drink," she said, speaking more to herself than to me.

"It's almost midnight," I said, as if it were too late to have a drink.

Maeve went into the kitchen anyway. She used to have a drink at bedtime whenever she had menstrual cramps, but she was past that now. She returned with a thick tumbler of whiskey in her paw, took a swallow and set the tumbler — an old marmalade glass, actually — on the mantel. There was a clink-clink of brass dog tags from the dim corner by the door as Rover yawned. Then he shuffled up to Maeve and her hand automatically scratched and combed his old head. She took another drink.

"Want me to get another log?" I asked, for she seemed more yielding now and I thought we might linger into the night.

"No. — What are you reading?"

"A book about photography by a stupid Frenchman."

"Oh, *photography*." Maeve glanced about with a slight frown, then gave innocent Rover a short kick meant for Roxane. He padded back into the shadow, slumping down heavily with a sighing grunt.

"Are they asleep up there?" I asked. We wouldn't carry on if the kids were awake.

"Long ago. Did you want me to get you a drink when I was in the kitchen?" That was her overture and if I said yes, it meant I would take her up on it. But that little kick had made me wary.

"No," I said.

"Nothing at all?"

"Not a thing."

She took a swallow of whiskey, then sat in the chair on the other side of the fireplace and placed the glass on the floor beside her. I was frustrated by not knowing whether to go forward or backward, so I whacked the logs with the poker, sending up a fountain of sparks, and began to rearrange the broken coals. "Are you angry about something?" she asked a moment later.

"No." It came out more abruptly than I had intended. I brushed off my hands and sat down. "Are you being antagonistic?"

"You seem awful surly."

"Because I said I didn't want a drink? We had plenty Friday night."

"We haven't talked all weekend. I just thought we should talk."

"I don't mind talking. I just don't want to argue," I said.

"Neither do I. But I don't think we drank too much Friday night. After all, there were four of us."

"I didn't say we drank too much. I said we had plenty. At least, I had plenty. I won't say anything about you."

"I enjoyed myself. I enjoyed the company." She took a sip and set the glass back on the floor. "I enjoyed Felix. He's interesting."

"He ought to be."

"You seemed to be having a good time," she said.

"I was."

"Well, Felix is interesting," she told me.

"Yes, you've said that."

"Well, I like him," she said, her voice as simple as a drop of water.

"So do I, but probably with less intensity."

"I'm not *intense* about it. I like him a lot, that's all."

"That's all?" I said. "All these weeks he's been coming around to see *you*, not Nina!"

"Do you mind?"

Of course I minded. "Why should I mind? Is there something going on I should mind about?"

"I don't know," she said.

"You don't know! Now what does *that* mean?"

"It means I don't know what would bother you these days."

"*These* days? *These* days? What's so special about *these* days?"

Maeve had started to drink and now with her mouth full she paused and shot me a compressed look, as if she were about to spit in my face. "All right all right all right! Forget I said that." I knew what was coming.

She swallowed the whiskey and took a breath. "*Roxane* seems special to you these days! I'd say *Roxane* is what's so special these days!"

"All right, Maeve."

"But nothing is bothering *you*."

"Don't be a bitch, Maeve!"

Her eyes flared and her mouth became a straight line. When she was younger her face could be handsome with rage, but she was no longer young and at this moment she looked plain ugly, and I felt cheap for making her look that way.

"Look," I said. "The things that would bother me, if you did them — This is ridiculous! We've been over this before. Just keep me informed. All right? I don't want to be the last to know."

"I haven't done anything to know about," Maeve announced crisply.

"Neither have I!"

"Not yet, you mean?"

"The same as *you*, Maeve!"

Rover's dog tags clinked and he padded out of the shadows. He slouched morosely down the length of the living room rug and went out the door, his nails clicking quietly on the stone floor as he passed into the kitchen to get away from us.

"We're too old for this," I said after a while.

"I'm not," she said mildly.

"You're not what?"

"I'm not too old for this." She turned to me. "And neither are you. And that's the trouble."

She had begun to lift the back hem of her robe with both hands, hauling the heavy cloth up to expose her heels and calves and thighs to the heat, and now she stood in her gold high-heel sandals, her fists on her bare hips so the thick gather of cloth about her waist would fall forward and down in stiff folds to her toes, while her moon colored rump (a handspan of talcum on the underside) glowed warmly above the fire.

"Does it have to be trouble?" I asked.

"I don't know. In the past, I would have said — I don't know. What do you think?"

"I don't want trouble."

"Neither do I. I never want trouble," she told me.

I looked at her long calves, the tightened backs of her knees, her thighs and the heavy round of her buttocks in the small light of the fire. She was watching me, but her face was deep in the shadow of that turned-up collar with only two sparks to show her eyes.

"Do you think they'd wake up and come down?" I asked quietly.

"Your guess is as good as mine." Her voice was low and warm and she stood very still, her hands on her hips and the cloth in a stiff cascade to her toes, watching me while I looked at her.

"We don't have to make a lot of noise," I suggested.

"I can do something for you that won't make any noise at all," Maeve said.

37

In the morning, after Morgan Kathleen and Nico have gone off to school and Nicolo has left for the university, the house grows quiet once more and the rooms, emptied of sound, grow larger and more spacious, and each emptied room stands open to me, and I am free to be myself, alone and by myself, anywhere. I can draw the shades so the sun seeps around the edges and opens like a fan upon the ceiling, as if reflected from the shimmering waters of a Venetian canal, while I stroll naked and open through the hushed living room and naked mount the stairs, formal as a courtesan or oriental concubine, and stretch my white self on the dark blanketed bed to be taken by whoever I choose. More likely, I can wrestle the soiled clothes from the hamper and load them into the washing machine. Out on the terrace Rover dozes with his old gray chin on a warm flagstone and sleepy Calico lies curled in the long grass against the wood pile. The washing machine thrashes away in the next room. And I get down to work.

By eleven o'clock I'd completed the scribbling jobs, answered the phone half a dozen times, while the lozenge of sun had swung about and lay on a narrow wedge of table by the window sill. I lit the burner under the coffee pot, scooped the clothes from the drier and spread them on the living-room sofa to be sorted later, then I poured an inch of coffee into the mug and brought it to the table where I luxuriously gave myself up to thinking about Felix. *Why Felix?* Why am I drawn to him and not to some other Tom, Dick or Harry? He has a head of crazy ginger hair that never would have moved me in the past, and a wide upper lip I would find unattractive on anyone else, and when he looks at me I feel pleasurably taken, trapped in his amber gaze. But to be honest, it wasn't Felix who caught me, it was I who caught Felix. And a dozen years ago it was I who caught Father John Gabriel Sullivan, not the other way around. Only with Nicolo there was no catching either way: everything happened so fast there wasn't time for flight or pursuit. The morning I saw Nicolo he had already seen me and my heart was a cinder before I even heard the crack of the lightning. That evening when I laid my cheek on his warm chest we had already made love, but I was still only half way there and didn't catch up until the second time, out of breath, kissing his mouth, his jaw, his throat, saying, "Splendid man, you splendid man," and by then he was asking me to marry him. "Yes," I said. "My mother is dead but you can meet my father. Yes." Because I had already said yes, had been saying it ever since noon when I discovered that the rest of the world was only what was left over. The sound of his voice and what he was saying, every thought and movement of his heart, his touch, the scent of his skin, the smooth taste of him on my tongue — things were happening so fast the miracle is I wasn't giving birth the day we married. But you can't learn why you love someone by carefully picking him to pieces and studying each piece up close, otherwise you end up saying you love him because of his cock or his mind, and that's never quite true. Because it's not merely the pieces you love, but the way they're all together and the way they're together is himself and now you're back where you started, knowing you love him and not knowing why.

That's the way it was for years and years and I never gave it much thought, because I never had to. I was happy. Then I saw Father John and discovered that loving Nicolo as much as I did made it easy to love someone else too. I knew it wasn't supposed to work that way, but it did. That's when I began to think about love, think about what it was I knew when I said I loved Nicolo and what it was I meant when I said I loved John Gabriel. I saw myself loving Nicolo first and forever, loving Nina and Morgan Kathleen and Nico differently but forever and no less, and outside of them was the rest of the world. John Gabriel was close, but not so close as us, not inside, and though the love that went to him was the same as went to them it was diminished by the distance. God knows he was a sweet young man, fresh from the seminary like a chick just out of its shell. But not even God knows whether he lusted after me or some version of the Holy Mother he thought he saw in me. It began the day he came out to baptize Nico, for during the ceremony Nico had begun to cry and my breasts had begun to flow at his crying, dampening my blue dress, so afterward I walked off a ways from the guests and sat under one of the apple trees. And young Father John strayed down to the orchard and got lost among those cloudy boughs and found me in the long grass with my back against a tree, the baby asleep in my lap, my breasts bare, wet. We looked at each other and it was so quiet, even the bees stopped buzzing. He lunged and smacked his head on an apple branch, sending a flutter of blossoms down on me and the baby, then he staggered around and made his way back to the baptismal party. His heart was a terrible ruin, he told me days later.

Maybe there's no sense asking *Why Felix?* because maybe what's important is never just the man but when he comes along. A dozen years ago John Gabriel Sullivan came along just when I knew Nico was my last baby, and I was going to breast feed him way beyond his proper time simply because I didn't want to dry up. There was a logical step from weaning Nico to beginning with John Gabriel, and I understood that step and felt it as surely as I would feel a solid stone that I would step to in the middle of a creek to get to the other side. Of course, it's fair to say that John Gabriel came along the same time as Grace Greentree, and if Nicolo hadn't gone after Grace I wouldn't have let myself take John. And we might as well add that the time was right. I was beautiful at thirty-four and I knew it, enjoyed it, showed it around — why not? Everyone stopped by our house that summer and we had an endless picnic, eating in the shade of the grape arbor, drinking May wine and entertaining each other with stories about Watergate, as if we were amorous Florentines sitting out the plague. One hot afternoon in the barn John asked me to take off my wedding ring before we knelt down in the hay and I told him, "Oh, no, this never comes off." After all we'd done he was shocked and the game was over, just like that. I haven't seen John or even Grace in a long while. That's the way it is with people you're not married to — they drift off the map and all you have of them is a three faded photos and some records to play when you're feeling blue and want to make yourself weep. We ought to wed each other more often.

Now Felix comes along when I'm in need

of comic relief. Of course, I could say it's because of Roxane, could say that when I saw Nicolo taking an interest in Roxane I looked about and found Felix to distract me. But that's not true at all, or no more true than if Nicolo said the same about me and claimed he was injured, was feeling hurt, claimed he was looking only for solace in Roxane. But Nicolo doesn't work that way, he doesn't get hurt and go fooling around — he really likes Roxane and would like her no matter what. Felix comes along when I'm feeling more spent, more used up and more tired every week. In a dumb way I thought it would get easier as the kids got older. Actually, it just gets harder and harder to hold it all together. Here's Nicolo and me revolving about each other while young Nico and Morgan Kathleen go circling around us in wider and wider orbits and beyond them is Nina — one of these days her path will straighten out just a wee bit more and off she goes like a comet. I'm told they come back at long intervals.

Everything is breaking loose, except me, and I'm forty-six. My mother never got to be this age and I think of that sometimes, think what it was for her to know she was leaving three children, including this Maeve, age eleven. When I was a kid I used to weep for myself because I had no mother, but as each of my kids turned eleven I wept for my dying mother. I remember pouring water from my beach pail into a hole I had dug in the sand while she sat on a towel in her swimsuit, watching me — you could see her breast was gone. And now I'm forty-six. You hear that age and think, *She's menopausal, that's her problem — fat as a spayed Collie or skinny rough like an alligator boot — poor old bitch*. I would have thought so myself, twenty years ago. But here I am, weighing barely more than I did the day I got married, my summer skin as smooth as olive oil. The scar on my breast has melted away, my hair is still thick and black where it matters. Nicolo was forty when the first gray thatch appeared on his chest, fifty before it began by his cock. The handsomeness of the young is mostly their solid health and energy. That's why you want to sink your teeth into them. Nicolo calls me a goddess who sweats, and he means it as a compliment, but only he could love such a thing. Anyway, it's not love I'm talking about, but just a holiday.

I once jotted down a list of reasons why a woman who was married to the man she loved might get involved with another man. It was short but satisfying work. Afterward, I folded it to the size of a bookmark and squeezed it way to the back of my junky pencil drawer where it hid with the baby teeth, a lingerie catalog and a cellophane sandwich bag of marijuana. That was years ago when I was too busy with the kids to be getting out much and Nicolo had begun coming home with these buccaneer girls — energetic young women with flushed cheeks and bright eyes who planned to become Nicolo, not Maeve, when they grew up. I think Nicolo was bringing them around partly to entertain me, though it didn't work that way. From time to time I'd be moved to turn the list into an essay, but I never got very far. I'd start off by saying that a woman who loves her husband needs another man because 1) she doesn't want to bore the one she's married to with complaints about, say, the printer who misread her entire layout and destroyed her week's work, or about the diaper that got stuck in the john. She needs someone new to talk to, that's all. And 2) because after a certain number of years you begin to wonder if he loves you from the heart or says those things only from habit, seeing that you're in his bed and have his kids and share his bank account. And, believe me, it's always a delightful surprise to hear those same words from a man who has no decent motive to say them, only his base craving to have you when there are plenty of other women around but it's you he's after. And 3) because a different body is full of surprises, unexpectedly heavy or light or hot, rough here and silken there where you didn't expect it, with a different odor and taste. And every part of him is a bit displaced from where it was, so the fit is different everywhere and your flesh is startled into awareness, creating a whole new geography, a new self. What's so bad about that? I meant to keep the essay short and to the point, like the Gospel, but even so I never finished it. I'd picture myself in a tryst with this or that young man and I'd see for sure that it was only earthly pleasure (no more or less than that, not a harmful thing), but when I'd turn the scene so it displayed Nicolo and a woman — the whipping flash of his buttocks, his shoulders glistening with sweat, his face growing dark — then it looked horrible. When I last cleared out my upstairs desk there was only a scrawl of rubber bands and paper clips back there and a vibrator forgotten for a decade. I unscrewed the cap end of the vibrator and found one of the ancient batteries was corroded firmly to the inside of the cap and the other had leaked white stuff within the cylinder.

I don't *care* why Felix and I don't *care* why now and, as a matter of fact, I don't know why we love anybody except the children. But we are drawn to each other and this desire to cradle someone else's flesh is answered by the craving to be held. It's as simple as that and that's what all the fuss is about. Because I can stroll back and forth in my kitchen and feel this gaiety in secret, as if a choir of excited birds was perched on my ribs just under my breasts, trilling their wee hearts out. Because I can put away my pencils and pens, take out the lettuce and the colander, and go on smiling all the while, though no one is around to see.

Because the world still has its happy possibilities — like the morning Felix turned up at the door, knowing I'd be home alone at that hour, asking, "Do you like flowers like I like flowers?" and he unbuttoned his shirt and began to pull bunches of daffodils from his armpits and sleeves, and irises from his pants, narcissus, lilies and fern.

38

Saturday I drove to Roxane's and cantered up the stairway and said, "How about a drive in the country?" It always staggered me, how actual she was — those startled eyes, that wheat color hair. "Hello," I said, trying to recover.

"The hot water quit again," she said cheerfully. "I had to boil gallons just to wash the dishes. I want to take a hot shower. I crave and desire a hot shower." She held a small jar of yogurt and was spooning it around as she talked.

"You look clean enough to me."

"I did wash, Nicolo. — Want to share some breakfast?" she asked, licking the spoon.

"I don't think you eat right, Roxane."

"I know you don't. But this is healthy food. By the way, I want to buy a plant this morning. I'm tired of ferns."

"Are we going out or not?"

She handed me the yogurt jar and her spoon, saying, "Finish this for me. I'll be just a sec." Then she ducked into her bedroom. I took a spoonful of yogurt and made a stroll around the stringy rug — breathed in the clean odor that hung in the air like fresh laundry, looked at the tall oblong of yellow-green leaves and blue sky that leaned against the wall where the empty mirror had been, bent down to pat the galvanized washtub filled with audio tapes and discs — then put the empty yogurt jar in the sink and wound up by the door again. Here was a man fond of things simply because a woman he loved lived among them.

Roxane came in from the bedroom. "I couldn't make up my mind whether or not to put on perfume," she confessed. She yanked the door shut behind us and hurried down the hall. "I'm a shallow person, Nicolo."

She wasn't shallow and I told her so.

"You think you know me," she said, swinging down into the unlighted stairway.

I insisted I didn't know her as well as I wanted to.

"I know me all too well," she said, lifting her voice above the echoing clatter of our footsteps. "I'm another young woman with a camera and some pretensions, that's all. Once upon a time I wanted to be a model. Did I ever tell you that?"

"You'd make a great model."

"Sure. I want people to look at me and like me and want me without my doing anything to deserve it. What do you think of that?" She glanced back over her shoulder at me.

"*Watch where you're going!* — And you're

a good photographer. Maybe a great one if you give yourself time."

"Oh, I'm full of *theories* about photography. Or maybe they're only opinions. It doesn't matter."

We broke into the daylight at the foot of the stairwell. "You're all right, Roxane. You're healthy, intelligent, good looking —"

"You have no idea what it's like to be a nothing," she cut in. "I'm a zero. I really don't make a difference anywhere. And it's so strange. Because it seems it's always been this way and still I can't get used to it. I keep wanting to amount to something and I never do. I keep trying to *be* something, anything, anything at all. And I'm still a nothing." We were standing at the open doorway.

"You're important to me."

Roxane glanced at me. "Do real people have conversations like this?" she asked.

"Who cares?"

"How long are you going to care for me?" She looked square at me, waiting an answer. She wore three tiny wire rings in this ear and two in that one, and there was a little scar pit above her eyebrow where, she told me, she had picked at a chickenpox scab when she was nine. Her eyes were steady and gray, with flecks of green deep inside.

"Forever," I said. "Or as long was you want. Whichever comes first."

"I won't hold you to your word," she said.

She gently slid a hand inside my shirt and moved it searchingly against my chest, this way and that. "But did you say that because you knew I wanted to hear it?"

"Yes. And because it's true." I had taken her hand and was pressing her nails into my flesh, enjoying the pain of those stabs to my heart.

"You're a kind man. I hope we're taking your car, mine's a bomb."

We stepped into the sun. The air was sweet and mild and there was my father coming down the sidewalk beside the row of parked cars. "Oh, there's my dad," I said. I was surprised to see him wearing his old white ducks, white jacket and panama hat. The day wasn't hot enough for it. It was his favorite summertime suit from the 1930s, but it must have been recently bleached or something, because the cloth was blurringly and almost blindingly white, like a sunstruck photograph. He smiled at us and waved with a broad flourish, as if to embrace the sunny day, then he turned his back and tugged at the car door.

I turned to Roxane and said, "Come on. Let me introduce you."

She hung back a step, looking at me with her lips parted as if she had been about to speak.

"What?" I asked her.

"Nicolo," she said in a low voice.

"Don't you see him? Is it just me?"

"I see him. But he's a real person. He's not your father. He's not —" she broke off.

"Don't worry," I told her. "It's all right. Don't be afraid."

I jogged up the sidewalk. My dad was about to get into his car, but when he saw me he straightened up with a little smile. He was strong and more robust than ever, and that relieved me, made me happy. He smiled and said, "I'm getting so forgetful, I need to carry a list. I think I've taken care of everything, or almost everything. What about you? Are you taking care of yourself?"

"I'm all right. I'm fine. Listen, there's something I meant to do."

He slid behind the wheel with a certain effort and laid his hat carefully on the passenger seat and I caught the familiar cool odor of the car interior. He said, "Just try your best. Then relax and don't worry. That's all you can do." That was always his advice to me. "Everything will work out," he assured me. I peeped into the friendly old Ford. The instrument panel looked sadly old fashioned and some of the chrome on the horn ring was worn away, revealing the yellow metal underneath. He had started the motor and now he began to pull slowly from the curb.

"Wait! There's something I meant to say, something I want to tell you!"

Turning to me he gave a gentle nod and a wave to show that he knew all that I had intended to tell him, that he understood, that there was no problem, then he drove serenely up the street. I watched as the beat-up car slowed and then turned the corner and vanished. "Shit!" I said.

Roxane had come up. "Are you all right? Nicolo? Hey, are you all right?"

"Sure. What's the matter? Don't I look all right?"

She watched me closely but didn't say anything.

"What?" I asked her.

"Nothing," she said at last. "Are we going for that drive in the country?"

So we got into my car and I drove down Dublin Street and made the turn out to the highway. Roxane rolled her window down all the way and let the wind blow her hair. The traffic was flowing smoothly and it was easy to drive along in the sun. I made the turn onto the bridge. The river was cobalt blue with gentle swells of dark green and I thought of my father and how one winter he and a friend had walked across from Back Bay. It had been like walking on thick glass and when they were more than half way across they had heard *crack-crack-crack* — "Like a buggy whip," he said.

"Where are we going?" Roxane asked. She had clapped her hand on my thigh and rubbed once, as if to get my attention.

"What?"

"We're heading into the city, not the country."

"God! I hadn't noticed. I'm sorry."

"That's all right. Boston's all right." She let her hand rest loosely.

"My father was born on Hudson Street, down by Fort Point Channel. I never actually visited the place. I have a photo of it and I know the number and I always meant to visit it."

"All right," Roxane said. "Let's go there."

39

My father was born at home at 55 Hudson Street and went to school around the corner at Quincy Grammar. I saw the place where he was born once when I was a kid. It happened when my father took me to buy my first real suit, one of those exceptional days when he and I were alone with each other, off together, away from home. Whenever we went to do something, just the two of us, my father would become more ebullient or eccentric or reckless, or perhaps he merely took bigger steps and drove faster, or maybe he just revealed more of himself because he showed off a bit when we were alone, but whatever it was that he actually did I knew that he became more masculine and whatever we did was itself more masculine than if my mother had been along with us. But this particular outing didn't work as well as others had. I was happy about getting the grown-up clothes, but the store was unfamiliar to me and I was disappointed by the shabby look of things, the disorderly bolts of cloth heaped on an old table, and the way the ancient wood floors creaked under foot.

Afterward I was ready to go straight home, but my father was buoyant and drove crazily up this narrow street and down that one, jigging us here and there and talking about the good times he had spent playing with the kids on Hudson Street. I got bored. We were coasting slowly along an endless row of dull brick fronts, houses three or four storeys high. "That's where I lived! Right *there*," he said. But they all looked alike to me and I told him so. My father laughed and when we came to the end of the street we turned onto an avenue and sped away. He never showed the house to me again. He still talked about it, the same as ever, but my father never drove there with me again.

"Actually born there? In that house and not in a hospital?" Roxane asked.

"Born there, delivered by a woman is all he knew. Maybe a woman doctor, maybe a midwife. He told me he once asked her where he came from and she told him she had found him in the woods."

"No. That's wonderful."

"He had never seen a woods. He thought the world was covered over with asphalt and cobble stones, except for places like Franklin Park or the Public Gardens."

Roxane read aloud from the map, directing me this way and that in zigzag steps across the city. The streets began to take on a known look, the aspect of streets in those dreams where I am back in a long forgotten neighborhood, lost amid familiar surroundings. My father had loved this place more than any other.

"We might go inside," I said. "If we talk to them, the people living there might invite us in. Then I could be in the same rooms as my dad."

Roxane looked up from the map and smiled agreeably at the jumbled mess of store fronts. "It's the next street over. Turn down here."

I turned and drove slowly along. There were only a few cars on the street. "That's it!" I said. "There! That's his first school." Quincy Grammar School was a plain square brick building, just as he had described it, but now I saw above the second-floor windows there was no great carved name, only an oblong scar where the stone letters had been chopped away. Over the door hung a sign in Chinese or Japanese characters: a meaningless hash, like those dictionaries Nina was studying. "What?" Roxane asked me. I told her I was surprised that the name was gone, too. I drove along for a while, turned the narrow end of the block and coasted around the corner into Hudson Street. It was empty and quiet. On this side stood a solid row of russet brick house fronts, three and four storeys tall, and a deserted sidewalk. The other side of the street was gone. There was only a sagging chainlink fence that had trapped a sheet of yellowed newspaper and some white plastic cups, and beyond the fence ran the massive incline of a ramp to the Expressway. I drove slowly. "What was the number of the house?" Roxane asked, breaking the silence. I told her he was born at 55 Hudson. "Then it's still here some place. Because this side has the odd numbers," she said. I pulled to the curb and parked. I looked up at the blank windows, the stone sills rubbed smooth by the arms of all the men and women who had watched this street.

"Are you all right?" Roxane asked.

"Me? Sure. I'm all right."

"Well. Are you going to get out?"

"I thought it would be different. I thought there would be kids playing in the street. The houses are empty and everybody's gone."

We got out and walked along, reading the door numbers. On the way down to 55 there was a space where some houses had been demolished, and further on we could see the blank side of the next building, like a huge slate grave stone on which somebody had drawn the roof line of a missing house. We walked past the open place to where the row began again, but the numbers there were too low. My heart had begun to thud in my chest.

I walked back to the open place to look around, but there was nothing to see, only a few junky cars parked on the hard yellow dirt. "Are you all right? Nicolo? Hey, Nicolo!" Roxane said. She grabbed my arm and held me up for a second until I caught my balance. "I'm okay," I told her. We walked back to the car but when we got inside I put my head down on the wheel and began to cry, so Roxane drove us down Hudson Street and around the block up past his old grammar school and then out of the city.

40

On examination he is a healthy-appearing man in no distress. Pulse 80, blood pressure 130/70. His discs are flat and clearly outlined with good venous pulsations seen. He sits in a somewhat stooped position with a notable stare on his face. There is marked facial masking and occasional drooling. Speech is soft in a fine monotone without inflection. Blinking is very infrequent, yet he is unable to inhibit a blink when he is tapped on the forehead. There is slight cogwheel rigidity of both elbows, none is present in either wrist. The knees are somewhat rigid in flexion without appreciable cogwheeling and his neck is somewhat flexed forward and with some rigidity. It is notable that he had to urinate twice while waiting in the waiting room. There is a very fine resting tremor 4-6 cycles per second in the right hand, none in the left hand and none in the leg. Mental status testing reveals him to be fully alert, oriented, cooperative, speech monotone but fluent. Praxis intact. Memory intact. Visual fields full without extinction. There is marked masking of the face but facial, sensory and motor are otherwise intact. Tongue is midline and there is no slurring of his speech. Deep tendon reflexes are hypoactive throughout but present with bilaterally flexor plantar responses. Finger-nose-finger testing is done slowly but without ataxia as is heel-knee-shin testing. Motor power 10 out of 10 throughout. He is unable to stand with his feet together even with his eyes open. His gait is stooped, with short steps and sometimes he will stop, walking in place for a few seconds. Diagnosis: moderately advanced Parkinson's Syndrome, probably of idiopathic type.

He had Parkinson's disease, the palsy, the shakes — call it what you want. His eyes burned, his taste went flat, his appetite shrank, his bowels locked. Little by little his features changed. The dome of his head grew more prominent, his face thinner, his ears fleshier and his nose longer. One day his hip bone broke and he dropped to the kitchen floor in a heap, baffled, almost without pain. A surgeon deftly replaced the shattered end. Rafe and I stopped at the nurses' station to ask which room Mr. Pellegrino was in, and we were directed to the end of the hall, to the windowed pavilion. There were nine beds, but no one lying there looked like my father. Yet, there was my mother standing by that bed with its side rails up. Her hands rested on the silvery railing and she gazed sadly at the old man in the bed and her face was the face of Mary when they lowered her son to her from the cross. She lifted her hand and stroked — oh, ever so softly she stroked — the white fringe of hair about his ears and caressed his naked head. They had braced his legs apart and had tied him loosely to the side rails with strips of sheeting or bandage cloth, but still his arms jerked and his hands trembled in fitful circles, as if he were swimming on his back desperately, his long nose just an inch above water. His eyes gazed up past the large plastic hose which they had thrust into his mouth and down his throat. I leaned over him and croaked, "Everything will be all right. We'll take care of it. Everything will be all right." And Rafe said, "Nicolo, he can't hear you." Dad's head rolled slowly this way and that and his wide open eyes, glassy bright, stared up past me. I had not thought God would permit this.

At home Daisy or Maeve always set a plate at the head of the table and one of them or one of the kids would sit there across from my mother at mealtime, but not Rafe and not me. Dad recovered and sat in a chair by the hospital bed, and there my mother would read his get-well cards to him and set them in a row on the big window sill. The therapist taught him to exercise his arms which he would need to use more now. Some days his mind could not focus. "Do you know where you are?" the nurse asked him. He looked at her intently, his eyes round with wonder or fear. "In this hotel," he whispered at last. From the hospital he went to the rehabilitation center and there they taught him how to use crutches. Rafe and Daisy brought their kids to cheer him up and the kids played there, turning somersaults on the exercise mats among the maimed and limbless. Dad struggled five paces on the crutches, then they lowered him backward into the wheelchair. A nurse grew annoyed because dad could not remember how to work the wheelchair brake. Later we all sat around a table in the dining room and had cupcakes and coffee and tea. Dad looked up and saw Nico and smiled at him, a strange sweet monkey smile. Later he peed in his pants, but it didn't matter, and I didn't wheel him back to his room until we had to go home.

As soon as there was no more improvement in his condition he was discharged. Mother wanted him home but she was exhausted to the verge of illness, so we found a nursing home where father could stay temporarily. It was even harder now to understand his speech. "The car," Rafe said. "He wants to remind mother to keep enough gas in the car. — Yes. We do. We will. We're taking care of everything. Here's mother now," Rafe told him. He shared a room at the nursing home with another ailing man, and one day father had to wheel himself down to the nurses' station to tell them that the man had slipped from his chair and needed help. The last time I spoke to him I asked, "Are there any pains? Does it hurt anywhere?" He was slumped in the wheelchair, in pajamas and maroon bathrobe, and a belt ran under his arms to hold him more or less upright in the chair. He looked up at me, as if to puzzle out my question. "No," he whispered in his soft rasping voice, barely audible. "No pain." We looked at each other a long moment and then I asked him, "Is there anything you want? Is there anything I can do?" And he said, "Home. I want to go home."

Maeve drove us to the nursing home. The corridor had a sweetish odor of shit. They led us to a room, not his room, but another at the far end of the hall. There mother sat in a straight-back chair, her eyes red and puffy. Her sister Candida sat in another at her side, holding her hand. "I told him you were coming," mother said. "He knew you were coming. I held his hand and said Nicolo is coming, Rafe is coming. And he squeezed my hand. He knew you were on the way. But I don't know if you want to see him. He is so —"

"Where is he? Where's dad?"

Maeve touched my arm and nodded toward the white cloth screen. I walked around the screen and there was the bed with an ancient stranger dead in it. I walked to his side, who did not look like my father, but rather like his own gaunt father, the grandfather I knew only from old sepia photographs. His face was lean and hollowed, and had a yellowish color. His nose, longer and thinner than ever, curved down like a blade and his toothless mouth, with the lips folded in, stood open. His eyelids were not quite closed and showed a crescent of dull brown iris. There was a fine, almost invisible stubble on his chin and jaw — how like sandpaper it was when I sat in his lap and rubbed my cheek on his! His face had simplified to a pair of blanked-out eyes, a long nose, a slot mouth: the face on the old slate gravestone in the cemetery where Rafe and I used to play as kids. I was turning to stone and had to race to get through the *Hail, Mary* and to bless myself, then I walked back around the screen to mother.

That evening I talked to Rafe in the kitchen at the old house. "I want to kill somebody. Somebody has to *pay*," I told him.

"Take it easy," Rafe said. "Who are you going to kill? The doctor? The people at the nursing home?"

"I don't know. But *some*body has to pay."

He looked at me a moment, dead tired. "Eat your food," he said at last. "You're too exhausted to kill anyone."

Two days later we had a good long dinner for everyone who had come to the funeral. The next morning mother and Rafe and I went to the cemetery for the burial, and when we got back to the house Daisy and Maeve made a light lunch for all of us, and I took my place in father's chair.

41

Roxane and I went for a drive one afternoon. This time she had bought a bunch of grapes, some hard-boiled eggs, and a warm loaf of bread. "I'm ready to go anyplace," she said, twisting the heel from loaf. "Anyplace where we can eat in peace. — What are you laughing at?" she added. "I know a very quiet place," I told her. That was the day we drove around to the old burying ground where I used to play as a kid.

We walked under the black pines and arbor vitae, the soil damp and soggy as ever, and came to the bright sunlight inside. A bird sang two long notes on the warm air. The dirt road faded to an end and all about us stood the old slate markers and the bright shaggy grass. The bird sang the same two notes again and then again. It was sunny and quiet and as I looked around I began to recognize the slates, the features coming back from memory little by little, each stone unique in its bearing, but all replying to my gaze with the reserved and reproachful look of a discarded plaything, doll or teddy bear. In my witless way I marvelled at how patient they were to have waited, all in their proper places, waited for years.

"Good God! It hasn't changed at all! It's just like when we used it for a playground," I said, amazed.

She looked around, shading her eyes with her hand. "This isn't so bad for a grave yard. It's not what I thought it would be," she said.

"It's just as it was! It's *exactly* the way it was."

Roxane smiled, not understanding that my surprise was at being able to walk into an unchanged acre of my childhood. She opened the wax bag and peered inside. "Are you still hungry?" she asked me.

"I can't get over this. It's like going back to when I was ten. The world hasn't changed in here."

"Hey, look at this," she said. She had come across the Childs marker, that wide slate which had been cut to resemble a row of six smaller slates standing side by side. The row was tilted more than ever and everyone seemed about to fall down backward: Sarah Childs, Eunice Childs, Abijah Childs, Abigail Childs, Benjn Childs, Moses Childs. In the blank above each inscription was the small neatly carved face, each face more or less like each other, still wide-eyed and bearing no grudge against the world. "All in two and a half weeks. What do you suppose happened?" she asked.

"Small pox or some other lousy thing."

I don't know how many times I had read the stone as a kid, but today as I stood there eating grapes I saw that the first to go had been the youngest, Moses, who *Died AuguSt 19th 1778 Aged 3 years wanting 8 Days*. And it touched me as it had not done before that each age was written to the very last day — Sarah, the oldest, *Died AuguSt 28th 1778 Aged 13 years 8 months & 11 days* — moved me that by this calculation some one, surely the mother or father of these children, had tried to carry each life a bit further.

We wandered here and there among the short, uneven rows. As a boy I had not glimpsed anything in the ages of the husbands and wives, or the groupings of family stones. I had taken no more interest in those things than in the hues of the slates themselves, which had looked plain gray to me, though now I saw that some were veined with white and others were rose color or blue as smoke, and lichens bloomed on the stone in a living stipple of yellow and green. We came to the square stone pillar that supported the stone urn with its looped stone drapery and its stone flame. That was old *DAVID FISK*, who had died Feb. 14. aged 87 years. and his Descendants. I recalled the Fisks' cast-iron fence and cast-iron gate, a crumbling piece of 1856 fancy work with elaborate spear points, leafy volutes and finials, but all that remained now were the granite stumps it once stood upon. A few steps further along we found the rust-color table-top stone that announced HERE LYETH JINTERRED YE REMAIN OF MR BENJAMIN ESTABROOK A.D. 1697. But instead of resting on a great brick box as high as your chest, the slab was down in the grass, lying on a mere two courses of brick, so there was no longer any question as to whether the REMAIN was above ground in the box or deep beneath the sod.

We came to the dark slate on which the stone cutter had revealed death in two blank eyes, a line nose, a slot mouth. "I'm sorry, Nicolo, but I hate that one," she said. And, of course, I pointed out the oldest marker, a chunk of slate just two feet tall, showing a winged skull above an hour glass with crossed bones to the left and right. It belonged to Isaac Ston, Deceased 10 of December 1690. "The oldest stone is Isaac Ston," I told her.

"I hope that's a joke left over from your childhood and not something you made up now." She looked into the bag. "There's one egg left. Want to go halvesies?"

We walked across the open oval of grass where I had played scrub baseball and, a few years before that, had sailed my ocean liner on a crystal sea of melted snow. I felt again the cold pressing grip of my rubber boots as I waded in, remembered the grass rippling gently beneath the water like make-believe seaweed. Roxane paused to tap-tap-tap the hard-boiled egg on a slate. She began to peel away the shell. I looked out to where the sunken hay field and the apple orchard had been. I tried to find some familiar landmarks, but there were rows of neat white houses and I couldn't make out anything. I could see cars beyond the houses, whipping silently along a road that lay where the margin of the woods used to be. On the far side of the road there were some low brick buildings and behind them the land rose up to a ridge sparsely covered with trees. Outside the boundary of the grave yard, the world was all changed.

"This is sad," Roxane said.

"What's that? What's sad?" I turned to see what she was talking about.

She had just taken a mouthful of egg and now she waved a hand at the nearby grave stone. It was a small slate, not quite knee high, with a few bits of Roxane's egg shell lying about it on the grass. The emblematic winged skull and decorative borders left only a small square of slate for the inscription and the stonecutter had worked hard to squeeze in all the words.

> HERE LYES Y^e BODY
> OF MARY LOCK
> WIFE TO WILLIAM
>
> LOCK AGED 21 YEAR^s iuner
>
> & 15 DAYES DIED 1 month
>
> FEBRUA^ry Y^e 21 1710
> ALSO A SON BORN MARCH
>
> Y^e 7 1709 BURIED BY HER
>
> & A DAUGH^tr BURIED WITH HER

"I don't remember that stone. I don't remember it at all," I told her.

Roxane looked at the slate a long while without saying a word. "She buries her stillborn son one year, then gets pregnant again and dies in childbirth," Roxane said meditatively. "And she's younger than I am."

I had grown up with this old burying ground for my backyard and had played among the slates, knowing and not knowing what they signified, and not caring anyway. It had never been a gloomy or fearful place, but just another field to play in or to cut through on the way to someplace else, and the only unusual thing about it was that nothing there ever changed except the weather. The slates stood in small patient groups while the sun shone on them and the cold rain beat on them and the snow blanketed them, but when the snow melted and the sun returned the slates were still gathered there, unchanged, waiting. If time had stopped in Eden when we left it, then it would look like this when we went back. It was strange to stroll through the place now in the middle of this sunny day, to stand inside the circle of stones and look across at the kitchen windows where I had stood to gaze at these same stones almost fifty years ago, or now to look the other way at the meadows and woods where I had gone for adventure — I mean, where the meadows and woods had been years ago. Time had taken many things away and aged what was left living and, of course, I was older, too.

42

Roxane got her bath. Her little bath room had no tub, but only a rusty shower stall, the size of an up-ended coffin. We emptied the big galvanized washtub of all the audio tapes and disks, hauled it to a sunny place on the carpet, then carried pots of steaming water from the stove and poured them in until the tub was almost full. "This is impossible," Roxane said, then she yanked her jersey over her head and flung it somewhere. She was wearing a plain white bra. "Or is it possible?"

"God, yes. Yes, yes, yes."

She had begun to gather her hair, sweeping up the strands from the nape of her neck again and yet again, a large tortoise-shell hairpin clamped between her teeth. She was only mortal flesh and blood, but still it was hard to look straight at her.

"I'll scrub your back," I said, dizzy, sitting back on the window sill to watch.

She took the tortoise-shell pin from her mouth. "You're an easy man," she said, smiling. Then she folded her hair into a knot and pinned it.

"What do you mean?"

"To undress for." While she looked at me she unclasped her bra and shrugged it away, letting it fall to the floor anyplace. Without taking her eyes from mine, she unbuckled her jeans and shoved them down defiantly, pushed her underpants down and lifted her knee, rolling the skimpy band of apple-green cloth down her shank and off this foot — one hop — and off that foot, all the while watching me watch her.

What is there to say? Roxane was a young woman and her flesh glowed like a cloudless sky at daybreak. She was smiling broadly. I was hot with shame for my saggy old self.

"I'm old," I said.

"I know. Did you think I hadn't noticed?" She laughed. "You're way older than I am. Maybe that's why this is happening."

I looked away, fell into the mirror where another Roxane, unaware of us, was testing the ringed water with her toe. "Aiii!" she cried. "This will take getting used to."

I didn't have the courage to undress this aging body in front of Roxane. So I ran around, snatched up a bar of soap and a wash cloth and tore a huge towel from the bathroom, then settled down behind her. Roxane crouched cautiously into the washtub, braced her hands on the tub floor and seated herself with a *thump*, so the water surged and sparkled within inches of the rim. "How did they ever take baths in these things? How did they fit?" she asked. Her knees were forced almost to her breasts.

"They used two of them," I said, handing the soap and cloth to her from behind. "Tail in one, feet in the other."

"I've changed my mind," she announced. "This will never work." She looked around her shoulder at me. "It's impossible."

"You do the front. I'll take care of the back. It's possible." I was vibrating with hope.

She looked doubtful, then she turned away and began vigorously to scrub her ankles.

I tore off my shirt and threw it on a chair and hid behind her again. A moment later she passed the soap to me, then returned to scrubbing her shins. I poured water from my cupped hands till her flesh shone, then I slid the bar of soap from the turn of one shoulder to the turn of the other, and back again and across again and over once more, studying the strong sweet nape of her neck.

"Do you think it's possible for us to stay friends, or whatever we want, and not get hateful," she asked. "Do you think it's possible for us to keep in touch a long while?"

"Of course!"

"You say *of course* as if it were the most natural thing in the world for people to stay friends. But it's not natural at all. They never do. In the end people always get away from each other."

"It doesn't have to be that way. We can stay in touch for as long as we want."

"I mean a long, long time."

"We can try."

"I mean forever," she said.

"Why not?"

No monk ever read a text as devotedly as I did Roxane's back, inch by inch, not skipping a word or a letter or a minuscule or muscle from her cervix to her coccyx. She folded her arms on her knees and said, "That would be so nice." I pressed my thumbs into the groove of her spine and forced them slowly upward while she pressed back, groaning with pleasure. At the top I swept the loose fine threads of hair up from the nape of her neck and rinsed away a handspan of suds. I had a crazy desire to sink my teeth into her.

"Who do you love most in the world?" she asked.

And I said without thinking, "Maeve."

"*And?*" she said, waiting.

"How many people can a man love *most*?" I sat back, clawed at my shoelaces, tore off my shoes and socks, stood up.

"You know what I mean!" she cried. "Oh, This is impossible." She smacked both hands flat into the water, sending a flock of brilliants into the sunny air. "I'm not in love with you."

"I know. I know. That's why all this is possible. Because you're not in love with me. And I'm crazy about you." I threw off my pants.

"I can't believe this is happening," she muttered. Roxane put a hand to the floor of the washtub, gave herself a shove forward, stood up and stepped out, turning. And here I was, naked and rising. She gave me a skittish look up and down while the water still heaved and panted behind her. A flush had come to her cheeks. She gave me a second look, even bolder, then glanced up to say, "What curious legs you have. Now I'll do your back."

I sank myself in the merciful clouded water and hurriedly worked up a lather.

"Remember that time last fall when I walked into DaPonte's Café and you were sitting there alone?" Roxane said, fetching a pot of hot water. "I could have gone anyplace, but I walked all over town in that downpour until I got there and when I went in and saw you waiting I knew it was the right place." She emptied the pot on my neck and shoulders. "Because it felt like I had been looking for you and you had been waiting for me to come back. Want to help carry the futon to the floor?"

The futon was that thin cotton mattress Roxane kept draped over the bare oak sofa frame to make an upholstered surface. Roxane, the young gymnast, wore nothing, but shy me wrapped himself in the big towel. We dragged the futon into the slanted oblong of sun. Just as I threw aside my modesty towel she knelt back on her heels and cried, "Maeve is going to find out and hate me, I can't —"

"Look," I cut in. "I've been married half my life and — "

"She probably already knows, for Christ's sake! She's going to hate me."

"If she's going to hate anybody she'll hate me, not you, and she's —"

"I actually *like* Maeve," she wailed.

"Everybody likes Maeve. It's one of the things I put up with."

She shoved her hands back into her hair, saying, "Look at this place. It's a mess. It's a *mess*. I live in a *mess*!"

As a matter of fact, it was a mess. The futon sprawled in the sun with the empty wood outline of a sofa on one side and the galvanized tub of water on the other, wet footprints everywhere, cassettes anyplace, three running shoes half way to the door, my crumpled pants (shorts snugly inside) by the tub, Roxane's striped jersey on the breadboard in the corner, her apple-green underpants here, her bra there, the mirror by the window, the geranium on the sill. And there was Roxane herself on her knees in the sun, her flesh shimmering and shadowless, her hair coming undone. She dropped her hands to her thighs with a slap. "I live in a mess."

"No," I said, kneeling down with her. "That's just the way life is." Then I removed the big tortoise-shell hairpin and her hair fell open like a shining fan, streaming over my hand and her back. My arm closed around her warm shoulders.

"I know what I want," she said, her mouth on my mouth. "But you have everything. What's in it for you?"

"Oh, Roxane," I whispered, my hand at the hot inside of her thigh, my blood coming to a boil. "You —"

You take an older man, he can make it last and last, but even with a man who wants to make love forever it comes to an end in time. Now I lay on my back in the sun and here was Roxane on her side, up on her elbow, looking at me, a shine of sweat beneath her eyes.

"I would like, so much —" She paused, out of breath.

"Yes? What would you like?"

"No, it's foolish —" She got to her knees, thrust a cassette into the player by our heads, and crashed down on her side again. Some frisky operatic music sprang into the air. "What I want is —"

"What?"

She drew to my side, threw an arm across my stomach and laid her head against my chest. I put my arm around her. Little by little her breathing grew slow and deep.

"Is this what you want?" I asked.

"Yes. And most of all I would like us to last forever," she murmured.

I gave a long hug and looked up beyond her head to the ceiling. A quicksilver web of light played there, unfolding and refolding where the sun reflected from the shaken water in the washtub, and I stared up at it, thinking how wonderful it would be for us to go on forever. The music was rich and optimistic, and in my stupid brainless way I wished that Maeve were here to enjoy it, too, while lying like this in the sun. I wondered where she was and what she was doing just now, and it came to mind that she might be visiting Felix or that Felix might be out to the house. My arm jerked from a cramp. Roxane lifted her head and looked at me. "Don't you like opera?" she asked. "Overtures by Rossini?"

43

Roxane was crazy about opera. No one in her family had taken her to an opera when she was growing up, no one in that house listened to music of any kind. Away at college she collected rock albums, but for the past two years she had been listening to opera. Everything about it was new to her, fresh and pure and exciting. When Roxane heard an aria she heard only the words and the music, and no overlapping resonance from a hundred other occasions of the same song. When she listened to *M'appari tutt'amor* she didn't also hear my mother telling her how Caruso, despite the doctor's orders, had begun to sing, had called to his wife and begun to sing — oh, ever so softly, ever so gently, almost whispering, like this, *M'appari tutt'amor* — and at the end of an angelic note a blood vessel burst in his throat and he died. Nor, as Roxane listened, could she see my grandfather hairy-chested at the great porcelain bathroom sink, trimming his beard and singing that same aria accompanied by that same Caruso whose voice, sounding small and faintly nasal, was coming from the graceful horn on the Victrola phonograph in the master bedroom.

I had stopped at Roxane's late on a Monday afternoon and that's what we were talking about. She told me she had almost wept at the close of *La Boheme*. "The snowy roofs of Paris outside the garret window, the good times all gone, Mimi coughing her lungs out. Well, it's so — Did you almost weep?" she asked. I told her no, I had not wept when I first saw it. I was twenty years old and too hard-hearted for that. And nowadays when I hear those final minutes where everybody is back together again — Musetta, Marcello, Schaunard, and now Rodolpho, not realizing that Mimi is dead, holds the cloak against the glowing skylight so she can sleep a bit longer — I weep, weep not for the young Bohemians on stage but for us enthusiastic rowdies in the cheap balcony seats thirty-three years ago (Harry, Alan, Ellen, Cathy and me) and what has happened in between.

"You mean I'm too young," Roxane said.

"Is that what I mean?"

We were seated on the floor, facing each other across the sawed-off coffee table. Roxane drained her espresso cup and set it neatly in its little saucer.

"Yup," she said. "You mean I can't hear the same arias as you hear, because the music picks up emotional echoes as you go along and get older, so you hear something quite different from me because you're older. And I'm young. Right?"

"You *are* young." She was wearing the green sweatshirt and had pushed up the sleeves, lifting the blond hairs backward so they blazed in the sunlight, announcing how beautiful and how young she was.

"I did weep, actually, but it was a different opera," she confessed. She looked down at her own hand, watching as she slid it slowly across the table toward me. She separated my fingers and laced hers through mine. "Can we talk about anything or are there forbidden subjects?"

"Anything under the sun," I said, closing our hands into a fist.

She smiled. "Anything under the sun. What a lovely phrase."

"What did you want to talk about?" I was flooded with pleasure, for she had lifted my hand to her face and was rubbing my knuckles slowly against her cheek.

"About us?" she asked, looking at me.

"What about us?"

"Whenever I think about Maeve, I die. I mean, I know — I know — I know how I would feel if I were in her place," she said.

The blood in my arteries had gone cold and my heart contracted. When she let go of my hand I cautiously leaned back against the sofa frame, afraid something was about to go smash.

"She used to like me," Roxane said. "A little, anyway. Didn't she?"

"She still likes you." That wasn't the exact whole truth, of course.

"She does? Really?" She wanted to believe it.

"Yes," I said.

She came around to my side of the coffee table and sat beside me, took my faithless hand again. "I had all day yesterday to think about us," she said very calmly. "All of us. You and me. And Maeve. As a matter of fact, that's all I did. It made for a gloomy Sunday." She laughed briefly.

"What conclusion did you come to?" My mouth had gone dry with fear, but my voice sounded quite ordinary, though weirdly distant in my head.

"No conclusion. I just went round and round in circles," she said quietly. She had lowered her face and lifted my hand to her mouth and now I could feel her lips on my fingers and her warm breath as she spoke. "I don't want us to stop. I don't want to. I don't want to stop."

She dropped my hand, got to her knees, slammed a cassette into the player and sat down beside me again. The room began to fill with irresistibly flowing music and then one soaring voice and another and another. I put my arm around her shoulders and rolled us to the floor while Roxane whispered, "Right? Am I right? Am I right?" breathless and insistent.

"What?" I slipped my hand beneath her sweatshirt and floated my palm on her warm flesh, pressing harder now against the gentle edge of her rib and upward. "Right about what?"

"Am I right we have to stop?" she said, her mouth moving against my mouth, my jaw, my throat.

"Oh, God. God. God." She was wearing no bra and my hand swept against her breast, silken and heavy, lifting. I shoved her sweatshirt up and rolled my face in the fresh warm odor of her flesh.

"We can," she gasped, out of breath.

"Yes, you're right." I yanked the futon from the sofa frame onto the floor, dragged it into the sun while Roxane knelt up, pulled off the sweatshirt, stood up and stepped from her jeans. I tore off my shirt. The operatic trio had been joined by yet another singer and all four were moving around us, their voices rising and falling through each other like colliding waves. Roxane had knelt on the mat in front of me and was unbuckling my belt, her strong fingers delicately arched, tugging awkwardly in her haste. I knocked her hand away, tore the buckle open and shoved my pants, shoes and socks off. For an instant I saw the red geraniums on the window sill, saw how the sunlight dappled Roxane's shoulder and cheek and I glimpsed the open-mouth look of surprise in her face, then I sank my hand into her hair, grabbed a fistful and wrenched her to.

I cannot recall the first time I heard an operatic aria or the first time my mother said, "Listen to this, Nicolo. Listen. This is where —" And then came a gossipy tale of passion and betrayal, violence, death. She would tell me again about Turiddu, killed in a knife fight with Alfio for fooling around with Alfio's Lola, or poor Canio who stabbed his faithless Nedda and then whirled around to bury the knife in her lover's heart, or tell me about any number of comic old men, like Dr. Bartolo, who thought they could keep a pretty woman like Rosina upstairs forever. These bits and pieces tangled themselves in my imagination with tales she told about our relatives and friends. For there was the story of my mother's cousin, beautiful Alba, who went to a glittering dance at the Copley Plaza the night before she died of TB, and there was foolish old Canzanetti who raged so loudly at the young Irishman who came to see his daughter that he didn't hear her open the bedroom window and crawl onto the porch roof, didn't hear her climb down the trellis and slip into the young man's coupe, didn't even notice she was gone until eight the next morning when she didn't bring him his coffee. Above all, there was the tale of Emanuel, when he was dying, how he looked at his wife Amelia — he knew all along that she fooled around behind his back — how he looked at her and said, *Adduma le candele che il Signoruzzo te la fatto la grazia. Light the candles, little Jesus has given you your wish.* Then he died. "As for Amelia," said my mother, "She cried the rest of her life." I was a kid making ships out of walnut shells at the dining room table when I first overheard that story. I don't know how many times I listened to it, but I still kept the notion that the tale was opera and that *Adduma le candele* was a line like *La comedia è finita*, something spoken on stage as the curtain comes down. Years later I discovered that my grandparents had known Emanuel and Amelia, that the story was true and that everyone in the North End knew it word for word.

"You have more aunts and uncles and cousins than anyone I know," Roxane told me.

"These are true stories," I said. This was while we lay naked at noon on the mat in Roxane's apartment. I was looking up at the wet green leaves outside the window and listening to the soft fall of the rain.

"What a strange — I mean, what kind of a childhood did you actually have?" she murmured.

"I had a happy childhood. I'm told all my problems can be traced back to that." I omitted it was Maeve who told me.

"That sounds like Maeve." She laughed,

then frowned and jerked herself free of my arm in a confusion of feeling.

I didn't want yet another talk about Maeve, so I began brushing the hair from her eyes to distract her. I lost myself in touching her cheek, delighting in the fine weave of her skin. Roxane was generous that way: she would lie utterly tranquil while I ran my finger over the ingenious workmanship of her eyelid, or would suffer me to gaze at this and that secret immaculate part of her until I had got it by heart. "You're a beautiful young woman. Did your father ever tell you that?"

"No. And you were going to tell me how to go back to repair my childhood. Remember?"

"Oh? Did I say that?"

"Ages ago. Something like that. Yes," she said.

"I'm sure I never said you could go back."

"You said it was possible to redo the past. I'm positive you said something like that." She rolled over, got to her knees and began to search among the odds and ends on the window sill. "I wish I still smoked," she muttered.

"The only place to redo the past is the future. Have children. Make them a happy childhood. There's your second chance."

"That's it?" she said, sorting through a handful of postcards and audio cassettes.

"You don't get a third chance."

She slipped the cassette into the player and

came back to the mat. I told her I hoped it was rock music. She said it was hors d'oeuvres or desserts, something by Rossini. "He wrote it when he was old, like you." She pulled my arm around her shoulders and lay half on me again, not saying anything for a few minutes. "Oh, Christ, Nicolo! When are we going to *stop* this —"

"Stop what?"

"Stop fucking," she muttered into my chest.

"You ought to clean up your vocabulary, Roxane."

"That's not all I ought to clean up." She said nothing more and for moment I thought she had actually dozed off, then she said, "Maybe the only reason I do it is so we can lie this way afterward. Did you ever think of that?"

"Yes. I thought of that."

"So. We could try just lying this way next time. Just lying like this and not, you know —" She trailed off.

"Not what?"

"You know. Not fooling around."

"Is that what we've been doing? Fooling around?" I began to laugh.

"I'm cleaning up my vocabulary. And you know exactly what I mean, Nicolo. Fucking. Screwing. Sodomizing each other. Stop laughing." She had begun to smile. "You. Damn. You old man."

"I love it when you say that. I don't know why."

Roxane got up and stepped from the room, reappeared a moment later with a camera.

"Hey. No! *Wait!*" I cried, rolling over. I scrambled around on my hands and knees, searching for my clothes. She dropped down, aiming the camera while I grabbed my pants and shirt.

"Relax," she said, her voice falling in disappointment. "The film is too slow. The rain makes a nice silvery atmosphere, but there's not enough light." She put the camera aside.

I got dressed. Roxane pulled on a loose red sweater, nothing else. She folded her arms and walked idly to the window. We had been so happy just a minute ago but it was fading fast.

"And now you're driving home in the rain," she said lightly. She had bowed her head, pressing her forehead to the streaked window. It was strange to see her half dressed, to look at the red sweater and that flawless bare bottom and to hear the music flooding into the room with so much happy energy and to feel only this shame, this sense that I was betraying her and Maeve, too, by going home.

I didn't know what to do. "That's the way it is," I told her.

"I know how it is." She looked over her shoulder at me a moment, her eyes as gray as the rain. "Drive carefully is all I meant."

Those hours with Roxane were saturated with music. I wanted to play rock, but she couldn't get enough opera and liked to play the same things I had heard so many times when I was growing up. There are passages in *La Traviata* that fill my head with the odor of basilico and simmering olive oil, because my father liked to prepare our Sunday dinner and as he worked in the kitchen he enjoyed listening to opera records, singing with everyone from the tenor to the basso while encouraging the orchestra with his free hand. Roxane was enchanted by the amorousness of opera and by the sound of Italian in song. "They go together, those love songs and that language," she told me. Of course, my parents and relatives spoke English plain as day, spoke it everywhere outside the house and almost all the time at home, and only when their voices dipped softly, because what was coming was scandalous, or when their voices soared in rage did they break into Italian. I knew from the start that it was the language of secrecy and sensuality and violence. The luxurious women lolling naked in ART FROM THE RENAISSANCE spoke Italian, and the costumed heroines in *Opera News* — splendid women, heavily made-up, tragic, imperious and demanding — they were singing it. The eroticism was heavy, the way velvet is heavy when you lift it from the dye vat, the way the sun is heavy on a hot summer day, the way your parts feel when you realize it's happening yet again. It was close and familiar and secret, like Gina years ago, her warm breasts against my bare back as I stood eating a cantaloup and looking out the window to Gloucester harbor, Gina singing *E tu non sorgi ancora, e puoi dormir così?* "And you're still not up, still able to go on sleeping?" That was Italian opera.

"I just like the way it sounds," Roxane said. She was standing naked at the tall mirror by the window, brushing her hair.

"I'd rather play the Beatles or the Stones." I had picked up my shorts, but instead of putting them on I stood there watching her, enchanted by the rhythmic twist and shimmer of her back as she pulled the brush through her hair.

"I grew up with that stuff. And, frankly. I don't know why you think it's so great. Wait here a sec," she added, going off toward the bedroom.

I caught a glimpse of myself in the mirror — aging ape face, hairy chest, limp dick — and turned away. "Because at my age you get tired of history," I called after her. "And that stuff has no memories attached to it."

"None for you, maybe," she called back.

I pulled on my shorts. My pants were in a tangled heap and I was shaking them out when Roxane returned with one of her damned cameras.

"What are you getting dressed for?" she cried. "It's not late. You'll just get stuck in traffic if you leave now."

"Don't aim that thing at me."

"Available light, Nicolo. It's wonderful." I grabbed at the camera, but Roxane was already spinning away. I reached around her from behind, reached under her arm, her smooth shoulder grazing my chest, her hip and then her firm silken buttock in my groin, distracting me. She had lifted the camera high in both hands and now over our heads the shutter went *click*, the film-advance made a raspy *whirrr*. "Wonderful. I just took a photo of the ceiling," she said.

I snatched up my pants, pulled them on.

"Come on, Nicolo. Look at the light in here. In a couple of days the sun will be too high up to come through the tree this way. I don't want to waste it."

"If you don't want to waste it, let me take pictures of you."

"Nicolo."

"What?"

She took a photo of *Bare-chested Man Standing With Arms Folded*.

"Why are we doing this?" I asked her.

"For the historical record. — Now move closer to the window. Did you realize that photographs always show history? I bet you never thought about that. Photographs are historical documents. — Now put your shoulder against the wall there. That's not true of symphonies or novels or even of paintings. But every photo is historical. Think about that."

Roxane took a photo of *Man Standing With*

Hand On Window Latch and *Man Leaning Against Wall* and so on, even (my folly) *Man With Woman's Lemon-Yellow Underpants Tucked In Belt*. She was right about the light, of course. At that hour the sun was broken up, refracted and reflected a million different ways by the glistening fresh leaves that hovered outside the window, and it filled the air in here with a weightless and rippling green hue, as if we stood in a grotto by the sea.

"You're young and beautiful, Roxane. And you're naked. So why are we taking pictures of me?"

She lowered the camera and peered at the film counter, frowning. "Because I want a memento. Because I want a keepsake." For a while she continued to fuss with the camera, twisting the lens ring this way and that with absent studiousness. "Because I'm fond of you. Because —" She looked up at me, the color coming to her cheeks. Then this handsome young woman who had been walking around stark naked, brushing her hair, chatting, taking shapshots, fell silent and smiled hesitantly because she was embarrassed.

"*Memento mori*, perhaps. One of those heads carved on a graveyard slate. Let me try the camera."

"All right," she said, her face clearing. "You want me this way? Or shall I put on one of my costumes?"

I can't recall now if it was that afternoon

or some other that we spent fooling around with the camera. Roxane liked to play dress-up in old fashioned gowns with high lace collars and pearl button cuffs, or glittering black corsets and spike heel shoes, or milk-maid ginghams all disarrayed, the hem tossed up and the laces undone. And I was happy to take snapshots of her — not very good ones, apparently — while she instructed me on f numbers and depth of field and why you couldn't take a photograph now that looked like one taken a hundred years ago and how polite nude photos obliterated the personality of the people in the picture but casual dirty photos did not, and so on. But that was the kind of talk we had on any afternoon. I do remember the tender green lettuce color of the leaves outside the window, some rock group screaming *she is outta sight*, and the air blossoming with the scent of coffee, because she was showing me a portfolio of photos she had taken since last December and while we were looking at them the espresso boiled over.

44

This is how it stopped. I had driven from work to Roxane's one noon and when I got there she said, "My period began today." Oh, I said, well, oh, and I asked her how she was feeling. "Heavy and ugly. How do I look?" She was wearing a blue leotard top and a black skirt and had her hands buried in the skirt pockets. It's true, she did seem a little muddy around the eyes. But she looked fine to me and I told her so.

"Do you want to fool around or —" She trailed off.

"Whatever you want. What do you want?" I asked.

"Not much. Give us a hug and a kiss."

"Come here," I said, reaching for her.

Before we let go she asked, "Friends for life?"

"Absolutely," I said. Then we sat on the futon sofa and sorted through her portfolio, arranging the photographs first in this sequence and next in that one, while she talked about the chances of getting a show at a Boston gallery, or maybe at a smaller place here in Cambridge.

"I love you," she said.

She had spoken as if she were going to say more, as if she intended those words to explain or forgive what she was about to tell me. But more words never came and she went on sorting photographs without glancing up. In the long silence I looked at her studious profile, a sheaf of bright hair slanting across her cheek, and I wondered what it was she could not bear to say after that announcement, and then I knew she was saying goodbye. "I know what you mean," I said at last, drawing back a strand of hair and tucking it behind her ear. The words had come from my mouth but I felt nothing, nothing at all, only this numb ice-like clarity.

She lifted her head and looked at me a sober moment. "Yes. You probably do."

I had know all along that we were going to reach this place and I suppose I have no right to say it came as a surprise, but still it felt like the blood was rushing out of me all at once. "And you want to get on with your life. You need to move on," I said mechanically.

She gave a heavy sigh. "Well, we can't go on fooling around forever. I know that much."

I had to clear my throat to talk. "This is as good a time as any."

She didn't say a word but compressed her lips and nodded her head, yes.

I don't recall what happened next, how much time passed. I know she dropped whatever she was doing with the photos and tossed herself back into the sofa, saying, "This is impossible! People don't break up just because a certain day of the month rolls around."

"We're not breaking up. We can still — We're going to see each other. We're going to talk to each other."

"We're just quitting sex forever. That's all."

"Not because of some day in the month," I said.

"No. We're quitting sex so we won't have to break up. That's a joke. That's a better joke even than menstruation. I can't believe this is happening."

"Roxane —" I began.

"I don't know what I want!"

I had started to put my arm around her shoulders but she knocked my hand away, saying, "I'd like to know why we can't keep doing what we've been doing! *I* like it. *You* like it. So far so good. Why don't we keep doing it a while longer and —"

"This is a fallen world, Roxane. It won't let us."

"Well, I don't know if I'm *ready* to stop. How are we going to do it? I mean, how are we going to *not* do it? This is impossible." She was gasping. "I can't believe this. Sane people don't talk this way. I can do what I want!"

"You want to go on fooling around and —"

"Yes," she cut in. "Fucking and sucking and everything else! That's what we're talking about." Her eyes were glistening. "And Maeve hates me. And why not? Oh, shit." Her eyes had begun to flood and abruptly she went to the kitchen counter, snatched at a box of paper tissues, wiped her eyes and blew her nose. She didn't turn to face me.

"Look," I told her. "You were the one who said we couldn't go on this way and —"

"Well, we *can't*," she cried, whirling at me.

"All right all right."

"But last time we made love wasn't exactly perfect, you know. It's a rotten way to leave it. We can't just stop and leave it that way. — Don't get that look!"

"Roxane, it's never —"

"And don't tell me it's a fallen world, Nicolo!"

"I was going to say that life isn't that way, it isn't exactly perfect."

"Oh, you sound so old when you say things like that."

We talked a bit longer and when it looked like a good time to leave, I said, "Want to come out to the house for dinner tonight?"

"You're out of your mind."

"You have a standing invitation."

"No." She knelt down by the sawed-off table and began to gather up the last few loose photographs, tucking them into folders. "I'm going to take a couple of aspirin and go lie down. Phone me tomorrow?"

"I'll stop by."

"No. But phone, will you?"

"Sure thing," I said.

I got into my car and drove down Dublin Street. I felt hollow and heavy at the same time, as if my body were a husk of old bones and skin. I don't know what I was thinking. I parked and dragged the dead weight of my carcass up to the Square. The café was crowded outside and some rock group had set up a microphone and was getting ready to play. I sat with my coffee, thinking about Maeve and then I remembered that she was at a meeting somewhere in town. I thought about going back to my office, but classes had ended a week ago and since my promotion had been turned down there was nothing I needed to do there and, besides, I wanted to see Maeve. The band had begun screaming *she's so fine and I wish she was mine* and I drove home.

45

I made the turn into the driveway and there was Felix Stout's rusted white VW, looking like a rotted egg shell. I had forgotten about Felix. I coasted over the gravel and pulled up beside Maeve's wagon. And I had thought she was at a conference in the city. Stupid me. I sat there a moment, not wanting to deal with any of this, then went inside. Rover lifted his gray chin from the kitchen floor, thumped his tail once in greeting and yawned. Maeve's dog, not mine. The pod of whales floated motionless over the table and the only sound anywhere was the *caw caw caw* of distant crows. "*Anybody home?*" I waited a while, then clomped noisily up the stairs loud enough to wake the dead or amorous. All the bedroom doors were open, our bed a smooth blank. I tossed my briefcase, went downstairs and out to the back terrace. The ancient apple trees were in full blossom, making a dense white cloud on the long slope down to the creek. There wasn't a soul in sight. The crows wheeled silently downward, settling into the woods.

I began to walk down the central aisle,

looking and not looking. The grass was deep and glossy. This had been a wagon path long ago, but now the snowy boughs brushed your shoulders as you walked. I could see the pink flush on the apple petals and breathe their sweet scent with the odor of the soil and hear the subtle humming buzz of the bees, see them hovering there and there and there, or watch a blurred bee resolve into its small shaggy self while it curled inside a blossom. And here was a man's yellow-striped jersey hung from a flowering limb. I stumbled over a man's shoe nested in the grass and then saw two rumpled socks further on. A pair of tan slacks had been draped over the crotch of the next tree. A few more steps and I came across a man's under shorts hanging limp from the tip of a branch. And at the open end of the aisle stood Maeve herself, tall and proud in her white linen business suit and white high-heel sandals, her fist on her hip, watching me.

"I thought you had a meeting in town today," I said, walking down to her.

"Obviously, I didn't get to it."

"What are you doing down here?"

"I might ask the same of you," she said, lifting her chin. She had put her hair in a French roll — it wasn't as neat as she usually made it, but it wasn't actually mussed, either.

"I came looking for you. I found the house wide open and no one home. So I came looking."

"Roxane seeing somebody else today?" She drew a loose strand of hair back and tucked it into the roll.

"Why didn't you go to your meeting?"

"The car wouldn't start," she said.

"You should have phoned me. I could have driven back, picked you up. I'm not busy these days, you know."

"I did phone. I phoned your office, looking for you. Then I phoned Roxane's place. She said you had just left. And she sounded like she had been crying. What did you do to her?"

"I didn't do anything to her. We talked. That's all. She likes to talk."

"And you? What do you like to do?" Her voice was light but brittle as glass.

"What are you getting at?"

"I know you, Nicolo."

"I hope so. I hope you do. Where's Felix?"

"The last I saw of Felix he was standing right where you are. That was about two seconds before you came sauntering down here." She glanced around, squinting against the sun.

"What were you doing?"

"I wasn't doing a thing," she said, shading her eyes with her hand.

"For God's sake, Maeve —"

"Don't for-God's-sake me!" she cried, snapping her head toward me.

"His Goddamn fucking clothes are all over the place! They're in my apple trees!"

"I wasn't expecting him!" she cried. "He

just turned up. He came down here and he was already taking off his clothes."

"*He* was expecting something!"

"He's that way."

"So you just stood there."

"What was I supposed to do? Run away? Hide my eyes? He's a romantic. He likes to make romantic gestures. So what?"

"Oh. Great. You just happen to be standing here by the creek and Felix just happens to park in our driveway and come strolling down here, taking off his clothes as a romantic gesture. *Shit*. How long has he been doing this?"

"What was Roxane weeping about?"

I lifted my voice and called out, "*Felix*." I turned to her. "I don't know. We just talked, that's all. She wasn't crying when I left."

"I like Felix. He cheers me up," she announced.

I stooped down and peered here and there under the sagging branches of the apple trees, searching for him. The trunks were twisted and leaned every which way, as if they were about to collapse from holding up the enormous weight of the blossoms. "*Felix. You can come out now!*"

"I don't regret anything. Not a thing," she informed me.

I looked at her. "You never do. Or at least you never admit it."

"Well, why should I? I haven't done anything you don't do."

"Is that right? What have you been up to? What have you been doing the past few weeks?" I crouched down to survey again the igloo space beneath each snowy tree.

"What's done is done," she said.

I straightened up and looked at her. "What does that mean?"

"It can't be undone. Anyway, it's over with," she added. "All done."

"Over with? You mean finished? What do you mean?"

"What did you say to Roxane to make her cry?"

"Why not ask her?"

"You still love Roxane?"

"I'm not making love to her, if that's what you mean."

"You've stopped fucking her?"

"Sure! When I do it, it's fucking. When you do it, it's only a romantic walk in the meadow. I take it you've finished with Felix."

"You've stopped fucking her," she stated.

"That's right. You two ought to get together, you and Roxane. You'd understand each other real well. You speak the same language. — *Come on, Felix. All-y all-y in free! I've got your pants. You can't go anywhere.*"

"He's in the tree," Maeve told me. "That one. Over there."

She squared her shoulders and headed back to the house, striding through the grass in her high-heels as if she were swinging along the pavement in downtown Boston. I walked around to the next tree and there was Felix, perched on the left-hand branch just where the trunk divided. We peered at each other through the blossoms, neither of us moving. "How long are you going to stay up there, Felix?" He didn't answer, but sat hunched like an owl and stared glumly out at me. "The kids get home from school about now," I told him. "If the kids don't find you, one of those bees will." At last he dropped to the ground and came out and stood facing me, more or less at attention. The bronze hair had a thick nap on his chest, but it went skimpy on his pubes and his legs were skinny as spindles. I turned around and led the way to his clothes and, to discomfort him, I watched him get dressed. He plucked his under shorts from the tree, jerked them up. He shook out his pants, yanked them on, pulled on his jersey, then thrust into this sock, that sock, this shoe —. Now he hopped about on one shoe, looking for the other. I wondered if he had been able to hear much of Maeve's conversation with me. He found the shoe, knelt to lace it tightly, and stood up.

"It's time I got married," he said crisply.

"You have anyone in mind?"

"No," he said, frowning. "But that's beside the point. I've been thinking about this a long time, thinking about marriage. Only the time has never been right. Until now."

We began to walk up the wagon path

through the apple trees to the house, the cloudy boughs sweeping our shoulders. "And now?" I said.

"It just came to me while I was sitting in the tree. I thought, What am I doing up here? Why is it me up here and them over there? Why is it always *me* up a tree or out on a limb? When do I get to be *them*? When do I get to stand by a brook, talking to my wife? It's time I got married."

"You're out of your mind." We walked in silence a while. I couldn't sort out my feelings about Felix or Maeve or Roxane or even about myself. The warmth of the late afternoon air, the scent of apple blossoms, their flushed colors, the odors of the earth, the drowsy hum of the bees — everything had melted together and swam in my head all at once. "You don't know a thing about marriage, nothing, *zero*!" I told him.

"On the contrary, I've given it a lot of thought. It fascinates me. I'm obsessed by it. I have a theory —"

"You would! If you ever get married, you'll have fewer theories about it. Wisdom comes when you abandon your final theory."

Felix was still talking when we emerged from the orchard and drifted to a halt a short distance from the back of the house. Up on the terrace, Morgan Kathleen was in her shiny blue swim suit. She had unfolded the old lounge chair — a wobbly aluminum frame and some frayed nylon webbing — and was now supine in the full sun, her lax arms and legs glistening with oil, a *Glamour* magazine spread open on her face as a shade. Calico was curled up beneath the chair, dozing in its shadow. A tennis ball rolled from the big shade-filled doorway, dropped onto the terrace and came to a confused halt, apparently blinded by the sun. Nico came out with a ball in each hand, scooped up the one which had escaped and ducked back through the doorway.

"At a certain age you discover there are two kinds of people," Felix was saying. "The married and the single. I mean, you always knew there were these two kinds, but on a certain day in your thirties you discover that married people are actually very different from single ones. Because married people have been single and have out-grown it. They've left it, gone on. Single people don't know how to do that. So they become what's left behind. They become left-overs, the garbage."

"What are you telling me this for?"

"Because you're married and this is a discovery that only single people make."

"You discovered a lot up in that apple tree."

"I've know this for years, especially about women. There are two kinds of women."

"Don't tell me virgins and whores."

"Married and unmarried, Nicolo. And I've never gone for an unmarried woman."

"Oh? Why not?"

"Because I never know how to begin. And I never know what to do. Because she's only another left-over like myself. I don't do single women."

In a moment this buffoon was going to clamp his hand over his heart and cry, *I might make love to my friend's wife, but never to his daughter!* "Why is it I think you're lying? Why is it I think you'd try a snake if you could figure out how to hold it down?"

"Oh, I've *tried* single women," he said. "But the romance never works out. It's all blunders. It ends in confusion and hurt feelings, some kind of horrible mess, every time."

"And with married women you avoid all that?"

"Married women don't take me seriously, Nicolo."

"And that's the way you want it?"

"That's the beauty of it."

We had begun to walk again. I wouldn't trust this clown speak the facts, but I was curious about him and even if his little discourse on himself was a fiction, still it would tell the truth in the end, so instead of turning up to the terrace I turned idly down the path between the next two rows of apple trees. I don't know how many times we wandered toward the hidden creek, startling the crows to flight, and then climbed back to the house again. We never actually reached the margin of the water, but always turned back just before it came in sight. Because they loomed in my mind, those meetings of Maeve and Felix on the long grass on this side of the creek, or on the other side in the ferns in the shade of the woods, and I had no desire to witness the place and make myself sick. I soothed myself by listening to him talk about his misadventures and eventually we came up and found the lounge chair empty, *Glamour* magazine forgotten on the flagstones and Calico gone. We went into the kitchen, into Maeve's "I say we take a break and try some of this." She had changed from her business suit to blue jersey dress, held a new bottle of wine in one hand and a corkscrew in the other and was talking not to us. For there at the sink, shaking a colander of drenched lettuce, was Roxane. I was knocked back a step and Felix crashed into me from behind.

"Hullo," Roxane said, brushing her hair from her eyes with the back of her wrist. "I took you at your word and here I am."

There was a *pop* as the cork came out. "What about you, Felix? Can you stay long enough to have dinner?" Maeve asked.

46

We all talked loudly at once. I grabbed four wine glasses and lined them up (no two alike in our house) on the counter, and Maeve — her hand trembling in a way to make me heartsick — poured the May wine which Roxane had brought and Felix, lifting his glass, cried out some foolish toast. We all drank, then looked around at each other in silence. For here are Maeve and Nicolo standing alone in the middle of the kitchen while over there is Roxane, clinging with one hand to the sink by the window, and over on this other side is Felix, like a barrel someone had forgotten in the doorway. I wondered how long Roxane had been here and what she had confided to Maeve, and I knew that Maeve, looking out at me and Felix in the orchard, had wondered what he was telling me. I could see Maeve's chest quicken its beat, but only her guardian angel knew if it was the prospect of losing Felix or the sight of me and Roxane in the same room that made drawing breath so hard. Now to break the silence Maeve said, "Well," as if she were going to say more — for the color was beginning to show high on her cheeks and the wings of her nose flared as she took those rapid breaths — but she didn't say more and at last I said, "So," and that was all there was. Then Felix eased himself in from the door to ask, "How's your photography these days?"

Roxane looked startled. "What? Oh! Great. It's great. How's your book?"

"It's great, too. — About finished. Over with. All done," he added abruptly.

And Maeve, catching this deliberate echo of her words to me, shot a look at Felix, but to hide himself he had already thrown back his head and was draining his glass.

"Well. That's good," Roxane said politely.

Morgan Kathleen shouted from upstairs, asking how soon we were going to eat. Maeve turned abruptly, escaping to the foot of the stairway where she would speak a few plain words to Morgan about shouting in the house. "Want to see me juggle?" Nico asked us, coming in from the long room. His innocence threw us into confusion, but we were eager for distraction and quickly said *yes, show us; let's see you do it!* So Nico juggled three tennis balls and it was a reproach to our colliding lives, the way he got the balls to fly up and return, but to never bump or fall away — each miniature planet miraculously rescued at the last instant and released upward once more, safe on a trajectory which would return it to one of those busy shuttling hands. But the tennis balls drifted always forward, compelling him to walk slowly through the kitchen to keep under them while we snatched a stool and then a chair out of his way. Then he banged into Maeve's desk, caught two of the balls in the air and the third splashed into Calico's saucer. "Hey, you really can juggle," Roxane said, surprised. "I've always wanted to do that." Felix said it was an excellent demonstration of the cascade and asked Nico if he also knew shower juggling. Nico said no, said he had never heard of cascade, either, and then he smiled, in case Felix were making a joke. But it wasn't a joke and while Felix went on lecturing I took my first full look at Roxane. The flesh beneath her eyes had the tender discoloration of a bruise, but she gave me a hot defiant stare, as if she were a rebellious prisoner here, or maybe it was as if she belonged here and was daring me to say no, or maybe it was something else — I couldn't tell. The confusion pumping through my heart was so great I thought maybe Maeve was right when she said love was lunacy that got us to this condition. Then Maeve herself returned, the large French roll in her hair somewhat sloppy now, as if her inner agitation were shaking it loose. "Morgan wants to go out with Lisa and Wendy right after diner, so why don't we all eat now?" So Felix and I moved the kitchen table until it stood at the open door, looking out to the orchard, then we pulled the cork from another bottle of wine and set out the dishes while Maeve and Roxane pieced the dinner together. It was a crazy-quilt feast — Greek salad, cold chicken, miso soup, five artichokes, as much pasta as you wanted, a big bowl of wild rice, half a dozen cheeses, two loaves of French bread and a third bottle of wine. Roxane and Nico sat at my end of the table, Felix and Morgan at Maeve's end. Morgan Kathleen came to the table in eye-liner, an oversized sweater that left one shoulder bare and, thank God, a decent skirt. "Where are you going tonight?" Roxane asked her.

Morgan gave her attention to the slice of cold chicken hanging perilously from the tines of her fork as she lifted it to her dish. "The Graffiti," she said. Then she took up her knife and cut into her chicken, apparently not caring whether the conversation continued or not.

"It sounds good," Roxane said frankly. "What kind of a place is it?"

"They have some good bands there. It's a dance place," Morgan said, glancing at Roxane for the first time.

"Who's driving?" I asked.

"Lisa. And no drinks," she told me. I groped through memory, trying to recollect what I knew about Lisa and whether or not she was a prudent driver. Morgan Kathleen turned back to Roxane, saying, "We just go there and if there's some kids we know, we dance. Or we go some place else. We meet guys. I like to dance," Morgan told her.

We heard the front door swing open, slam shut and here was our Nina, her face white and her eyes glistening and her mouth a small straight line. "Nina!" Maeve said, jumping up to give her a hug and a kiss. "Sit down, I'll set a place for you."

"What happened?" I asked, getting up as Nina came over. "You look as if you had a near miss on the highway."

"Nothing," she said. We had a hug and a kiss. "I'm fine, just tired," she told me.

"Come join us. Sit down. — Nico, move over a bit," I said. Roxane had grown as still as a marble statue since Nina entered.

"Oh, hi, everybody," Nina said distractedly, letting her knapsack of books fall to the floor. "Hi, Roxane. Hi, Felix." She sat on the corner of the bench beside Nico, spent.

"How did you get here?" I asked her.

"How have you been?" asked Felix.

"Fine. I just finished. Last exam this morning." Nina spoke as if she were out of breath.

"What exam was it?" Roxane asked. The blood had risen to Roxane's cheeks, giving her a flush so slight it seemed rather like a haze or veil over her face, masking her. It gave me a dizzy moment, like putting on the wrong glasses, to see that our love making and our frenzies on the floor of her apartment haunted her in the presence of Nina far more than when she faced Maeve.

"Japanese History and Culture. — You've

changed since last time. I like your hair down that way," she told Roxane.

"And you've cut yours," Roxane said, smiling. I suppose I was the only one to notice that Roxane was breathing with such caution you might think she were made of glass. "It makes you look — What's that look?" she asked Nina.

"It makes her look Japanese," said Morgan Kathleen, her voice crisp. "I'm going to get my hair cut, but not that way."

"Who gave you the ride out from the dorm?" I asked Nina.

"Finley," she said, unfolding a napkin into her lap with an exasperated wave of her hand.

"Fin? Why didn't you ask him in?"

"Because the story's over," she said brusquely.

"Did you get my letter?" Nico asked her.

"Yes and I loved it. Especially the drawings." She smiled and rubbed her brother's shoulders.

Maeve had arrived at the table with a bowl of miso soup for Nina, saying, "What's that about Fin? I haven't seen him in weeks."

"It's over, mom, it's over!" she cried. She threw her napkin onto the table and jumped up from the bench, flinging *Excuse me* over her shoulder as she rushed from the room. We heard her run up the stairs and slam her bedroom door.

I felt the same ache under my ribs as when

I stood in the front hall last year with my arms around Morgan, her books and papers sliding to the floor while she wept, because on the way home from school she had learned that this boy she was fond of had invited not her, but an acquaintance of hers to the junior prom. Maeve bit her lip, then lifted the bowl of soup from the table and poured it back into the pot, a studious frown on her forehead all the while. Roxane had lowered her eyes to her plate and was carefully turning her fork in the pasta. "Would that be the same Finley Fisher?" murmured Felix.

"The same," I said. "I'd like to twist his delicate neck."

"Nina *knew* it was happening," Morgan informed us. "They even *agreed* about it. That's what she told me over the phone weeks ago and frankly I don't understand why she's so —"

Maeve cut in, saying, "Morgan, have you ever thought that your sister might have told you things that she doesn't want you to tell anyone else?"

"What did I say?" asked Morgan, her hand with an artichoke leaf paused in mid air.

"The salad is delicious!" Felix announced, changing the subject. "Delectable. Luscious. Amazing. Stunning."

Maeve laughed and said, "You can come to dinner any time you want."

"Who says the Irish can't cook?" Morgan asked.

"On the other hand, there's nothing Irish on this table except that glass bowl," Maeve said.

"How Irish *are* you?" Roxane asked her.

"My parents were born here," said Maeve.

"She's Irish enough," I said. "Her grandparents were born at the bottom of a lake in County Clare."

"Poulivan is hardly the bottom of a lake," said Maeve.

"Maeve celebrates Beltane, that's how Irish she is," I said.

"Beltane?" asked Roxane.

"A festival," Maeve told her. "And Nicolo is only talking. Not even God knows what the Celts were doing outside on May first back then."

"What were they doing out there on the first warm day of spring? I could make a good guess," said Felix, his eyes bright.

Morgan Kathleen started to laugh and then looked around. "Does he mean what I think he means?" she asked.

"They probably celebrated being able to go outdoors without getting rained on," said Roxane. "They probably dug holes in the bogs, planted Maypoles."

"Another phallic symbol," Morgan told us.

Felix drank down half a glass of wine and then paused to look at Maeve. "Can you remember —" he began, his voice unnaturally light and careless. "Can you remember doing things in the fields on the first of May? That's not so long ago."

"We can look at the calendar to find what you were doing," Nico told his mother.

"You stay put," his mother told him. "There's nothing on the calendar. Felix is making a joke."

Maeve went to the stove where she lifted the lid from a pot and glanced inside, apparently forgetting his question. I knew her better than that.

"You must have been doing *something* outdoors," he insisted slyly. "I know that I was." I watched him and began to wonder just how far he was going to take this.

Maeve adjusted one of the burners, saying, "I suppose I did lots of things that day. Morgan?"

"What?"

"Would you like some soup?"

"Not that Japanese gruel, thank you."

"Let me tell you what *I* was doing," Felix said, jumping to his feet, his glass in his hand. "I was celebrating spring in the fields. I was under the spell of the goddess of everything green, a beautiful and pitiless —"

"You were enjoying your food a minute ago," I said to cut him off.

He drained his glass. "A beautiful and pitiless and immortal creature in the shape of this Maeve here."

"Did he say immoral or immortal?" asked Morgan.

"Immortal. Immortal creature," Roxane told her.

"Pitiless because she is im-mortal, and im-mortal because she is beautiful," Felix went on.

"No speeches, *please*," Maeve told him. The stove or something else had made her face sweat more fiercely and the fine loose hairs by her temple were curled and damp.

"This is love, damn it!" he cried.

"Sit down," I said.

"Listen. Listen to me. I'm in love. I'm in love with her." His voice had an operatic sob in it.

"Oh, everyone's in love with mom," Morgan reminded him.

"I have rights! Unmarried men have rights, too, you know."

Roxane, her fork poised above her plate, understood the goings on between Felix and Maeve and her lips parted in surprise.

"Odd man out. Rules of the game. Sit down," I said.

"Please," said Maeve. "Before you embarrass the children. Sit down."

But Felix was already half way to the stove where she stood. "This Maeve is one of those Irish, one of those supernatural women who lures you into their pastoral games, one of those women who keeps you enchanted for as long as she wants to play with you and then wakes you up when it's over." By then he had turned on one of the gas cocks on the stove. "When you wake up, that's when you discover you've lost half your strength and you're thirty-something years old and still unmarried."

Now Felix threw open the oven door, crashed to his knees and thrust his big head inside the oven. Maeve screamed "Felix!" and lunged at the stove, trying to turn shut all the gas cocks at once, while I had cried "You fool!" and grabbed him around the neck, struggling to yank him backward from the oven. A great luminous blue wave like a ballooning sapphire burst from the oven with a soft explosive POOM and Felix lay face up on the stones with his lids shut, his lashes gone and his eyebrows singed. My right arm began to sting and I saw that it was scorched. Nico and Morgan Kathleen and Roxane had rushed over. Felix looked up at us, stunned. "Did he bang his head?" Roxane asked. Felix shook his head and croaked, "No." Maeve went to the sink and ran cold water through a dish cloth while I studied his eyes. He looked up at us and appeared somewhat confused by the new perspective. "Ass," I told him. Maeve knelt on the floor, tenderly cradling his head of corkscrew curls in her lap, and pressed the damp cloth to his lids and his forehead. "Bliss," he murmured.

Nina had come into the kitchen. "What's going on?"

"Felix tried to blow himself up," Nico told her.

"Felix is such a romantic," Morgan Kathleen said, returning to the table.

We went back to our places (Roxane still had her fork in hand) and a minute later Felix lifted his heavy head from Maeve's lap and joined us. Maeve dropped the dish cloth into the sink. Nina carried a bowl of soup to the table and slid onto the bench next to her brother. We talked about a dozen different things. "May is Mary's month," said Maeve. Her hair had come undone and now lay uncoiled in loops and tangles over one shoulder. Felix recited, "All things rising, all things sizing, Mary sees, sympathizing."

"Ugh, not the Virgin," said Morgan Kathleen. "Gag me with a spoon."

"But it's a lovely poem," Roxane said. "— With that world of good, nature's motherhood. Something like that."

At some point Roxane asked Morgan Kathleen what she was planning to do this summer after graduating from high school, and they got into a discussion of jobs and colleges. Morgan was pleased by Roxane's interest and told her, "Nina and I are alike in some ways — right, Nina? — but actually we're quite different in other ways. Before I go out I'll show you my room and you'll see what I mean." Roxane said she'd like that a lot. Nina was eating her rice and vegetables with chopsticks and Felix exclaimed, "*Hashi!*"

And Nina said, "Good for you, Felix. *Hashi* is chopsticks. You remembered."

"Of course I remembered. You think I have a mind like a sieve? I remember *neko*, the cat. I remember *denwa*, the telephone. Also *shimbun*, the newspaper. And *beddo*, the bed. And *neko*, the cat. Did I say that? And that's all."

"Does *beddo* really mean bed?" Roxane asked.

Nina began to talk about Japanese, about *hiragana* and *katakana*.

"May I be excused?" Morgan asked me, very uninterested in Japanese. "I've got to get ready. Lisa and Wendy will be here any minute. — Want to see my room, Roxane?"

So Nico went off to play some labyrinthine game on the computer and Morgan Kathleen took Roxane upstairs to view her bedroom.

(The door to Morgan's room displayed her carefully lettered quote from Pink Floyd about the dark side of the moon, and the walls showed her varsity letters, her prize certificates, a Who album cover, a placard announcing *Antigone*, another about Miss Piggy, some fashion designs by Ertè, a mirror she had framed in eighth-grade shop, three of her own watercolor sketches of our orchard, a tennis racquet, a coronet of dried flowers from the Greek festival at St. Sophia's, a big black-and-white glossy of Maeve from Maeve's old modeling portfolio, a pencil sketch of a photo of David Bowie, a sepia snapshot of my mother at eighteen — cloche hat, bobbed hair — and a cork bulletin board studded with notes, appointment cards and newspaper clippings. Her sister's wind-chimes hung by one window, a red satin heart-shaped pillow dotted with slogan buttons hung by the other. The top of her bookcase held a collection of stones begun when she was seven, a row of bracelets, a cluster of lipsticks, some empty beer bottles, and on the bedside table stood her alarm clock and a jumble of small junk, including a framed snapshot of herself being violently kissed by some kid at a party.)

Now Maeve and I and Felix and Nina lingered at the table, eating a bit of this or that, refilling our glasses, talking. The doorbell rang, Morgan Kathleen rattled down the stairs and swept through the kitchen, saying, "Wendy's here. I'm going now. Home by midnight or the car turns into a pumpkin. Bye-bye, you guys." Roxane came to the table, sat down and began to peel an apple. Nina had begun to talk about Fin Fisher. "I know you have the wrong impression," she told us. "You think I'm unhappy or that I was having a bad time, but you're wrong. I had a wonderful time. I'm glad."

There was a long moment when no one spoke, as if we were still listening to the echoing resonances of her voice, for it had a clear ringing note in it, much like a fragile goblet.

"Well," Maeve said. "That's all right."

"You don't understand!" Nina said. Her eyes had begun to water. "I mean, I know it's my fault you don't understand, because I created the wrong impression. But if you think I regret anything, you're wrong. I had a good time, a wonderful time. I did what I wanted to do."

"No one's going to debate you," I said. "You know whether you were happy or not. You're the expert on that."

Nina rubbed the heel of her hand into her eye. "This is ridiculous," she murmured.

Felix was looking at her, his chin on his chest, his eyes half-lidded and melancholy.

"No one thinks it's ridiculous," Maeve told her.

"He's going back to Scotland, you know," said Nina.

"When?" I asked.

"I don't know," she said.

"He hasn't told you?" I asked.

"What difference would it make?" she said heatedly.

"He sounds like a shit to me," I said. I drove my chair back from the table and then wrenched it forward, all to release the furious impulse in my arms and legs.

"That's why I didn't tell you guys about this. I knew you'd say that. Excuse me a sec."

Nina used the heels of both hands to wipe her eyes. "My eyes are doing this by themselves. It isn't me."

"It's the season," Felix said, his voice surprisingly gentle.

Nina laughed briefly. "I'll outgrow it, like hay fever, don't you think?"

"Eventually," her mother said. "Who wants coffee?"

"Let me get it," Nina said, getting up. "Come on, Roxane, tell me what's new in your life. I need to be distracted."

We cleared the table and set a few chairs out with the busted lawn furniture on the terrace, so we could have our coffee there. The terrace was like the rest of this collapsing property. Years ago I had spent a summer building a grape arbor and heaping the soil here, raking it smooth and grading it and then laying down these slates, some of them the size of a checker board and others as big as a table top. Now a few gray bones of fire wood were stacked at one end, and at the other end there was a monstrous grape vine, a huge looping tangle of brown lines and pale green blotches, as if the poor oaf who had begun the arbor — still unfinished, by the way — had given up in frustration and had tried to obliterate his handiwork with this messy scrawl, and everywhere underfoot the grass and violets grew thick between the stones. Maeve and Felix were standing at the arbor, debating the proper ways to trim the grape vine — apparently there were two great systems of vine pruning, and Felix knew them both. Nina and Roxane were still in the kitchen, their voices floating out to us oddly flat, like diminished music. Nina asked Roxane if she were still seeing that computer entrepreneur or whatever he was.

"He's gone, thank God," Roxane said.

"I knew something had changed," my daughter said. "I could tell it was more than just your hair. Are you seeing anyone new?"

"Not really," Roxane said.

"What does that mean?"

"No prospects. No prospects for, you know, the future. Do you have a little pitcher I can pour this into?"

"You like talking to my father?"

"Oh, *damn*." Roxane murmured.

"Don't worry about that. The cat will love you for it."

"Wait. Let me wipe it up."

Maeve turned her head ever so slightly from Felix and sent me a look to show that she was listening to the kitchen conversation, too, though her face was so near blank you would have sworn she could hear nothing but Felix's lecture on viniculture.

"He's good to talk to," my daughter told her. "He raves about your photography. He really likes you."

"He said something about your going to Japan, maybe."

"It depends on the Japanese government, if they give me the money," Nina said. "I'm really sorry we haven't seen each other in so long. But you know how it is. I meant to visit you, but this Fin thing —"

"Sometimes it just doesn't work out. One thing or another."

"Yeah. That's true. Fin's older, but at least he's not married," my daughter said. "At least I didn't get involved with a married man. I've seen what that can do."

"Where abouts in Japan would you go?"

"Kyoto. I don't know what you're mopping down there. You got it all the first time. You've left nothing at all for Calico."

"All done."

"Here we are," Nina announced, coming onto the terrace bearing a tray with cups, mugs, spoons, milk and sugar. Roxane followed with the coffee pot.

At that hour the air was quiet and the light which had shimmered in the warmth of the afternoon now hung stilled, suspended all around us. The orchard was bunched between our terrace and the woods like a messily tossed pink-and-white quilt or a freshly shoveled snowpile. Those apple trees were old. Two had died and fallen to pieces and when you stumbled across their shattered trunks and broken limbs you felt you had discovered the ruins of an elaborately worked artifact, a tree of tarnished silver for a jeweled bird to sing in. But the living apple trees were even more astonishing, their ancient trunks twisted like corkscrews — hollow as a barrel, some of them — the bark scaling from the decrepit branches, and all the dried-out sticks and brittle twigs and sprouts, all of them loaded with blossoms, thick with blossoms, heavy with blossoms, making the sweet scent that floated through everything seem the air of enchantment.

"There's a wedding here in a month," Maeve remarked. "But all the blossoms will be gone by then."

"Wedding? Wedding? Who's getting married?" asked Felix, with the confusion of a person who fears a trick is being played on him.

"My cousin's daughter," I told him. "Aurora Dawn. She's marrying a shipwright from Marblehead and they want an open field to get married in."

Nina had dropped herself listlessly into a lawn chair with her leg dangling over the arm. "I would prefer not to go to that thing, you know," she told her mother.

Her mother told her it was a month away, and maybe she would change her mind by then and, after all, it was going to be an enjoyable outdoor party for a whole afternoon and evening, and a lot of friends and relatives we hadn't seen in a long time would be there and, by God, she hoped it would be sunny.

Nina was swinging her leg back and forth now. "Roxane, you could come to this thing and keep me company," she said.

Roxane replied that she was sure Aurora Dawn wanted only her close friends at the wedding.

"I haven't seen Aurora for years. We're practically strangers," Nina said. "You could come and take pictures."

Felix asked who in the world had come up with the name Aurora Dawn. I explained that it came from my cousin Arianne who had been in California when the baby was conceived and had only herself to please in choosing a name, because by the time the baby was born, the father — a splendidly built surfer — had vanished to Hawaii in his quest for an endless wave.

"Listen, you guys," Nina said. "I've got to go upstairs and lie down. I'm really out of it tonight."

"Hey, wait!" I said. She had started to push herself up and now she paused, looking to me to continue, and I wanted to tell her (this child, my daughter) *Stay here, be solaced here in my sight, there's no need to take your grief to bed, everything will work out for the best*, but there was no way to say that any more. "Are you all right?" I asked her.

"Yes, dad. But this Fin thing is driving me

crazy. I'm going to my room, take a couple of aspirin, lie down." She listlessly flung herself out of the chair and went into the house.

47

I asked did anyone want a drink and everyone said no. I went to the kitchen to get one for myself. We had used all of our proper glasses at dinner and now what remained was a row of big glass jars which had come to us a year ago packed with my mother's marmalade. I took one of the marmalade glasses, filled it with bourbon and water and went back to the terrace. "I changed my mind," Maeve told me. I took a large swallow and handed her the bourbon. The sky over the woods had taken on a tranquil violet color and directly above us there was a thin gold jet-trail, like a scratch on the firmament. It had come about that Maeve and I were seated next to each other, with Felix on the other side of Maeve, and Roxane here beside me. After taking a drink, Maeve set the glass jar cautiously on the terrace stones between us. "We were talking about Aurora's wedding," she told me.

"Nina and Morgan Kathleen will be having their own weddings in a couple of years," I said.

"Morgan Kathleen has a few years to go," said Maeve.

Roxane asked when we got married. Twenty-six years ago, I told her. "The year I was born," said Roxane. I took up the glass. There wasn't any point in announcing that she was half as old as I was. In the long flat light of evening the woods were beginning to lose their depth, were becoming a black decorative border at the foot of the sky. The bourbon had a pleasingly corrosive taste. Maeve and Felix had gone on talking about Morgan Kathleen and Nina, but it was a tedious effort to follow them and I ceased trying. "There's no point to the story. They grow up and leave," I said to Roxane.

"And that bothers you." She had turned to me with a face so calm and happy that I wondered if it were a trick of the evening light.

"Yes, it bothers me."

"But why?" she asked.

"I don't like goodbyes. In fact, I hate goodbyes."

"But *you* left home. You got married."

"Naturally. And I expect them to leave home. I expect them to marry. I miss them when they move to another planet, of course."

"You're being unfair to her," Roxane told me. "Japan isn't another planet."

"All right, so I'm being unfair. But I'm beginning to catch the drift of things, the way things go. When you get married, you begin to

349

put the world together. And when you bring up children, you get on with the job and put the world together the way it was best, when you were a kid, with a mother and a father and lots of other kids around. But just when you think you have it all together, it begins to fly apart. — Have I drunk too much?"

Maeve turned toward us. "Why? What's happening?"

"He's saying things about marriage and children growing up and leaving home."

"In a minute he'll begin to worry out loud about his mother," Maeve told her.

"She's living alone, Maeve. She eats a lot of meals alone. She —"

"Your mother prefers to live alone now. She wants to be independent. You know that," Maeve said.

"Yes, yes. I know. And I do phone my mother and I do invite her over here and I do go see her."

"And you see your father, too," Roxane added, with a fleeting uncertain smile.

"Oh," Felix said. "And I had thought your father died a few years ago."

"He did," Maeve told him.

"Ah," Felix said slowly.

"Yeah. Well," I said. "You know, Maeve still finds old things around the house that her mother has set out for her. Rings, combs, things like that. And her mother died when Maeve was eleven."

"That hasn't happened for a long time now," Maeve said, reflectively. "I wonder why."

"Eleven years old," Roxane murmured. "God. How awful."

"I think it stopped when your father died," I said.

"Is this the way you two live?" Felix asked, starting to laugh.

"Is there some other way to live?" Maeve asked him. "If you know it, for God's sake tell us. I thought this was the way everyone did it. I thought this was the only way there was."

"What did she die of?" Roxane asked.

"Cancer," Maeve told her, drawing her hand in a light caress of her own breast.

Felix laughed and spoke across us to Roxane, as if privately. "This is what happens when the Irish and Sicilians get together, this hobnobbing with the dead."

Roxane had leaned slightly forward to hear him, and in a flash of possessiveness my arm unfolded to lie along the back of her chair before I even thought of it.

"Oh, that," Maeve told him, tossing her head a bit to catch him back from Roxane. "We can't avoid death and dying, but I was hoping you meant there was some way to avoid all the work and the aches and pains."

Maeve's hand drifted down toward the terrace stones, groping, and I gave her the glass of bourbon.

"Isn't that why people fall in love?" Felix

asked, his voice artfully casual. "If not to conquer death, at least to avoid pain? Or to get over it? Or to make it bearable?" The deepening blue shadow in which we sat made it impossible to detect if he were serious or mocking, and maybe he took it as an advantage.

"You make love sound like a tactic," Maeve said. "You make it sound like a round-about maneuver to avoid misery. You ought to know better than that. There's so much pain in it. Love isn't some way we go by choice. Why do we love this person and not that one? Or why only this one and that one, why not a dozen? And knowing what we know, why do we marry? Why have children?"

"There's instinct and then there's human invention," Felix said pedantically. "And they're not the same. There's love and there's sex."

"Hey, wait a minute," Roxane cut in. "I'm getting confused. Is it love or is it fucking that's the instinct?"

"I'm not so sure about the fucking, but love is instinctive," Maeve remarked.

"Quite the contrary, love is some kind of human invention," Felix said.

"You think it's an *invention*?" Roxane asked him.

"Sex is instinctive," he went on. "But love is this ramshackle thing rigged up by us mortals. That's why it's so flawed. Nature doesn't make things that badly. We do."

"Love is as natural as all this talk," Maeve insisted.

"Ha! You call this natural?" Felix asked her.

"Did you ever meet a person who wasn't born to talk?" she retorted.

"It's human nature, is all it is," I said. "We fall in love for no reason at all, but only because we're human. We fall in love against conventional wisdom and our own better judgment. It's a terrible force of nature, human nature. We shrivel up and die if we don't go along with it."

"Sex is what we do and love is what we make," said Maeve. "Does that mean anything or am I drunk? I hate clever remarks. Anyway, this teeny tiny glass is empty," she said, looking into the marmalade jar.

"The love that parents feel for their children — when the children are young, I mean — that must be a natural instinct," Roxane suggested, leaning forward a bit to Maeve.

"I've always supposed so," Maeve said. "But when I held Nina at my breast for the first time I didn't know what I was feeling. I tried to feel and to understand what I was feeling, but it was so odd. We had been living together for nine months, Nina and I, and when I looked at her face she was a stranger and I thought *Who's she?* Now, whether I love them or want to kill them, it all feels natural."

"My mother and father must have —," Roxane broke off. "I don't know why I keep thinking about my mother and father all the time. I even dream about them. Isn't that strange?"

She had shifted her shoulders, had bumped my arm where it lay along the back of her chair, and now my muscles ached, though whether they ached for her touch or more deeply to solace her in an embrace or both those together I could never tell.

"How about the love of God?" Felix said from the dark, the yellow stripes of his shirt almost invisible now beyond Maeve. "Is that an instinct?"

"You *have* to love God," I said. "That's why he made us. It's all in the Catechism."

"I have a hard time loving a God who never sat up with a sick child," said Maeve.

"You don't think he keeps track of each sparrow that falls?" Felix asked her.

"Maybe he does," she said. "But I notice it's Nicolo who rescues them from the cat and puts them back in the nest, even if it takes all day."

Roxane's shoulder had brushed my arm and now it returned, lingering.

"You're a terrible Catholic, Maeve," he said, his voice merging with her, she had him so close.

"My father hated priests," Maeve told him. "I learned it from him."

"God, look at those stars. There's so many tonight," Roxane said. She leaned back in my arm, resting on me, and I didn't care how my Maeve had Felix at her side.

Maeve laughed. "My father used to say that the face of God is serene and meaningless, like a beautiful woman's behind."

"He was a theologian?" Felix said.

"And a man about town," Maeve told him.

We talked about these and other things while the stars floated over us in a great slow tide. Nico went to bed. The light in Nina's room went off. Morgan Kathleen came home to bed. As for Roxane and Felix — no, they did not spend the night. Roxane drove home in her car, and Felix (his engine racing like a freshly wound watch) drove off just behind her. And when I went to bed that night I remembered how it had been one other night long ago, or not so long ago, when my mother and father had come for Thanksgiving dinner and to sleep over. After the last one had gone to bed on that other night, I had walked from room to room on the first floor, quietly testing the windows and rattling the doors, and then I had climbed the stairs to our bedroom and felt them sleeping all around me — my mother and father and Maeve and Nina and Morgan Kathleen and Nico — and, as I lay in bed and pulled up the covers, the waves of love spread out in circles from me and my home to touch first Maeve's brothers and their wives and kids in nearby New England, and then my brother Rafe and his wife Daisy and their kids way down in Washington, and I knew I had them all in one fleet, together and safe. And I was happy.

48

Late Monday morning I was at the washbowl when the stream of faucet water abruptly thinned and I knew that Maeve had opened the hose out back. I finished and went out to the vegetable patch where the sprinkler was running. In the orchard a lot of blossoms had fallen and in a day or two they would all be gone. A trail of footprints in the long, dew-drenched grass showed where she had walked down between the apple trees. I walked through the nearest aisle toward the creek and just before I got there I saw her and stopped. At that season of the year the creek is still too wide to jump across, but only six inches deep, and there was Maeve, standing in the middle of it in that thin white dress that looks rather like a chemise. She gazed down stream and with the dreamy slowness of an enchantment she lowered herself until she was seated in the water. Then she drew her hair forward over her shoulder and sank back impassively on her elbows to watch the idle water moving along her hips, washing under and between her thighs, soaking in and out and away through the pale garment that clung in darker handholds on her legs and buttocks, or floated just at the surface, as if she sat in a pool of milk.

I walked back through the orchard, shut off the sprinkler, went upstairs and began to shower. The bathroom was blurred with steam when she knocked at the door. I said *Come in*. She was naked now, emerging from the cloud in vivid flesh the color of a candle flame. I yanked the curtain aside and she stepped in. "I slipped at the edge of creek," she explained. "Got a little muddy."

"Join me."

I stood between her and the shower, so she could get used to the scalding water, her cheeks already growing red under the hot mist, her eyelashes thick with drops. She handed me the soap and turned around. She had pinned up her hair, leaving her neck exposed. I soaped the hard nape of her neck, her shoulders, her back, all the while feeling myself grow heavy and pendulous. The water poured over my hand, sluiced down the deep groove of her spine. She moved, sliding her glistening haunch against me and I sank my fingers into the thick folds of her hair, getting ready to rein her in. "Do we need to explain every little thing?" she asked, sliding past me into the scalding downpour.

"No, I don't think so."

The water was bursting over her shoulders,

streaming over her breasts and belly, wrapping across her thighs.

"What do you think?" I asked.

"I think explanations are trash."

I reached past her and turned off the shower. The air was quiet now, white as a cloud, and all that was visible was our freshly washed selves. "Do you want to talk or do something?" I asked her.

"We can spend the rest of our lives discussing things."

"Right. The rest of our lives."

"Let's go do something," she said.

49

My father rarely told stories about his past and when he did, it was in the lightest and most off-hand way. When I was growing up I sometimes wondered what he had been like as a boy and young man, and now I have a certain amount of evidence. As I write this, I have here on the kitchen table a snapshot of my father taken in the summer of 1928, a few weeks after his wedding. He's in a white shirt with a starched collar, but he hasn't bothered to put on his necktie, and now he has folded his arms and is resting a shoulder against the wall beside a window, smiling as he waits comfortably for his bride to snap the picture. This would take time. The camera was an Ansco Vest Pocket Speedex No. 3, a lovely instrument bound in black leather — you opened the front downward, like a drawbridge, then cautiously pulled the lens and bellows forward on a miniature track — but it carried a tricky view finder perched beside the lens mechanism. You had to peer straight down into it to bring the figures (marvelously small) into sight, then they would hover and drift in the convex glass to the tiniest tremor of your hand. My mother paused until the image of my father was just where she wanted it, then she pressed the wire plunger — *there*! And *here's* the evidence, a small sheet of celluloid (2 1/4 x 3 1/4) bearing a thin emulsion mixed with the same light that filled the hotel room that morning, and here is the photographic print itself, positive proof from the year 1928. My father is a happy young man on his wedding trip.

I have other exhibits, too, for when I was hunting for my snapshot of Judy Clark — apparently lost with the rest of 1948 Gloucester — I came across a thin manila envelope with ancient photographs of my father, photographs I had never seen before. They were studio portraits embedded like fossils in their decorative cardboards. They had lain pressed one upon the other so long that it was a delicate job to pry the strata apart, but while most everything else had been destroyed these delicate squares of paper had slept beneath a silt of bank statements and cancelled checks, safe as sea shells in sedimentary rock.

The earliest one must have been made about 1898 or 1899, perhaps on my father's first birthday in 1899. He's dressed in a white gown which rumples up around the nape of his neck and falls in ruffles over his shoulders and over his arms like the petals of a singular white blossom, so that only his head shows (the wide alert eyes, the mouth open to smile) and one bare hand reaches from the lovingly fashioned pleats and lacework while he leans forward to look more closely at the photographer.

The second is a slate-like tablet showing a wildly mixed group — four men, five women, two girls, two infants, three boys and two patient farm dogs. That's sixteen people, including my father's mother, standing second from the right in back, and my father's father, seated on the far left, all gathered in front of a grape arbor. The women smile, even the little old one dressed in black whose cheeks fall in for lack of teeth, and some of the younger women squint as if the old yellowish light reflecting up from their blouses is still too bright. The young show-off on the right has plugged a cigar stump into the corner of his mouth and stands with his feet planted wide, negligently displaying the long barrel of a shotgun in the crook of his arm, but the other men (even the stout fellow with the baby cradled in his arm) have taken on more convivial poses and flourish wine bottles, holding them aloft to offer us a drink. They're on a mid-summer outing in Massachusetts, this crew of Calabrian banditti, and there on the far left, posted beside his father (wistful eyes, black mustache, smile) stands my dad at age six. He's wearing a cap with a tiny visor, a check shirt, knickers and big laced shoes. The shirt is too small and his wrists dangle far below the cuffs, and the knickers — which have been cut from adult trousers — are comically voluminous. While the bigger boys wrestle with their dogs down front in the dirt, and while the boisterous sweating men hoist wine bottles, this sweet-tempered kid stands properly beside his father and smiles at the camera with a look of such openness and trust that it wrenches my heart.

The next one displays my father at seventeen in the parade uniform of his high school regiment, dark jacket and white trousers. He stands proudly in Stiller's photographic studio, the white gloved fingers of his left hand resting precisely against the sword sheath that slants along side his leg, the ornate hilt just barely visible in the slight space between the sleeve and the body of the jacket. On his sleeve there is a gracefully curved chevron which reaches to his shoulder, a thick twist of gold braid sits on each shoulder and a two-branched garland of gold leaves decorates the front of his cap. I used a magnifying glass to make out the school's fancy initials on the cap face and, later, while moving it over the photo, I noticed the faint crease across the bottom of each trouser leg where the cloth had been let down to make the pants fit the growing young man.

The topmost photograph in this little deck presents my father at twenty. It's a smooth amber head-and-shoulders portrait of an intelligent young man, self-assured and ready and somewhat amused. He doesn't look vain, not at all, but he does appear to know certain things. He's just completed four years' work in three, has graduated from the Massachusetts Institute of Technology and Harvard University (those academies having joined forces during the Great War), and now possesses a joint degree from both. He's discovered that he's wonderfully adept at structural design and analysis, he's delighted by the symmetry that links the iron railroad bridge to the toothpick truss of an aeroplane wing, the submarine to the airy dirigible. The prospects are pleasing.

The next time Nicolo turns up is in the hotel room, waiting beside the window that looks onto 1928, while his bride Marissa snaps the picture. That piece of evidence has already been marked and recorded. Now here is Marissa in her plain negligee and Nicolo in his open shirt and the camera itself, all facing us above a breakfast tray on which there is a coffee pot, two cups, a rumpled napkin — the whole scene within the mirror frame. In the other little snapshot we're outside and he smiles broadly. He's wearing glasses (big perfect circles outlined with black rims), wearing them with the air of a man in disguise, the young aviator. One hand lingers on the guard rail, and now he grabs at his straw boater while his neckties blows across his shoulder, flapping. Down below the balustrade there's a turbulent shimmer, a cloud, perhaps, or a city park as viewed from the cockpit of an open aeroplane.

The remaining evidence is circumstantial. These are three pamphlets which used to be wedged into the bottom of my father's bookcase, jammed between a row of stout Baedekers (foldout maps, green provinces, fabulous cities) and the tall thin atlas at the end of the shelf. The first is a black-and-gold program from the Théâtre national de l'Opéra comique for a performance of *La Vie de bohème* and *Paillasse* on Dimanche 8 Juillet 1928. A long time ago someone put the ticket between these pages, a slip of green paper: *40 fr. 50. Soirée du Dimanche 8 Juillet 1928. Fauteuil d'orchestre. Côté droit. No. 118. Les dames ne sont pas admises en chapeau.* The other two come from the same summer. The first has a red paper cover with *Programme* written in gold script, and an oval window cut through to reveal a woman's face (pencilled eyebrows, sidelong glance) so that when you open the cover there's the photo of her, Smolenska, in a white feathery boa, beneath which it says *Folies Bergère, 22, rue Richer, Tél: Gutenberg 02-59*. The show began with *Le Cortège du printemps* and ended with *L'Éternel Féminin*, comprised two acts with a total of sixty tableaus. There are a few photographs of the performers, including one of Josephine Baker, but nothing to compare to the souvenir album. The Folies Bergère Album is a large flat booklet of shimmering photographs, the men in cache-sexe and the women in sequins, which I used to study while sitting cross-legged on the floor by the bookcase when nobody was home. I was fascinated by these naked gymnasts — this young man wearing a jewelled woman lightly on his shoulder, this girl in a beaded loincloth who crouches to pounce — was puzzled by the women, the slave girls bound with ropes of pearl, the Empress in a glittering fountainous crown, Eve with a silver apple, a jaunty aviator suspended in a fantastic biplane, the rows of dancers. The photographs have a soft silver hue and the pages are made of glossy smoke-white stock which adds an opalescent sheen to the pictures, sealing them against too clear a view. They are just as they were at first, the dance and play go on forever, the ageless savage and debonair athletes bedding those dazzling women naked amid the diamonds and feathers and pearls.

50

Here it is. It wasn't lost, after all. The snapshot was taken the summer I was working at the bakery shop in Gloucester. The girl is Judy Clark, age fourteen. The breeze has filled her shirt (actually her father's shirt) and is blowing her hair as she squints in the sun and laughs. The black-and-white photo makes her hair look dark, but actually it was light brown with flaxen streaks where the sun had bleached it. That's a mast to the left of her because she's sitting on the bow of a beached sailboat, her legs hanging over the gunwale and below the margin of the picture. The photo was taken at the end of the summer (at half past two, if the watch on her wrist is still accurate), but we had met at the beginning of the season on a path in a meadow that rolled down from a dairy farm. I stepped off the path and waded in the grass beside her, told her that the open car down there at the side of the road belonged to my aunt — that was my aunt herself, sitting in the shade beneath the tree and the kid pulling her to her feet was my cousin Arianne. She pointed at a cluster of roofs down against the sea and told me which one belonged to the cottage that her parents were renting for the summer. I told her I was here for the summer, too, and that I was leaving for college in the fall. She had gray eyes and the bridge of her nose was sunburned, the skin peeling like fine tissue paper. We arrived at the bottom of the field where a kid in red swim trunks was coming up the road, hopping on one foot. He paused to look at us, then turned and began to hop quickly away on his other foot. "That's my brother," she said, smiling. "He's going to ask mother who I'm talking to."

We went swimming together almost every afternoon, and a couple of times her father let us take the small sailboat (*The Birch Island*) in which we tacked slowly back and forth in Annisquam Cove. My last day in Gloucester went according to our private plan — I packed my suitcase in the early afternoon and loafed on the beach with my aunt and cousin while Judy went shopping with her mother and spent the late afternoon memorizing her irregular French verbs. Then in the evening we evaded our friends and slipped away together for a walk at sunset. She was wearing shorts and a jersey with faded yellow stripes and I carried a flashlight. Once we stopped by a shadowy grove of trees and I kissed her and she hesitantly put her arms around my neck, unsure of herself. I kissed her again, holding her and not quite touching her, feeling the weave of her jersey beneath my fingertips, and she kissed me. We walked up the path into the dark meadow where we had first met. The hay had been freshly mowed and the stubble prickled our legs when we sat down. We talked and talked and when we lay back the stars plunged at us, halting an inch above our outstretched hands. It makes no sense now to bring back her words and mine, or the fresh odor of the soil beneath the dusty stubble, the press of her stiff breast against my palm, the plain taste of her skin. We lay in each other's arms, that was all, and when it was time for us to get up she put her head on my chest and wept. (For a year after, I kept my shirt from the wash.) Outside her door we said good-bye, she touched my cheek and I ran home wild with triumphant grief. She was fourteen then, must be fifty now.

51

The two weddings took place in back of our house on the lawn between the terrace and the apple orchard in the sun and heat of the early afternoon. I don't know the exact number of guests, no one does, not even Gina who with her granddaughter Aurora had arranged the feast and mailed the invitations. Aurora and Jens had invited all their friends. Then Gina had invited her brothers and sisters and their spouses — that would have made sixteen more if everyone could have come — and Arianne had invited all thirty-five of our cousins, plus their partners and children, though fortunately not all of them could come, either — and because it was going to be held in our own back yard Maeve and I had invited some of our friends, too.

It was my job to call the guests to the terrace, which I did, and then I put my head in the door and told the couples that we were assembled. When I turned around I saw that we were a larger crowd than I had thought. A moment later Marshfield Thomas came through the doorway, ducking his head to get under the lintel, then he straightened up and gave his arm to Regina as she came out, and they remained arm in arm while the judge, a friend of theirs, read the statutory text to them from a card. Marsh wore a blue yachting blazer, white trousers and white shoes, and he listened intently to each word, a glaze of perspiraton on his forehead. Gina stood beside him as steady and placid as a carved caryatid, the honey color of her flesh looking especially dark against the sunny white dazzle of her hair. Then the brief ceremony was over and the judge, by virtue of the authority vested in him by the Commonwealth of Massachusetts, declared that Marshfield and Regina were husband and wife, and we cheered.

I went to the door again, told Aurora and Jens we were ready and returned to my place. My chest flooded with joy, for there was my father in a light gray summer suit standing about half way back among the other guests and, like them, waiting with an expectant smile for the bride and groom to come through the door. His face held the same reassuring confidence as when I looked to him from the altar where I stood waiting for Maeve years ago. I searched hurriedly for my mother and found her right here in front, seeming shorter and frailer and somewhat more stooped beside Maeve, and wholly unaware of who was standing only ten feet behind her. I bobbed this way and that, trying to catch her eye, but it was no use. Then I spied Gina's first husband, John Campagnia, between my uncle Zitti's shoulder and the wildly exaggerated straw hat worn by my aunt Candida. I don't understand why I was so surprised to see my father in the middle of this gathering, or why I thought I would have been less surprised to observe him at the far margin, say, or on the more distant lawn where some children were playing (one little kid running around naked) as if they were not here at all. Nor could I understand why John's features, so faded in memory, were so clear today. And in the midst of all this I was distracted by a white handkerchief being fluttered by the stout woman seated on a folding chair almost directly across from me. During the first ceremony she had begun to dab her handkerchief at the perspiration on her neck and now she was waving at me, the cloth clutched in her hand, waving and smiling — my grandmother! — Marianna Cavallù who had died a few hours after seeing her own mother, the goddess, standing on tip-toe on a big scallop shell that floated off the shore at Mondello. Still looking at me, Marianna turned her head slightly toward the man behind her who leaned forward to catch what she was saying. He straightened up and peered at me, then he smiled to me, too, though he was certainly not my grandfather nor anyone else I recognized. But now the bride and groom, with the minister between them, came walking from the house.

Aurora in a pale green dress stood slender as a blade of grass and on her head she carried a fragile circlet of wood, a braided crown carved by Jens' grandfather in Sweden. Jens wore dark trousers, embroidered suspenders and a white shirt open at the throat. They had each written a declaration of love, which each in turn read haltingly but boldly before us and then, in response to the minister, Aurora and Jens took each other by the hand as husband and wife, for richer for poorer, in sickness and in health, to love and to cherish from that day forward until death would them part, and they exchanged rings as a token of love complete and eternal.

As soon as the ceremony was over I glanced across at my father and grandmother, for everyone was still there. The sun glowed on my grandmother's 1910 violet satin bodice and on the café-au-lait flesh of her breasts when she turned to say something to the man behind her, and I knew that when he leaned forward he would catch again the scent of her lily-of-the-valley cologne. But before he could move, the scene changed magically, flipped, turned over just as it does in an optical illusion — as in those plain line drawings of a stairway, or a cube, where you see that the cube is tipped up this way, but a moment later you discover that it's turned a different way and now you can't get back to seeing the first cube no matter how hard you try — that's how it happened. Even the folding chair, which had faced *this* way, now faced *that* way, and my pretty cousin Linda stood with her hand on the back of it, actually leaning on it as she twisted sideways to remove one of her high-heel shoes.

We had put up a canopy of yellow canvas at the edge of the orchard and set the food and drink beneath it on trestle tables. If you took your plate of food into the orchard you would surely come across four or five of the older guests seated in a circle, talking and eating in the checkered shade of an apple tree, and if you went beyond that group you would most likely come to another one (young men with their neckties loosened and jackets tossed aside, young women with their high-heel shoes kicked off) lounging on the shaggy grass beneath the parasol of the next tree. And if you went all the way to the creek you could watch some of the youngest kids playing in the leaky rowboat that Nico and his sisters used in their adventures long ago.

I walked past here with my cousin Arianne early in the afternoon, talking about this and that, mostly family matters. She worried about her daughter and Jens and how they would survive, and we discussed whether or not it mattered being poor if you were young, and we talked about Morgan Kathleen's graduation from high school and Nina's going to Japan (yes, Japan) and my mother's nice recovery from surgery and about Gina. Arianne smiled, saying, "How many women have seen their mother and daughter married on the same day?"

Everyone gathered at the yellow canopy to watch Aurora and Jens cut their wedding cake. Someone rang a glass with a fork to call for quiet, then Jens' father stepped forward to read the couple a letter written by his own father, Jens' grandfather. He gave each sentence first in Swedish, then in English. The little note told how happy the grandfather was that his grandson was marrying today a beautiful girl with a beautiful name. He remembered the summer when Jens had come all the way to Sweden to visit him, how much fun they had had sailing together in the harbor. And now Jens was no longer a boy but a man, and a craftsman like his grandfather. He hoped that Jens would always remember that the family came from Oland and that Olanders made the best fishing boats. He blessed Jens and his bride Aurora and he hoped that they would visit him next summer, because he longed to hug him one more time as he had when Jens was a boy.

After they had cut the cake, I talked a little while with Jens' father, for I had been moved by that old man in Oland writing to this distant grandson whom he feared he would never hold again — even the unfamiliar Swedish had sounded woeful to me. Later I went looking for Mercurio but ran into Gina instead. I told her how handsome she and Marsh looked during their wedding. She said it was all in the point of view. "Who's the young woman taking the pictures?" she asked.

"That's Roxane Beach. Would you like to meet her?"

"We've already met. We met just before the ceremony. She seems like a nice person. I just wondered where she came from."

"She's a friend of ours," I said.

"*Your* friend, I'll bet. And the man with her? The one with all those cameras hanging around his neck. I suppose that's her assistant?"

"Yes. That's Felix Stout."

"He's an interesting looking man," said Gina.

"Would you like to meet him? He's a friend, too."

"Oh, no. I wouldn't want to interrupt. He's far too busy with your Roxane person. — Say, your mother tells me that Nina is going to Kyoto."

"Which is far, too far away," I said.

"Don't be sad, *caro*."

"I'll miss her."

"Be happy. She's beautiful and full of life — just like you, when you were her age." Gina smiled, looking into me and wrinkling the corners of her eyes, though anyone who saw us would say she merely squinted in the sunlight. "You can still remember yourself at that age, can't you?" she asked.

I smiled. "Sure. Sure I can remember."

"Good." She laughed and glanced away. "I wonder where I left my cigarettes."

"Smoking is going to ruin that beautiful voice of yours."

"I'm going to stop. Don't worry. I've already made plans."

Afterward I found the table where Mercurio was seated. There was a bottle of Asti spumante, some loose crackers, a couple of cheeses and a small white box of *confetti* — almonds with a glossy white sugar coating as smooth and hard as marble, the traditional candy at Italian weddings. Mercurio had grown a beard which filled in the hollows of his face, so that he had the appearance of a gaunt but healthy long-distance runner, except for the depth of his bright eyes. I asked him how he was doing.

"Not bad," he said crisply. He laid a soft wedge of Bel Paese on a cracker and popped it into his mouth, crunched it vigorously, then washed it down with a swallow of Asti. "If I get tired of sitting, I walk around a bit. And if I get tired of walking, I sit down."

"Good," I said.

"I stopped the treatments," Mercurio announced. "No more medicine for me. Some pain killers, of course. But no more medicine."

"Well." I groped for what to say. "Well, that's the way you want it, then."

"I had a friend — oh, she was a lovely woman — who had these radiation treatments, chemotherapy treatments. But in the end, when she was dying, I saw what they had done to her and she told me, so —" He shrugged lightly.

"If you can get out and enjoy life a little —"

"Well." He laughed. "I can enjoy food, anyway, and drink."

Nico had joined us at the table and now he began to crack and grind the sugar-coated almonds between his molars.

"Did uncle Mercurio ever tell you about the time his bomber burned up and he had to jump?" I asked.

"Nope."

Mercurio was watching him with mild interest, a tired smile on his face.

"Mercurio was a waist gunner on a B-24," I said.

Nico looked at Mercurio's eyes. "Where was the war?" he asked politely.

"Oh, it was all over the place," Mercurio told him. "It was everywhere."

"Tell him the whole story," I said.

Mercurio shook his head. "That story is history, ancient history." He uncorked the Asti and refilled his glass, snapping the bottle upright with a turn of his wrist to keep the last drop from the table cloth.

"I love that story," I told Mercurio. "Do you remember telling it to me in Gloucester? It was summer. Years ago."

"No." He pressed a bladeful of Brie onto a cracker and worked it for a while, lifted it slowly to his mouth, then hesitated. "All I remember about Gloucester is the smell of fish. And I recall your father asking me to find out what you were doing there. He wanted to know if you were in trouble with a woman. He knew something was going on." Mercurio snapped up the cracker and cheese.

"My father?" I said.

He took a long swallow of wine, then looked reminiscently at the glass as he set it down. "But I don't remember telling anything about any war stories."

"My father thought something was going on?"

"A woman, he figured. We could only guess who." Mercurio glanced at me, his eyes black but with a soft liquid glitter, like water at the bottom of a well. "I came back from Gloucester and told him not to worry, you'd be home in a week. —And I wasn't just a waist gunner," he told Nico. "We were trained to fire from any position. Waist, tail, belly."

"What did my father say?" I asked him.

"I told him you'd be home in a week. And

you were. I don't recall your father saying anything. He loved you."

"What happened to the B-24?" Nico asked him.

"It fell into the Mediterranean," Mercurio said.

"And then what happened to you?" Nico asked.

Mercurio Cavallù fell out of the clear blue sky after a bombing run on the rail yards at Rome (19 June 1943) when the shredded B-24 on which he was a waist gunner caught fire on route back to its base in North Africa, bailed out just as the starboard wing vanished in a sunburst, a swirl of incandescent junk like a cloud of burning feathers, and Mercurio came to himself in a slow somersault through the empty air, the pale blue sky and brown land and dark blue sea rolling gently past again and again and yet again, though he must have pulled the rip cord at last because the parachute rattled out behind him, yanked him upright, halted his fall and let him drift through the wail of an air raid siren and the distant *poom poom poom* of anti-aircraft fire, drift down toward the dun buildings and faded greenery that spread out so much like any other city that it was not until he watched the solitary mountain loom over him in the shape and color of a giant loaf of bread that he realized he was falling not into Africa but into Sicily, falling past Monte Pellegrino and into

Palermo, falling beyond a row of army trucks toward a wrinkled blanket of palm trees and fig trees and grape vines and over a tiled roof into the Via Imperatore Federico where he slipped free of the chute harness, loped down the sidewalk and vaulted over the wall into the garden just as his father was coming up from the back of the villa. "*Papà, it's me, it's Mercurio!*" he shouted, running past his father and up the stairway to the terrace. "*I've got to hide!*"

His father came stumbling up the stairs behind him. "How did you get here? The Americans are supposed to be on the other side of Sicily."

"Tell them I ran out the back!" Mercurio cried, crossing the terrace.

"You're in danger! Where's your gun? There are still some Germans left in Palermo."

They halted, embraced at the doorway, then Pacifico turned and started down the stairs to the garden, shaking.

"Tell them I ran through the garden and out the back," Mercurio called after him. Then he swung into the kitchen and found his sister Lucia standing at the table with a coffee pot in her hand, staring at him.

"Mercurio! I *knew* that was your voice. Well, well, well. What are you doing here? We thought Patton was only in Caltanisetta."

"Parachute. I'm in the Air Force. —They're

going to be here in a minute," he said, crossing the kitchen toward the hall.

"You're a paratrooper? The paratroops are coming?" she asked, following.

"No, damnit! I'm in the Air Force, the Air Force! I'm a gunner on a B-24, a bomber. — Tell them I ran out the back."

"This is my brother Mercurio," Lucia said, turning to the young woman seated at the table.

"They're out there right now," Mercurio whispered. Pacifico's voice floated up with the voices of some other men — Italian soldiers who had run in from the street. "Go down there and play dumb."

Lucia was already crossing the terrace toward the stairs, the coffee pot still in her hand.

Mercurio stood in the center of the kitchen and looked across the table at the young woman, taking in her sea-green eyes and the wild mass of bronze ringlets held back by a ribbon over her head. "I should go hide," he murmured, speaking Italian for the first time. But he didn't go hide. He looked at her and listened to the shouts and the rush of footsteps on the gravel pathway through the garden. He was still looking at her when his father came in out of breath, silently snatched up the three empty coffee mugs that stood on the table between Mercurio and the young woman, and went out again. Mercurio listened to the quieted voices of the soldiers accepting the mugs of coffee from Lucia, the voices growing clearer as they came back up the gravel path through the garden. Later there was some laughter, then some thank-yous. At last the voices dwindled away. The solid wood gate to the driveway made a secure *thud* as it closed. Who knows how much time had passed while Mercurio stared into that wild hair and those wide green eyes?

"I think they're leaving," he murmured, still looking at her.

The young woman stood up smiling and reached across the table to shake his hand. "My name is Coral. A friend of Lucia's. My room's just down the hall and you can hide there any time you want," she said quietly, seeing that he had fallen out of the sky and into her life forever. "Don't tell your sister."

Pacifico came in, lowered the coffee pot gently to the table and sank onto a wood chair. "My God," he said, dropping a hand on each knee, "I thought when I tore up your damned flying helmet that you were through with that nonsense. My God." Lucia came in and flung her arms around Mercurio and gave him a kiss, accidently cracking the mugs together behind his back. "Something had to get broken. There's a war on," she said, picking up a chip of porcelain.

"What happened to you?" Coral asked Mercurio. "You look as if you were sunburned. Even your clothes look sunburned."

Mercurio looked down at his uniform and noticed several burn holes about the size of a penny and a big charred hole on his pants where his thigh showed through, the flesh ruddy. "I don't know," he said, thoughtfully. "Is there anything to eat? I just noticed I'm hungry."

Three days later the US Seventh Army under General George S. Patton took Palermo. Mercurio eventually linked up with his group and discovered that he was the only one of the downed B-24 who survived. He finished out his service with the 98th Bomb Group of the 47th Wing of the 9th Air Force, flew a total of fifty-one missions (a Ploesti raid counted as two), received an Air Medal with three bronze clusters and two silver clusters and, of course, he married Coral.

Later in the afternoon Maeve and I made a slow meandering walk through the orchard, stopping here and there to talk with friends in the green shade of the apple trees. When we came to the edge of the creek we stopped to watch a bunch of kids playing with the old flat-bottomed rowboat. There must have been six or seven children, all ages. They dragged the leaky scow upstream as far as the tether would permit, then everyone climbed aboard and began shouting and rocking to free the bottom planks from the mud. We sat on the bank and watched them drift and inch or two in the honey-slow current, drift here and there and get stuck on the half-submerged stones, and shove off again and then again until the line was stretched downstream to the end of their ride. A couple of the older children tried to pull the loaded craft back to the willow by hauling on the rope, but the bottom ground against the pebbles and then slid to a dead stop in the mud. In the end even the big boys gave up and everyone disembarked at the bank where they had run aground. "Do you know any of these kids?" I asked Maeve.

"Hardly. The girl with the pale blond hair is named Ingrid something. One of Jens' nieces." All the children were trooping up to the orchard, except for the last one who stood in the stern of the rowboat and unbuttoned his pants. "And the little boy peeing into the creek is at least part Cavallù. Of course, at this distance —" She trailed off.

"That's my Maeve, all right."

The boy hopped onto the shore and trotted after the others.

"Come on," I said, getting up and giving her my hand. "I'll take you on a voyage. Away across the sea to China, come on." For we had told our children, when they were little, that this creek flowed into Dudley Brook and the brook flowed into the Merrimack River and the river flowed out to sea.

I shoved the boat from the mud and we

got in. The pole was still rattling around in the bilge, so I poled us upstream to the end of the tether. Maeve sat with her back against the bow and the sunlight falling through the willow leaves dappled her lacy white dress in a display that made the folds and shadows appear snowy blue. For a while it seemed we were motionless, as if I had shoved us onto a yellowed old mirror. The distant laughter of the wedding guests floated to us from the orchard, and here the mayflies danced in the heated air and the lazy creek water dozed in the sun and our noon spread out forever. We watched a couple of water-bugs skitter past us on the glassy surface, then little by little we began to turn and drift. Maeve had tilted her head way back and was looking up through the leaves at the sky. "If we ever got married again I'd like to do it outdoors in a field," she said, idly.

"Remember today when we were all together in a circle, just before the ceremony began?" I said.

"Yes."

"I saw the most —"

"Hey, you guys!" Nina called, waving to us. "How about a ride?"

She had just come from the orchard and was walking toward the creek. We waved to her and now to Nico and Morgan Kathleen who had come walking from the orchard, too. Nina turned to say something to Nico and we heard all three of them talk, though we could not quite make out what they were saying, then Nico laughed and Nina pushed his shoulder. Maeve and I listened, for the sound of our children talking together was sweet to hear. They wandered further away along the bank of the creek — Morgan Kathleen lifting the long hair from the nape of her neck, holding it up a moment to cool off — and then turned back into the orchard. A while later, Maeve and I pulled the old tub onto the bank and went up under the apple trees to join the others.

Printed by
Ateliers Graphiques Marc Veilleux Inc.
Cap-Saint-Ignace, Québec
in February 1994.